Praise for
MONEY, MURDER

There are two things I can't resist, the story behind someone receiving windfall wealth and a good mystery. *Money, Murder, Mayhem* delivers both. I expected a good story. What I got was a surprisingly funny and intense ride through the world of old money and intrigue. I can't wait for the Warwick's next adventure.

Ed Ugel,
author of *Money for Nothing*
and *I'm With Fatty*

Money, Murder, Mayhem is a brilliantly entertaining crime thriller packed full of mystery and intrigue. With smart twists and lots of laughs, you'll love every moment you spend with the Warwick family and their curious inheritance, right to the final page.

Rosie Walker,
author of *Secrets of a Serial Killer*
and *The House Fire*

A Lord and Lady Crosswick Mystery

MONEY
MURDER
MAYHEM

Tana L.H. Boerger

Altta Publishing
2 The Pointe
Sanford, NC, 27332

Printed in the United States of America

Paperback ISBN: 979-8-9873285-1-4
Hardcover ISBN: 979-8-987-3285-2-1
Ebook ISBN: 979-8-9873285-0-7

First Edition

10 9 8 7 6 5 4 3 2 1

MONEY
MURDER
MAYHEM

ONE

"**W**HAT WOULD YOU change about your life if you could pick anything?" Michael Findley asked, looking around the lavish dining table at his ten dinner guests.

"I want to go first! I want to go first!" A well-maintained, sixty-something woman fluttered her hand in the air, light bouncing off her ten-carat diamond.

"Tell us, Madeline, what would you change?"

She dabbed her napkin on either side of her mouth, then said, "I'd marry my second husband first!" She beamed at an attractive, much younger man sitting across from her, and blew him a kiss.

The table erupted in howls of laughter.

Conrad Reston, founder of the most successful law firm in the state, tapped his spoon on his wine goblet. The pretty tinkling caught everyone's attention.

"Okay, Conrad. The floor's yours."

"That's easy." The elegant septuagenarian arched a white brow. "Instead of working a hundred hours a week for the last thirty years to build a law firm that sucks the life out of me, I'd inherit my wealth!"

That drew a round of applause from the group of hard-working, successful diners.

Michael pointed to the other end of the table. "Go on, Philip, tell us, what would you change about your life?

Philip Warwick thought for several seconds, shrugged, and said, "Absolutely nothing."

The other guests hooted and booed; several threw their wadded napkins across the table at Philip's head.

Looking at her husband, Genevieve, his wife of forty years, blushed like a bride and grinned with pleasure.

"I can't imagine a better life than I live." He tilted his head. "Genevieve and I have a terrific son, a smart, loving daughter-in-law, and two hilarious grandkids. As entrepreneurs, we've worked our butts off and had our share of struggles, but that's been half the fun. We laugh a lot, rarely argue anymore, and we're still crazy about each other." His eyes caught Genevieve's. "Does it get any better than that?"

"If I had your life, I wouldn't change anything either," said James Wallard, one of Philip's oldest friends. James' stunning trophy wife, Lauren, sat next to Philip. She was thirty-two, more than three decades younger than Philip's wife, but with none of Genevieve's elegance. After forty years of marriage, Philip was still in awe of 'G,' as he had called her from the night they'd met at university. She was a second-year law student, he was about to complete his master's degree in art history. As he loved to say, "I married my trophy wife first!"

Now, seven hours later, Genevieve squinted, eyes reduced to slits. Having drunk her fair share of Champagne the night before, the reflection of the sun glancing off countless tiny waves on the lake was brutal. She leaned her thumping head back on the chaise and tilted her face toward the rising sun's warmth. The breeze coming off the water ruffled her hair, and a wisp tickled her nose. 7:30 a.m. It would be an hour before Philip stirred, too long to wait for coffee. Where was the butler when you needed him? Even as she mused about how difficult her life was without a manservant, her ears caught the sound of grinding coffee beans. She pried open her left eye. Through the window from the deck, she saw a lanky shadow moving about the kitchen. Grateful that her prayers had been answered, she hummed softly. She still thrilled at the sight of her husband. Though he wasn't a proper butler, he certainly was a handsome houseboy.

Genevieve teetered on the edge of a shallow dream in which Philip floated from the kitchen, took her hand, and handed her a steaming mug. The aroma of the brew was enticing, and it was only when Philip's lips brushed her forehead that she realized the coffee in her dream was on the glass table next to her. She sensed Philip lowering himself into the chair beside her.

"Good morning, pretty girl."

With effort, she opened her eyes to see Philip's lopsided smile. She chuckled and reached for her mug. "The service here is pretty good".

"Happy to take care of all your needs, Ma'am." He winked and fluttered his eyebrows.

Their deck was the perfect place to enjoy the early-morning

quiet. A heron strutted along the water's edge, stopping to look for a fishy breakfast. The home they had created suited them. Warm and inviting, it overlooked water and the endless green of a golf course.

Ceiling fans stirred the air, rustling geraniums in their yellow pots.

Philip stretched his long legs onto the ottoman and angled his face to the morning sun. "What did you think of Leslie's new face?" he asked without a trace of humor.

"Wow!" Genevieve said. "She got her money's worth! Who does she remind you of now?"

Philip knitted his brow. "Joan Rivers in a wind tunnel?"

Genevieve struggled to keep coffee from spraying out of her nose. She gulped then coughed before snorting out a laugh. As she pulled a tissue from her pocket to wipe her eyes, Philip's phone rang. He glanced at his watch. Eight o'clock on a Sunday morning. He pressed 'accept,' answering the unknown number.

"Philip Warwick. Yes. Yes." Silence.

Genevieve tensed. A call so early on a Sunday screamed "emergency," but Philip showed no signs of concern, just interest.

After a few minutes he said, "Let me talk to my wife, make a couple of calls…Of course."

She studied Philip's face for any sign of what the call might be, but it gave nothing away.

Philip listened; his forehead furrowed. "Yes. Yes. I understand, but it's critical to confirm all this.

Genevieve strained to hear but couldn't make out any words.

Should she be worried about their son, Duncan, his wife, Julia, their grandchildren Alexander, and Ella?

"Sure, as soon as the package arrives."

What package? Genevieve shoved herself from the chaise and began to pace back and forth on the deck, becoming more agitated by the second.

Minutes ticked by, punctuated by Philip's mumbles and nods. "Of course. Of course. I can verify all this with your New York office."

Genevieve tried to make eye contact with Philip, raising her eyebrows in a question. He ignored her. "This is quite a lot to take in."

Genevieve suppressed a groan of frustration. *What* is a lot to take in?!

At last, Philip said, "Let me make sure I have this right. You say he died ten months ago?"

Genevieve gasped. Who died? She couldn't believe Philip's detached expression.

"And you've been looking for the heir since then?"

Genevieve stood frozen, listening to the clues, trying to piece it all together.

"It sounds like a fantasy or more like a scam. Is the estate significant enough to warrant such a search?"

She crossed the deck to Philip's side, signaling for him to tell her what was going on.

At last, he looked at her. Surprise crossed his face as he suddenly remembered she was there. "I see. I see. Really?...

Hmmm. Really? Just a minute. Let me put you on speaker phone. My wife will want to hear this."

Philip pressed the speaker icon and put the phone on the table between them. "Genevieve, this is David Weatherington. He's calling from England, and he works for a law firm. Mr. Weatherington, tell Genevieve what you just told me."

"Good morning, Ms. Warwick. Or I should say, Lady Crosswick."

Genevieve's eyes widened. "What do you mean, Lady Crosswick? Why would you call me that?"

"Give Mr. Weatherington a chance to explain, G." Philip put his hand on her knee.

"Lady Crosswick, last November Jonathon Laney died. He was the 12TH Earl of Crosswick, and also your husband's distant cousin on his mother's side." Genevieve gave Philip a quizzical look, shaking her head as she listened to David Weatherington's posh accent. She stood and as Weatherington told his story, she wandered to a pot of geraniums, and started deadheading the old blossoms.

"He had no children and, it turns out, your husband is his closest living relative. Jonathon Laney was one of the richest men in England. Since his death, executors at Holmes Fitch Smythson Morrow have been confirming Mr. Warwick's identity and legal right to this inheritance."

"Inheritance?" Genevieve's attention whipped from the spent geraniums to the voice on the phone.

"More than £990,000,000, plus several properties."

Genevieve's look of shock met Philip's perplexed grin.

"You'll receive a DHL package shortly. It will confirm all this information. Did I leave anything out, my lord?"

Philip made a funny face at Genevieve and mouthed 'my lord.'

"I think that about sums it up, Mr. Weatherington."

Genevieve started at the sound of the doorbell then bolted into the house.

"I think the package just arrived. Genevieve's checking. Yes, I'll do that. Thank you, Mr. Weatherington. Of course, David." Philip ended the call and walked into the kitchen where Genevieve met him with a thick DHL envelope in hand.

"What a way to start a Sunday!" Philip searched Genevieve's eyes. "What in the world? Do you think this could possibly be true?"

"I have no idea, but I bet the information in the package will be interesting at the very least." She handed the envelope to him, her excitement growing. "Open it, Philip! Open it! I want to see where it says we're billionaires!"

He tossed the envelope onto the kitchen table and sauntered to the Nespresso coffee maker. He placed a pod in the head, put his empty cup under the spigot and pressed the button. While the machine poured out fresh coffee with a topper of thick foam, he turned around and leaned against the cabinet. He folded his arms. "You seem to be pretty excited, G."

"What is wrong with you?" Shaking her head at her annoying husband, Genevieve laughed as she threw a dishtowel at Philip. "Open the damn envelope!"

"Whoa! Lady Crosswick's getting bossy. The potential of becoming absurdly rich is making her drunk with aggression!"

"If you won't open it, I will." Willing to wait no longer, Genevieve reached for the DHL pouch but before she could snatch it, Philip grabbed her wrist.

"Not so fast, my lady," he said. "Look at the name on this envelope. Philip James Warwick. Do you see Genevieve Hayden Warwick written anywhere? It would be a federal offense for you to open my mail. In fact, it's probably a violation of international law since it came from England." Philip pulled Genevieve into his arms and tickled her showing no mercy. She squirmed and wiggled trying to escape his grasp, gasping for air between snorts of laughter. "I bet Interpol will knock down the door any minute!"

"Stop! Stop it, you beast!" Tears streamed down her cheeks.

"I'll stop if you say, 'Please stop tickling me, my lord.'" Philip found a new spot on her ribs to attack. "Go on. Say it, my little wench."

"Lady...Crosswick...is...not...a...a...wench!" Genevieve managed to wheeze out the words. "Please, Philip. Stop!"

"All right, all right. I've tortured you enough." He eased his hold on her and stepped back, gripping her shoulders until she was stable.

"I can't remember the last time you tickled me like that." She wiped her streaming eyes with a tissue. "You're terrible. Now would you please open the envelope?"

"My God, the woman is single-minded." Philip picked up the packet and his coffee and carried them to the massive kitchen island. He pulled out a stool and sat, nodding to Genevieve to do the same. "Okay. Let's see what's in this Pandora's box, my darling Lady Crosswick. Hand me the scissors, please."

"When you put it that way, it sounds a little ominous. You don't think this is going to open a flood of problems, do you?" Genevieve pulled the scissors out of the knife block and gave them to Philip.

"I was just trying to dazzle you with my command of literary references. Did it work?"

"Actually, it gives me pause. If we're trading literary references, how about 'Heavy is the head that wears the crown?' I bet there are a few burdens that come with a billion pounds. Can you imagine the scammers who'll come out of the woodwork?" Genevieve took Philip's hand, cradling it in both of hers. Holding his gaze, she said, "Until we know something different, Let's just take it step by step and enjoy every minute."

"Great plan, oh wise one." Philip held up the envelope and the scissors. "Shall we?"

"Oh yes!" Genevieve said, her enthusiasm bubbling over.

Careful not to cut the contents, Philip slid the scissors along the edge of the heavy plastic pouch. Genevieve was off her stool and hanging on his shoulder, stretching to see what was inside.

"G, could you please give me a little breathing space? I promise I won't hide anything from you." Though he smiled, Genevieve heard an edge in his voice that made her sit back down.

Philip pulled two inches of thick, cream-colored bond from the sleeve. On top was a letter of introduction with the name of one of London's oldest and most prestigious law firms: Holmes Fitch Smythson Morrow.

"Here we go," he said clearing his throat before he read.

Holmes Fitch Smythson Morrow
26 Upper Brook Street
London
W1K 7QE,
United Kingdom

Dear Lord Crosswick,

It is with pleasure Holmes Fitch Smythson Morrow write to confirm you are the sole legal heir to the estate of Jonathon William Wallace Laney, 12TH Earl of Crosswick, who, on November 18TH, died of natural causes at Margrave House, his townhouse in Kensington, in London.

The enclosed documents verify the information Sir David Weatherington provided via telephone. Sir David will be your principal contact going forward and will arrange your trip to New York to begin the transfer of your inheritance as soon as is practicable. In the meantime, enclosed for your review is general information about the estate and its holdings.

We will continue to serve you as we served your cousin, the late 12TH Earl of Crosswick and the five preceding generations of the House of Crosswick.

I have the honour to be Your Lordship's obedient servant,

Sir Mark James Holmes
Sir Mark James Holmes
Managing Partner
Holmes Fitch Smythson Morrow

"So much for perfunctory ass-kissing. Where is the list of assets?" Genevieve was anxious to see an inventory of the estate's wealth. She stood, reaching for the papers.

Philip scooped them out of her reach. "I've known you for forty-three years and I had no idea you were such a greedy girl." He gave Genevieve a sharp look and held the stack high above his head.

She plopped back onto her stool. "I'm surprised myself. This isn't like me, is it?"

Philip's eyes softened. "It's okay, G. This situation is unreal. I think we can give ourselves a little slack. We should give ourselves permission to feel however we feel for, let's say..." he looked at the ceiling then back at his wife. "Let's say we give ourselves until we get to Wilmingrove Hall. Until then we can feel greedy, excited, suspicious, happy, unhappy, miserable, thrilled—whatever we feel. But when we get to Wilmingrove Hall, you and I will have a serious conversation about what this all means and how we're going to handle it. Until then, we just enjoy the ride. Deal?"

Genevieve extended her hand, and they shook. "Deal," she said. "Now, show me the big fat list of stuff we're about to own!"

Philip flipped through page after page of the will until he got to the exhibits. "Aha. Here we go. This is what you want." He handed Genevieve several pages with the heading 'Property Inventory.' "Start with that." He continued scanning the pages. "Here are a few more." He put a dozen sheets with 'Art Inventory' next to the first stack.

"Wow. Just wow, Philip! Listen to this."

He dropped the papers on the counter and leaned back.

"We own a thirteen-room apartment in New York on Central Park West. We own the townhouse in London, Margrave House, where the Earl died. Evidently, Jonathon enjoyed living the good life. Thank you for that, Jonathon. We own Wilmingrove Hall, the family seat since 1882. There is an apartment in Paris on Avenue Foch, one of my favorite streets in Paris."

"Well, aren't you the lucky girl!" Philip smiled with pure joy as he listened to Genevieve, watching her excitement mount. To him, none of this would be real until they met with the lawyers in New York, but he was enjoying that Genevieve was embracing their possible good fortune.

"And we have a vineyard in St. Emilion. Do you remember when we visited several wineries there a couple of years ago? Wouldn't it have been funny if we'd toured Chateau Beaulieu, our vineyard?"

"That would be pretty amazing." Philip couldn't take his eyes off his wife's face. She looked twenty, cheeks flushed, eyes sparkling.

"And last but certainly not least, we own a horse farm in Lexington, Kentucky."

"A horse farm?" Philip began to absorb some of Genevieve's infectious excitement. "I wonder if we own any racehorses. I'd love that."

Genevieve stood up, put her hands over her head and stretched like an elegant cat. "Before I read any more, I need to go take a shower and let this sink in." She walked toward their bedroom, stopped and, over her shoulder said, "Care to join me?"

"I'll be there in a minute," Philip said, absorbed in a spreadsheet.

Genevieve walked through their bedroom into their spacious bathroom. She turned on the faucet and slid her silk nightgown off her shoulders.

Though she was sixty-four, a lifetime of exercise and great genes gave her a body defined by long, taught muscles and lovely skin. She was grateful how kind Mother Nature had been.

She stepped into the steaming stream, letting the water pound over her head. She heard the bathroom door open and felt Philip's presence.

He stepped into the shower and fitted his body against her back. He cupped a breast in each hand and leaned down, kissing her ear. "Darling girl." His voice was husky. "If this inheritance proves to be what it seems, our lives have just changed forever."

Genevieve turned in his arms and looked into his eyes, her lips just a breath away from his. "Last night you said you wouldn't change a thing about our lives."

"That was last night. This is today," Philip said, a smile on his lips and mischief in his eyes.

TWO

THROUGH THE WINDOW of the Bombardier Global
6000, Genevieve stared into a gray, wet wall, rain streaking
across the glass. Forty-eight hours ago, she and Philip were
nursing the after-effects of the previous night's party. Now, they
were hurtling toward New York City in their private jet to claim
a king's ransom.

Yesterday's call from their long-time attorney, Michael
Findley, confirmed everything David Weatherington had said.
Philip was the heir to Jonathon William Wallace Laney, the 12TH
Earl of Crosswick's immense fortune.

"Champagne, Lady Crosswick?"

Genevieve looked up into the hazel eyes of a leggy flight
attendant, holding a crystal glass filled to the brim with pretty
bubbles.

"Yes please." Genevieve accepted the flute, licking the side of
the glass where a small stream of Champagne had escaped over
the rim. She grinned, looking up at the flight attendant. "We
don't want any of this to go to waste."

The young woman gave Genevieve a wide smile. "Certainly

not!" she said in a posh English accent and extended a silver tray of hors d'oeuvres. "The salmon caviar bites are wonderful. In fact, everything is quite spectacular. Your chef is outstanding."

"My chef is outstanding... I have a chef," Genevieve thought to herself. Her lips turned up as she mouthed, "I have a chef." In her mind, fireworks exploded, and James Brown bellowed, "I Feel Good!"

Across the cabin Philip and Michael faced each other, their laptops open on a mahogany table between them. They had been talking non-stop since yesterday. In just a few hours, Michael had become the Warwicks' expert on the 12TH Earl of Crosswick. Philip and Genevieve wanted to have as much background as they could before meeting with the Estate's lawyers. The more they learned, the more interesting it became.

The Laneys' extraordinary family history unveiled generations of entrepreneurs and philanthropists. Now, Philip James Warwick, the 13TH Earl of Crosswick, and his wife, Genevieve Hayden Warwick, Countess of Crosswick, were the next link in the House of Crosswick chain.

Philip scowled at the sheaf of papers in his hand. He sat slumped in his dove gray leather seat, glasses perched midway down his nose. "The more I study these papers, the more complicated this inheritance seems to be. You have no idea how grateful I am you're here, Michael," Philip said.

"I just want you to remember that I knew you when!" Michael joked. The three of them had been friends since he and Genevieve were in law school, long before Michael became their attorney.

"It's exciting but mind blowing," Philip said. "I mean this guy is—well, was—seriously rich!"

Her Champagne glass in hand, Genevieve crossed the aisle to sit next to Philip. "And now, it appears, so are you. Tell me again what David Weatherington told you about your cousin."

"David wasn't at all surprised that my family didn't know about Jonathon Laney." Philip flipped through his notes and began to tick off entries. "He was ninety-eight when he died last November. He was an only child. He graduated from Cambridge, barely. His parents were killed in a car accident when he was twenty-three, at which time he inherited the Crosswick title and all the wealth that went with it."

Genevieve drank the last of her Champagne and hoped the flight attendant would take note of her empty glass. "Go on."

"At that point, he embarked on an earnest career as a jet-setting playboy, acquiring the Paris and New York apartments. When he was thirty-seven, he became engaged to an American heiress he met in New York."

Genevieve leaned forward, elbows on the table, chin cradled in her hands. "I love that he fell in love with an American."

"You're such a romantic." Philip brushed Genevieve's cheek with his knuckle and continued. "About a year and a half after they met, they were skiing in Sun Valley, Idaho, where he had an accident that left him paralyzed. He broke off his engagement and lived the rest of his life as a recluse in his townhouse in London, seeing only his small staff and few visitors."

"I'd prefer a happy ending." Genevieve looked at Philip and

Michael, eyes shiny with tears. "Please don't tell me that was the end of his love life?" Genevieve's said.

"I think David said something about an affair." Philip looked at his notes, flipping back a page. "Here it is. He engaged a young art historian to help him catalogue his art collection. She was doing a practicum with the Laney Museum of Art. According to the gossip, the professional relationship turned into an affair, but in the end, Jonathon encouraged her to find love elsewhere."

Genevieve sniffed then blew her nose. "Cad," she said.

Philip looked up from his notes. "David said unless someone in our family did a genealogy, no one would have any idea we were related to this very wealthy earl. I know my mother's ancestors were Laneys, a land grant family. They received land in the eighteenth century, but the information pretty much stopped there, at least as far as I was concerned. Believe me, If I'd known my cousin, Jonathon Laney, was holed up in a posh townhouse in London for sixty-one years, sitting on a billion pounds, I would have shown more interest in the family tree!" Philip grinned and looked over his glasses that had slipped to the tip of his nose. "I have to admit, this is getting interesting. As you know, I've never inherited a billion dollars...err...pounds before."

Genevieve's eyes sparkled. "It's been so exciting the last couple of days, talking about the great things we're going to do with this wealth. Believe me, darling boy, I'll be right by your side to help. I'm going to stick to you like glue." Laughing, Genevieve gave Philip a noisy kiss on the cheek. "I'm not going anywhere!"

When their plane touched down at Teterboro, the closest general aviation airport to Manhattan, the rainy day had turned sizzling and sultry, unusual for mid-September. At the bottom of the stairs a black Maybach limousine waited, motor running. When they saw the car, Philip caught Genevieve's eye. With a wry smile, he raised one eyebrow and said, "Of course there's a Maybach waiting for us."

Genevieve's shiny brown bob swished over her shoulders as she did a little jig ending with a bump into Philip's hip. "I think I'm going to like being outrageously wealthy!"

"Try to show some decorum, would you?" Philip said trying to hide his excitement.

Nestled in the luxury of the Maybach, they headed directly to the New York offices of Holmes Fitch Smythson Morrow on 6TH Avenue and West 49TH Street, where they would meet Sir David Weatherington for the first time. Though it was only thirteen miles from Teterboro Airport to mid-town Manhattan, it took almost an hour to navigate New York City's mid-morning traffic.

Except for classical music wafting from the Burmester sound system, and the low murmur of Philip and Michael talking, the car was quiet. Genevieve stared out of the window at the crowded sidewalks, lost in her own thoughts until the car stopped in front of a stone building with massive, carved wooden doors.

Their driver opened the car door and the three alit from the limousine. They jostled their way across the crowded sidewalk and pushed through the doorway into the imposing lobby.

An attractive, athletic man, about six feet tall, stood by the reception desk. His chestnut hair, graying at the temples, was fashionably long, curling just over the collar of his starched, pin-striped shirt. The moment he saw Philip and Genevieve, he burst into a broad smile as if seeing old friends. "Lord and Lady Crosswick, I'm David, David Weatherington. It's wonderful to see you." Striding forward to meet them, he extended his hand. "We're so pleased you could come to New York so quickly. I hope the flight was all right?" His English public-school accent seemed appropriate, given the baronial atmosphere of the foyer.

"When you're flying in your own jet, things seem to go pretty well." Returning his smile, Philip took David's outstretched hand, shook it warmly, then introduced Genevieve.

To her surprise, David grasped her shoulders and, in a much more Continental than English fashion, kissed Genevieve on both cheeks. "Welcome, welcome," he said.

"And, David, this is Michael Findley. Michael has been our attorney for twenty years and is a long-time friend as well. He'll be working with your group."

"I look forward to that, Michael. You'll find plenty of interesting estate law for all of us to share." Turning back to Philip and Genevieve, David said, "I can't tell you how splendid it is to meet you both at long last. After months searching for you, verifying your existence and your lineage, I feel as if I've known you forever."

"I'm glad you were so persistent," Genevieve chuckled.

"It's not every day I get a call saying I've inherited a billion pounds." Philip said. "In fact, I can't remember the last time that happened."

Their laughter bounced around the marble lobby.

"Shall we go up?" David gestured toward the bank of elevators.

Philip took Genevieve's elbow and guided her into the waiting car. "I have the distinct feeling once these doors close, our lives will never be the same."

"There's a significant chance of that," said David, punching the button marked P. "I hope you don't find the next few hours too dry or boring. There's a lot of legal ground to cover."

Philip scowled. "I can't imagine how anything about this situation could be dry or boring. What has just happened to us is not only shocking and overwhelming, but life changing."

"And thrilling," Genevieve added, her smile crinkling the corners of her eyes.

David looked apologetic. "Of course, you're right. As you said, this doesn't happen every day."

"It does not," Philip confirmed.

"Though Jonathon Laney was an invalid and recluse for the last sixty years of his life, I'm happy to tell you he managed his estate brilliantly." The elevator stopped. The doors slid open revealing a paneled reception room that looked more like an exclusive London club than a New York law office.

David ushered the Warwicks into the lobby. "So, while you are not taking on any financial terrors, there are hundreds of details to address: creating new wills, making decisions on charitable giving, overseeing a foundation, managing multiple homes, a vineyard and numerous other business interests, and getting a grasp on millions of pounds of artwork and antiquities: those owned personally and those held by The Laney Museum of Art, and the more recent Laney Musée des Beaux Arts, Paris. And, of course, security."

As David spoke, Genevieve looked around the genteel chamber they had entered. Wingback leather chairs were flanked by mahogany tables that Genevieve was quite sure were original Queen Anne pieces. At the far end of the room stood a large fireplace, its realistic gas logs awaiting a chilly day. She scanned the art hanging on every wall and smiled at the contemporary works of David Hockney, Georgia O'Keeffe, a crazy, rhythmic canvas by Anselm Kiefer and a massive Franz Kline, all a wonderful contrast to the staid elegance of the Georgian room.

"Wow, this is quite a surprise. Who's the collector?" Genevieve asked.

"Well... um, actually, the partners are great supporters of the arts." David looked down at his shoes then back at Philip and Genevieve.

"They have excellent taste," Philip said his voice full of admiration.

"They do, Lord Crosswick." David abruptly changed the subject.

"I understand that when you're finished here in New York, you're going to London to finish some legal work, then to Wilmingrove Hall. Is that correct?"

"That's the plan, right, G?"

"Yes. We're anxious to see this glorious family seat we've heard so much about. We can hardly wait to immerse ourselves in Laney history. Why do you ask, David?"

"If you don't mind, I would very much like to join you there for a couple of days." Lowering his voice, David continued, "I have several...uh...several concerns I want to share with you about the current relationship between Holmes Fitch Smythson Morrow and your estate."

Cocking her head to one side, Genevieve raised an eyebrow. "David, are these concerns things we need to know about sooner rather than later?"

"No. No." David said, but he looked unsure. "They can wait until the end of the week. It's fine. I shouldn't have mentioned anything until I came to Wilmingrove Hall. For now, just forget I said anything."

Philip narrowed his eyes. "Of course, now we won't be able to think about anything else!" He gave David a light punch on the shoulder just as a patrician man with a shock of white hair strode across reception.

"Lord and Lady Crosswick, what a pleasure to meet you at last. I'm Sir Mark Holmes, Managing Partner of Holmes Fitch Smythson Morrow." His voice dripped with arrogance when he emphasized *Sir* Mark. "Everyone in the firm has been looking forward to this occasion since David located you. Quite a story, isn't it? We had almost given up hope that we'd find an heir, and then…." He trailed off, leaving the sentence hanging in the air.

"Yes. As I'm sure you can imagine, it came as quite a surprise to us," Philip said. "A lot has happened in a short time. We understand we have a full agenda today."

"You do, indeed. This afternoon and tomorrow you have many documents to sign, then we will get into the interesting part of the estate: properties, inventory, investments, that sort of thing. I understand you plan to go to London and stay at Margrave House on Friday, before going on to Wilmingrove Hall. I don't think you will be disappointed in either property, but the Hall is particularly special."

With David's cautionary words still echoing, Philip said, "That's what we understand. We're anxious to confirm the family estate has been well managed and is in good shape." There was steel in his voice.

Sir Mark arched an eyebrow and drilled into Philip's eyes. "I assure you, Lord Crosswick, everything has been managed to perfection." His defensive tone confirmed Philip had made his point.

They made their way into a large conference room where floor to ceiling bookshelves were brimming with leather-bound volumes. Though the room was large, the low, coffered ceiling created a coziness. As they entered, twelve men of varying ages and shapes rose. Introductions were made one by one around the table. In addition to David and Sir Mark, Henry Fitch was the other partner who had flown from London to New York for the meeting. Henry was the son of now retired Winston Fitch, one of the name partners, and nineth in an unbroken line of Fitches in the law firm. Henry was cute in a Paul McCartney sense. He was a bit fleshy, his buttons straining the buttonholes of his shirt, his belly bulging over his waistband a bit. No women were among the brain trust, Genevieve noted with disappointment. She was the only woman in the room. Even the attendant responsible for the comfort of the meeting participants was a man.

After a few minutes of pleasantries, Sir Mark urged everyone to be seated. "Lord and Lady Crosswick, please sit here." He gestured to chairs on either side of his place at the head of the massive conference table. For the next three hours a steady flow of documents was presented, discussed, and signed. Questions were asked. Questions were answered. Estate taxes and how, over the years, the estate had been structured to pay the least amount of tax was presented at length. The partners' pride was evident as they explained to Philip and Genevieve how the firm had used every legal strategy available to estates as large as the Laney inheritance and how, through years of careful planning, they had minimized the taxes that must now be paid.

After hours of tedium, there was little energy left in the room. "There's one last subject we need to cover before we adjourn," Sir Mark said, fatigue obvious in his voice. "David, I believe you're going to address the issue of security."

Most of the day David had remained quiet, deferring to the two name partners who wanted very much to dazzle the new Earl and Countess. But at this point, he stood up, walked to a credenza, and picked up a remote control. "Lord and Lady Crosswick, the greatest and perhaps the only downside of your inheritance is that you also inherit the need for security. Because the previous Earl was a recluse, security was easy and minimal. For you and your family, however, that will not be the case."

Philip held up his hand. "David, let me stop you there. We appreciate that the estate is significant," he stopped himself and chuckled. "Well, enormous. But does it really put our family in jeopardy?"

Without hesitation, David said, "Trust me, my lord. It does, both physically and online. The moment we confirmed your identity as the heir to the Laney fortune, an entire world knew who you were and how wealthy you were about to become. Have you or the countess ever been scammed or had your credit cards hacked?"

"Multiple times, of course," Philip said.

Genevieve nodded. "It's part of life these days, isn't it?"

"It is, but this is quite different than finding an unauthorized charge on your American Express card. Just as there are elite athletes, there are elite criminals who spend every waking moment analyzing extraordinary fortunes and figuring out how to take as much money as they can from people with great wealth, even if they have to do harm."

"David, I appreciate what you're saying, but, unless Genevieve objects, I'd rather save this conversation until later. First give us a minute to embrace the idea of being billionaires. Then give us another thirty seconds to process the reality that everyone wants to take our fortune. Do you agree, G?"

"I do," she said. After the grueling day they had just had, the only thing she could think about was the glass of wine and dinner she hoped was waiting for them at their apartment on Central Park West.

THREE

"I'M EXHAUSTED." GENEVIEVE slumped against the marble wall in the lobby of the grand, pre-war building. The Warwicks arrived at their apartment after seven hours with their team of lawyers. During the marathon meeting, they covered the list of domestic staff in their properties, most of whom had been in the estate's employment for years, a comforting fact. Now, Philip and Genevieve were about to meet the first of that staff.

They entered the elevator and Philip fumbled with a small brass key as he tried to coax it into the slot next to 43E. He turned the key and Genevieve's stomach filled with butterflies as the elevator sailed upward.

"Are you nervous?" Genevieve asked Philip as the floor numbers sped by.

"Very. I mean, Mrs. Proctor has taken care of this apartment since 1974. I'm sure as far as she's concerned, it's her apartment. What if she doesn't like us? If she doesn't let us in, I guess we can afford to spend the night at a Hampton Inn."

Genevieve chuckled, grateful for the comic relief.

The reality of the huge roles they were assuming caused her breath to quicken.

"Do we really want to do this?" Genevieve sagged from her head to her toes, overwhelmed by fatigue. "Last week, our lives were our own. We were only responsible for our family. Today, we're shouldering the responsibility of hundreds of *other* people's lives."

Philip kissed the top of Genevieve's head. "I have to say, there were several times today when I thought we should just donate everything to MOMA and go home."

"My feelings exactly. But I was thinking the Guggenheim." Genevieve looked at him, relief in her eyes.

Philip offered a resigned smile. "But the thing I kept thinking all day is, we never wanted to spend our retirement watching the world go by. This inheritance gives us the opportunity to bring extraordinary resources to our passions, to the things you and I have been working on for years. The Laney Museum of Art is going to give us a huge platform to affect the art world. That alone will make this worthwhile."

"That, and the fact that we have our own private jet!" Genevieve couldn't contain her laughter.

For almost forty years at the Warwick's thirteen-room New York City apartment, Mrs. Proctor the housekeeper and Mr. Emory the houseman had worked as a team. They kept the apartment in immaculate condition, updating as necessary, answering only to the financial team that scrutinized every penny spent on the estate's multi-country holdings. It was hard to imagine the two would welcome the new heir with open arms.

The elevator slid to a stop. "Oh boy. Here we go," Philip said under his breath.

The doors opened and there, through a forty-foot wall of windows, lay a panoramic view of Central Park in all its glory, a green, lush canopy stretching before them. Neither Philip nor Genevieve understood where they were. It appeared, perhaps, they had arrived at a sophisticated lobby.

"Are we in the right place?" Genevieve whispered.

The doors began to close, and Philip stuck his arm out to stop them. He gave Genevieve a quizzical look and a slight shove in the back, nudging her out of the elevator car. They walked across the foyer's classic black and white checkerboard floor, looking for someone who could help them.

"Oh my! I am so sorry I wasn't downstairs to greet you," called an energetic voice with the polish of a slight English accent.

A willowy woman strode through the archway at the far end of the room. She was medium height with short, spikey, white hair. Her close-fitting pants accentuated her narrow hips. Genevieve recognized the woman's crisp, white linen shirt as designer quality and the gold cuff on her wrist as the work of one of Genevieve's favorite jewelry designers.

"We must be paying her well," Genevieve thought, suspicion overtaking her appreciation of the woman's style.

When she reached Philip and Genevieve, she stopped and bobbed a slight curtsy.

"I'm Harriet Proctor," she said. "You are, I presume, Lord and

Lady Crosswick. I can't tell you how thrilled we are to have you here! It's very exciting, the prospect of life and activity in the apartment." Her eyes sparkled.

Philip and Genevieve were speechless, so surprised were they by the warm greeting. In addition to expecting a chilly reception, they each had a mental image of their housekeeper as an elderly, austere woman.

The first to recover, Philip said, "As you can imagine, we're a bit overwhelmed."

"Who wouldn't be?" Mrs. Proctor rolled her eyes. "But trust me when I tell you: it will all be fine. You have many excellent people to help you along the way. Most of us have been with the estate for years and now that we have an active Lord and Lady, things will be much easier and much more exciting!" She clapped her hands. "Mr. Emory will be with us shortly. He's selecting wines for dinner, which can be served any time. I imagine you are exhausted after travelling so early and sitting in meetings all day. May I show you to your rooms?"

"That would be perfect. I'm dying to have a shower and change," Genevieve said, almost pleading.

"That can be arranged," Mrs. Proctor said, turning on her heel. "Right this way."

As they entered the living room, Genevieve's jaw drop. The view stretched from where they stood just off the foyer, across the acres of thick camel carpet, out onto a wide slate terrace, and across Central Park. Sounds of a jazz piano filtering through ceiling speakers filled the apartment. She grabbed Philip's hand and squeezed.

"Mrs. Proctor, this is magnificent." Genevieve breathed in the delicate fragrance of roses then spied a huge bouquet of vivid coral blossoms sitting on a carved credenza to the left.

"Lord and Lady Crosswick, if there is anything you would like redecorated, changed in any way, you must let me know." Mrs. Proctor stopped in front of a dynamic painting hanging over the fireplace. "I understand you two are art lovers."

"My God, is that a Motherwell?" Philip stared at a canvas dancing with burnt sienna, crimson, yellow and black. He leaned close to the signature and whistled under his breath. "It is. It's a Robert Motherwell. Does this belong to the Earl?"

"It does, my lord, it belongs to you." Mrs. Proctor smiled and continued across the living room. "Shall we?"

Speechless, Philip and Genevieve looked at each other, turned and followed Mrs. Proctor down a hall flanked on the right by a bank of French doors flung wide to the terrace, lined with pots overflowing with scarlet geraniums and periwinkle blue plumbago. At the end of the hall, double doors stood open to a large, sumptuous bedroom. The room reminded Genevieve of something out of a Kathryn Hepburn movie: understated old money. Every surface was polished to a sheen or luxuriously upholstered. Like the living room, soft grays, camels, and creamy whites worked together to create an irresistible retreat.

Mrs. Proctor stood to the side and spread her arms, encouraging Philip and Genevieve to enter. "Your clothes have been put away in the closet and drawers, and your toiletries are in the bathroom. I hope we have anticipated your needs, but if we have overlooked anything, please let me know. We want you to be very comfortable. Would you like a cocktail or glass of wine while you change?"

"I would love a glass of Champagne," said Genevieve. "It seems appropriate, doesn't it?"

"It does," Mrs. Proctor grinned. "And you, my lord?"

"I'll have the same, please. Is it necessary to call me 'my lord,' Mrs. Proctor?" Philip asked. "It makes me feel uncomfortable."

With a reserved smile and a twinkle in her eye, Mrs. Proctor said, "I'm sure you'll get used to it soon enough. Is there anything else, my lord? My lady?"

"No, thank you," Philip and Genevieve said in unison.

With that, Mrs. Proctor backed out of the doorway, pulling the double doors closed.

Within the hour, the Warwicks were refreshed, relaxed, and seated at a small table on the terrace. The evening had evolved from a sultry late-summer day into a balmy twilight. Candles flickered, their soft glow bouncing off cut crystal goblets filled with a delicate pink Bordeaux rosé.

Just as Mrs. Proctor brought plates of cold salmon with a peach coulis and crispy grilled vegetables, Philip raised his glass gesturing to his beautiful surroundings. Locking his eyes on Genevieve he said, "Here's to a great adventure and the only woman with whom I would ever want to share it." They clinked glasses and sipped the rosé.

"Mrs. Proctor, this wine is magnificent!" Genevieve said. "I love it! Where is it from?

"I'm so glad you like it, my lady. It's from your vineyard in St. Emilion."

Philip and Genevieve looked at each other, then at Mrs. Proctor. They raised their glasses toward her. "This is going to be a lot of fun," Philip said, and he took a rather large gulp.

FOUR

SITTING AT AN eighteenth-century mahogany secretary, Genevieve tapped on her laptop, organizing, making lists, evaluating. Just as she thought how wonderful a cup of tea and a cookie would be, Mrs. Proctor walked through the study door carrying a silver tray laden with a china tea service.

"You read my mind, Mrs. Proctor. How did you know I was longing for tea and treats?"

"That's my job, my lady, to anticipate your needs."

"Well, you do it brilliantly. If you have a minute, I'd love for you to join me. I have a million questions that only you can answer."

"Of course, my lady. It would be my pleasure to be of help any way I can."

Genevieve rose from her desk, moved to the sofa, and sat down, pulling her legs under her. She motioned for the housekeeper to sit.

"My first question is does the staff from each of the Earl's properties know each other?"

"No, though I speak with Bertie MacIntosh often. She's the

head housekeeper at Wilmingrove Hall. She's wonderful… and so very Scottish. I think you and Lord Crosswick will like her. She calls just to gossip now and then, or we chat about what's going on in the village, about all the events they're doing at Wilmingrove Hall."

"Events at Wilmingrove Hall?" Genevieve was surprised. "Why would they be doing events? No one lives there."

"Ah, of course. That must sound strange."

Genevieve detected a small note of condescension in Mrs. Proctor's voice and, for the first time since they assumed the earldom, she felt slightly out of her depth.

"Let me explain. As you know, Wilmingrove Hall is the manor house and family seat of the Earl of Crosswick. As such, there are many obligations the estate assumes regarding the county and the village of Wilmingrove, which grew, over the years, as a support village for the Hall. Year after year, the Lord of the Manor grants permission to hold certain events on the estate. Noblesse oblige, you understand."

Genevieve nodded, trying to grasp their future obligations. "So, what kind of events are we talking about?"

"There are fetes, gymkhanas —"

"What's a gymkhana?" Genevieve interrupted.

"A gymkhana is a local Pony Club event with competitive games on horseback. The Pony Club nurtures young riders, and their gymkhanas are always very well attended." Mrs. Proctor nodded, smiled, and carried on. The Hall also hosts charity balls, flower shows and all manner of fundraising efforts for the village and county. In addition, there are shoots, and *many,*

many, many country weekends for the partners of Holmes Fitch Smythson Morrow." As she repeated 'many,' Mrs. Proctor's voice dripped with disapproval. "Considering there has been no earl in residence at Wilmingrove Hall for well over sixty years, it's been a very busy place indeed." With that pronouncement, Mrs. Proctor tilted her head to one side and sat even more erect, waiting for Genevieve to reply.

"Hmmm," Genevieve said, not quite knowing what Mrs. Proctor wanted her to say. After a moment, she said, "Are you suggesting some people—the law firm or perhaps the village—have taken advantage of the fact there's been no one in a position of authority at Wilmingrove Hall to say 'No?'"

"Well, I'm not one to gossip."

Genevieve tried to hide her amusement. "Of course not, Mrs. Proctor." She leaned in, encouraging the housekeeper to continue.

"I'm just suggesting that it will be a very welcome change to have you and Lord Crosswick managing the estate. That is, for some." She left her final two words hanging in the air.

"Needless to say, Philip—um, Lord Crosswick and I appreciate your clear-eyed perspective on all these matters." Genevieve had no idea what 'these matters' might be, but whatever they were, she wanted Mrs. Proctor's viewpoint, even if it were only tittle-tattle between two housekeepers. Genevieve was sure that, as she and Philip delved deeper and became more involved, they would learn many unsettling things about the estate and who was doing what to whom. If a few people had taken advantage of the opportunity to enjoy Wilmingrove Hall or use it for charity or events traditionally hosted by the Lord of the Manor, they would sort it out in time.

Hearing the elevator door open, Mrs. Proctor said, "If there is nothing else, my lady, I need to check on lunch."

"Thank you, Mrs. Proctor. You've given me a lot to think about. Please don't ever hesitate to share your concerns with me." Genevieve looked over Mrs. Proctor's retreating shoulder to see Philip, sweat plastering his running clothes to his lean frame.

"Hi, you disgusting creature." Genevieve wrinkled her nose and scrunched her face in a look of revulsion. "Eeeuuu! Stay away," she giggled, as Philip strode towards her, holding out his arms for a massive hug.

"Come here, my dahling," Philip said in his best Bella Lugosi. "I vant to press my sweaty body against you."

Just in time, Genevieve stuck her foot into Philip's firm abdomen, holding him at bay. They laughed like kids as Philip grabbed Genevieve's foot in his two hands and proceeded to do "this little piggy."

Genevieve squealed, wrenching her foot from Philip's hands. "Would you please go take a shower? You're revolting!"

"Come in with me?" Philip leered.

Genevieve giggled as he leaned forward and licked the tip of her nose.

"Is that a yes?" he asked.

"Ugh! Absolutely not!" She pushed him away and grimaced as she touched his soaked t-shirt. "As tempting as it is, 'No' has to be my answer. Really, Philip. Go. Go take a shower and when you're clean, I'll tell you what I did while you loped around Central Park." Admiring his lean frame, Genevieve watched as he dragged his dripping body toward the bedroom.

Their apartment offered several wonderful places to dine, and Philip and Genevieve were having lunch in Genevieve's current favorite: a small room just off the kitchen, where floor-to-ceiling paned windows overlooked the south end of Central Park. Across the park's vast green expanse, one could see the upper floors of the Plaza Hotel. Though the apartment's interior was perfection, the view beyond the windows was the real star.

"Can you imagine sitting here in the winter during a snowstorm?" said Genevieve.

"Hmm?" Philip looked up from a sheaf of papers he was reviewing. "Sorry, G. What did you say?"

"I said, 'Can you imagine sitting here during a snowstorm?' What are you reading?'"

"Just more legal papers. A courier brought them while I was running. David's coming over this afternoon to talk about them." He flapped the pages at her. "You need to look at these. It's information about the foundation: its mission, finances, and the biographies of the people running it. It's interesting."

"Does it look as if it's well run?" Genevieve rose and walked to the sideboard where a bottle of white Bordeaux sat in a silver wine cooler.

"I haven't done a deep dive, but its endowments are growing at a respectable rate and the expenditures are pretty consistent from year to year. Why was that your first question?" Philip held up his glass for a refill.

"Mrs. Proctor seems to think the law firm is using Wilmingrove Hall as its own personal playground! Maybe they're diddling the foundation as well. So, what do you think of that, Lord Crosswick?" Looking smug, Genevieve plopped back into her chair.

"When you say the law firm is enjoying the use of the Hall, I assume you really mean the partners."

Genevieve nodded.

Philip picked up his glass and took a generous gulp.

"I know, I know." Genevieve rolled her eyes and bobbed her head side to side. "It probably was an arrangement Jonathon Laney made years ago with the firm and when I said it out loud, it sounded a tiny bit petty, but…."

"But you're new to this being-a-billionaire thing so you decided a few Londoners playing country squire, shooting a few of our squab and drinking a few bottles of our claret would put a dent in our finances. Is that about it?" Philip chuckled.

"Honestly, Philip, the way Ms. Proctor told me, in such confidence…" Genevieve twisted the yellow linen napkin in her lap. She looked across the table at Philip. "So, you think this is nothing?"

Still smiling, Philip put his elbows on the table, leaned forward and whispered, "I think, as lovely as she is, Mrs. Proctor wants to ingratiate herself. By offering juicy tidbits of insider information, she thinks she'll gain value in your eyes."

"Whoa! Look at you, getting all psychological, Lord Fancy

Pants! I think she has reservations about what's going on across the pond and she doesn't want us to be blindsided. So there!"

"Okay. We'll keep that in mind. In the meantime, David will be here any minute. I'm assuming we have some dessert we can offer him." Philip began clearing the table.

"Only what you made." Genevieve smacked Philip's butt as he walked by.

Walking in on the conversation, Mrs. Proctor said, "Did I hear something about dessert? How about chocolate souffles with fresh raspberries?"

With a dazzling smile Philip said, "Mrs. Proctor, you are, without a doubt, my favorite housekeeper!"

FIVE

A T 7:05 P.M. the Warwick's plane was wheels up. It hadn't taken long for Philip and Genevieve to decide they couldn't live without their private jet. After drinks and a four-course dinner, there were still a few hours for sleep during the seven-and-a-half-hour flight from Teterboro to London City Airport.

Quickly adjusting to their new life, Philip and Genevieve were unsurprised by the dark emerald Rolls Royce Phantom waiting on the tarmac to motor them through the Saturday morning traffic, into London, to their solicitors. Today's meetings would deal with issues that must be addressed on English soil.

As they passed the Tower of London, Genevieve watched rowers slide across the waters of the Thames in perfect rhythm. Across the river, the Eye gave visitors a bird's-eye view of the city. She loved London and all things English and had since she was a child. She pinched her palm just to make sure she wasn't dreaming. It was hard to believe she and Philip had abruptly become a part of English history. The Rolls threaded its way through the traffic until the Palace of Westminster loomed before them.

"Philip." Genevieve turned away from the window. "Do I remember correctly from our conversations with David that, because you're foreign-born, you can't vote in Parliament?"

"Exactly. So, in essence, my peerage is all play, no work. Not a bad gig." He beamed. "I think, however, from what we've learned so far, fulfilling my responsibilities as Earl of Crosswick is going to be a full-time job."

"There's no question you have big shoes to fill to keep the estate on a sound financial course, but you know, my darling, you're more than up to the task."

Philip touched Genevieve's cheek then took her hand. "I'm counting on you to widen the influence of the Foundation. I know you're excited about what we can accomplish with this new-found wealth and influence and you're just the girl to do it. Granted, it's not Bill Gates' or Jeff Bezos' money," they both laughed, "but there's plenty we can do with what we have. I can't wait to develop a plan and get moving."

They had no idea how to proceed, but they had plenty of clever people at their disposal who could help them figure it out and they had confidence David Weatherington would be at the head of that team.

An hour after they landed, the Rolls glided to the curb at 26 Upper Brook Street and stopped in front of an Edwardian building of white stone where window boxes overflowed with creeping jenny and wave petunias and fat pillars announced the entrance. Since 1864, the London offices of Holmes Fitch Smythson Morrow had been ensconced here.

Less than a week ago, Philip and Genevieve walked into the firm's offices in New York City unnerved by the mystery of what lay ahead. Today, they were collected and self-assured as they entered the elegant building. They were ready to assume their new roles. It was amazing what a difference a few days could make, and how quickly they had become comfortable in their new shoes.

"Hi there, you two." David Weatherington emerged from the elevator just as Philip and Genevieve entered the paneled lobby. "Have you got into any mischief since I left you in New York?"

"We've hardly had time. This estate assumption thing has kept us too busy, David." Genevieve beamed at their new friend. "And you're not helping. Forms, forms, forms, sign, sign, sign, fly here, fly there on our private jet, visit our posh properties, make sure everyone bows and scrapes when we enter a room. I mean, David, it's exhausting!" Genevieve flopped down on a sofa, flung out her arms, and threw back her head. "Simply exhausting! I don't know how long we can keep up this pace without buckets of Champagne!"

David rolled his eyes. A chuckle started in his throat, turning into a full-blown laugh. "My God! You've gone mad under the strain of becoming obscenely wealthy! Champagne, please, Mrs. Connley." He nodded to the receptionist as he ushered Philip and Genevieve into the elevator car.

"Are you ready for some fun?" David pressed the button for the fifth floor. "The partners who weren't in New York are all here to make sure everything goes smoothly. You're about to enjoy some major arse-kissing from some very pompous arses!"

Philip's eyebrows shot up, he said, "Isn't that rather risky talk?" Though their relationship had grown quickly to an "old mate" closeness since their first telephone exchange less than a week ago, David's cheeky candor was still a bit shocking.

Noting Philip's look of surprise, David quickly said, "Though some pompous men are waiting for you, a fine firm represents your interests. And you have some of the UK's sharpest estate law minds protecting your inheritance and minimizing your tax liability. And, best of all, you have me as your loyal dogsbody! As you can tell, I'm comfortable with you both, and I already feel a strong loyalty to you. I suppose it's because of all those months I spent chasing you down. I think of you two as friends. I hope the feeling is mutual and our relationship will last well into the years to come because, if that's not the case, I've just flushed my professional future in the loo."

Philip patted David on the back. "Now that you've called the senior partners a bunch of arses, I'm pretty sure you have to do our bidding forever! What do you think, G?"

"No question. Benedict Arnold had nothing on this guy. He's very lucky we already consider him an asset. Otherwise, we'd turn him over to the redcoats in a heartbeat!" Genevieve snickered.

"You two better be nice to me. I'm your inside man, your secret weapon." David sobered the conversation. "If it's still all right, I'm planning to come to Wilmingrove Hall this weekend. As I said in New York, I have a few things I need to discuss with you."

"We're planning on it, David. We can send the helicopter back for you." Philip scrunched his face into a crazy grin. "I can't believe I just said that!"

"Amazing how quickly you're adjusting to having obscene wealth. Now remember. Don't let on what I said about the other partners."

The elevator slowed to a stop, the doors opened and there stood Sir Mark, smiling like a Cheshire cat.

SIX

"ALL I WANT is a long soak in a hot bath with bubbles up to my chin." Genevieve lay her head back on the buttery leather of the Rolls' headrest. She closed her eyes against the evening London traffic.

"We'll be at the townhouse in just a few minutes." Philip covered Genevieve's hand with his and squeezed. "I'm ready for a scotch by the fire and dinner. There's no rush in the morning to get to Wilmingrove Hall."

Genevieve opened her eyes and looked at Philip. "You're right. The helicopter isn't going to leave without us, is it?"

"And that's why it's good to be us." Philip pulled Genevieve's hand to his lips and kissed her palm.

"After I get out of the tub, I want to wander through the house. From all the photos we've seen, it's quite beautiful, don't you think?"

"If you like old money elegance, it's alright I guess." Philip's smile was relaxed. "G, what would you expect after New York? Jonathon knew how to do it right."

The Rolls turned off Kensington Road onto Victoria Road.

Two blocks down, their driver stopped in front of the white, stately townhouse.

Walking through the black lacquered front door, they smelled the aroma of warm pastry and spices.

"Oh my," Genevieve sighed as she walked through the foyer into the quiet lounge. Sitting on the sideboard was an ice bucket chilling a bottle of something delicious, no doubt. On a silver tray, just begging to be eaten, were little pastry shells piled with cheese and bits of sausage still warm from the oven. Genevieve held out her hands, palms forward as she walked to the fire blazing on the hearth. She turned to warm her back and faced the living room. "Two weeks ago, we thought our lives were perfect," she said to Philip who slouched in the doorway watching her. "Boy, was I wrong. I had no idea how wonderful it would be to have people anticipate our every need. Jeeze, Philip! How did we manage?"

"Good evening, my lord, my lady. What a pleasure to have you here. I'm Mrs. Baker, your housekeeper." Short and sturdy, Mrs. Baker looked every inch the part of an English housekeeper. From her fuzzy halo of hair to her white starched shirt, from her cable knit cardigan to her tweed skirt, right down to her sensible brogues she was a character straight out of a cozy crime novel. "Cook thought you might enjoy a drink and hearty dinner after your busy day."

Genevieve beamed. "Philip and I have been looking forward to meeting you. What a treat to come home to a cozy fire and dinner waiting." Genevieve walked toward the chilling bottle.

"Allow me, Lady Crosswick." Mrs. Baker hastened across the

room to the sideboard. "Lord Crosswick, would you care for a glass of wine, or can I get you something a bit stronger?"

"Something stronger, please. For the last hour I've been thinking of nothing else but a scotch in front of the fire. Neat, please, Mrs. Baker."

Mrs. Baker delivered the drinks then passed the hors d'oeuvres. "Will there be anything else?" she asked.

"I can't imagine what it might be." Genevieve put her nose in her wine glass sampling the bouquet then drank. "This is wonderful," she said. "Is it ours?" It amused her how quickly she had adapted to owning a world-class vineyard.

"Yes, my lady. It's a blend from Chateau Beaulieu, your vineyard. I'm glad you like it. Please let me know when you're ready for dinner."

"I was going to bathe, but all of a sudden I'm ravenous."

Philip nodded. "I'm ready to eat any time."

"Shall we say fifteen minutes?" Mrs. Baker raised her eyebrows.

"Perfect."

"Well, this is pretty wonderful." Genevieve wiggled her shoulders deeper into the overstuffed sofa. She rolled her head trying to work out a kink in her neck. "I need a good massage. I'm wondering if Mrs. Baker does that as well. She seems to take care of everything." Genevieve looked at Philip, who was staring into the fire. "Philip, are you okay?"

"Listen, G. Something's been plaguing me this entire day. Sitting in the meetings, I got this overwhelming sense of being out of my depth."

"I don't understand." She saw a look on Philip's face she didn't recognize. "What do you mean?"

"I mean this is a vast, complicated estate and I don't know that I—that *we*—have the skills to navigate it."

"I think we've done very well over the years, don't you?"

"We have, in a big fish, little pond way. We've done very well. But this is swimming-with-the-sharks territory and, while we both have the capability, I don't think we have the experience for this."

"But Philip, we have this massive team of attorneys and accountants managing every aspect of the estate."

"And that's one of my concerns. The partners didn't miss any opportunity to point out how invaluable they are and how we can't negotiate this complex estate without them. They took great pains to impress upon us how we should leave everything in their hands and not worry our pretty little heads about anything but having a good time. Isn't that the fox guarding the henhouse? I'm sure you noticed Sir Mark's reaction when I told him I was going to have our lawyers in the states review the powers of attorney. I keep thinking about what Mrs. Proctor intimated about the firm using Wilmingrove Hall as their own playground. If they're doing something so obvious, why wouldn't we think they're taking money from the estate in more surreptitious ways?" He took a deep drink, lamp light bouncing off his facetted glass. "You're the first one who was suspicious. What happened to that?"

"I guess I felt a little silly when you made fun of me. And, as you just said, everyone at the law firm makes me feel that they know what they're doing. You're the one who convinced me to enjoy what we have and see where it takes us. Can't you just do that?"

"I don't know. After today, I don't I feel comfortable being blissfully ignorant. Before he left us in New York, Michael cautioned me to look at everything that's being done, supposedly on our behalf. I kept thinking about that today. That's why I'm sending him the POA's. We'll see what he says.

Genevieve sighed. "What do you think about David?"

"I like him, don't you?"

"Very much. Do you trust him?"

"Oddly, yes."

"That is odd given what you just said about the other members of the firm."

Philip put his empty glass on the coffee table and turned to look at Genevieve. "Look, G. I'm just trying to share my concerns with you. You're always asking me to tell you what I'm thinking. I just did. All I'm saying is let's not be complacent or captivated. Let's listen to our gut and yes, enjoy our good fortune, but we need to stay in control. We'll make some judgements and, if we have to make any changes, we will."

Genevieve opened her mouth to respond just as Mrs. Baker entered the room. "My lord, my lady, dinner is served."

SEVEN

GENEVIEVE'S PINK TOES peaked through the mounds of bubbles filling the claw-footed bath. Resting her head against the porcelain tub, she breathed in the woodsy, floral fragrance of her bath gel, her lids drooping until they closed. When at last she opened her eyes, her mind began to wander, wondering if Jonathon had ever made love to his fiancée in this bathtub. She imagined him with a white towel wrapped around his waist, lathering his face to shave, and looking at Katherine in the gilt-framed mirror above the sink.

Genevieve's mind floated from Jonathon to Philip and their earlier conversation. Philip was right. Since she had known him, the one thing she found most annoying about him was how taciturn he was when she most wanted to hear his thoughts. In their early married years, it was the source of more than one heated argument, always one-sided since he refused to jump into the verbal fray. Why did he choose now to be so forthcoming, just when she had shoved her earlier concerns about the law firm misusing the estate to the back of her mind?

"Life can be impossibly difficult when you're filthy rich," Genevieve giggled.

Goosebumps rose on her arms and she realized the water was no longer warm. As she stood, bubbles slid down her legs into the water. Wrapping herself in the warmth of thick terrycloth, she smiled. She loved that the English didn't like cold towels or dinner plates and always warmed both.

Cozy in a gray cashmere bathrobe and slippers, Genevieve brushed her hair back from her face and proceeded with her evening ritual. She leaned close to the mirror looking at the lines around her eye. "Can't you just stay away," she said to the crow's feet and dabbed elixir at the corner of each eye. Surveying her face, she tugged with her fingertips, coaxing the edges of her jaw up. "Hmmm, maybe just a little tuck wouldn't hurt." She opened a jar that smelled of lavender and marjoram.

Hearing the door open in the next room she called, "Philip, is that you?" Moisturizer covering her fingertips, her hand stopped mid-circle on her forehead as she listened.

"Philip?" she said again. She patted the remaining cream on her cheekbones as she walked into the bedroom.

The door stood wide. Genevieve shivered, startled at the cold air. "How strange," she said, crossing her arms for warmth as she stepped into the hall. Seeing no one, she came back into the room, latching the door behind her. Her nose caught the distinct fragrance of roses. She scanned the room, looking for a bouquet but saw none.

At last, she said to herself, "What is the matter with you? You think someone who wears old-fashioned rosewater came into your bedroom then turned around and left? Get a grip, girl. You have lots of things to think about and someone creeping into your room isn't one of them." She chuckled at her pep talk and headed back to the bathroom.

Finished with her regimen, she went in search of Philip who was still in the living room. Since dinner, he had been sitting by the fire with his briefcase open, surrounded by papers.

Genevieve kissed the top of his head. "Do you know if Mrs. Baker came upstairs while I was in the tub?"

"No, she was here talking to me most of the time. She has some great stories about Jonathon. Why do you ask?"

"I just had the strangest experience," she said. Eyes bright with excitement, she told Philip what had happened. "Do you think it was anything?"

"I don't know what you mean by, 'anything.' Do you mean was it something other than the bedroom door of a two-hundred-year-old house not closing properly and opening because of air movement from the furnace? Probably not."

"But what about the smell of roses?"

"Furniture polish?"

"Boy! You have an answer for everything, don't you?"

"Pretty much," Philip said, smiling a superior smile.

Feeling silly that she had been unnerved by a cold room and a pretty fragrance, Genevieve appreciated the logical explanations. She grabbed Philip's hand, trying to tug him out of his chair. "Come on. Take a break and explore the house with me, Mr. Smarty Pants?"

"You go ahead. I want to finish going over this stock portfolio.

At least this is something I understand." Philip looked up at Genevieve's scrubbed face. Marveling at her enduring beauty, he touched her velvet cheek. "Bring back something interesting to tell me," he said. "Do you want to take a glass of Port with you?"

"Great idea." Genevieve looked around. "Do you know where the Port might be?"

"Watch this." Philip moved his foot and pressed a button under the carpet with the toe of his shoe. Within seconds, Mrs. Baker appeared. He looked at Genevieve with a serious face but laughing eyes. "Mrs. Baker, could you please get Lady Crosswick a Port? She's going to explore the townhouse and thought it would be nice to take it with her."

"Tawny or Ruby Port, my lady?"

"Tawny, please. That would be perfect." She leaned over and whispered to Philip, "Great party trick."

Mrs. Baker returned with a Scotch refill for Philip and a small, stemmed glass containing amber liquid, which swished as she walked. "Your Port, my lady. Would you like me to come with you to explore the house? I'd love to share some of its stories. There is a lot of interesting history here at Margrave House."

"I would love that." Genevieve delighted at the idea of having a docent guide her through the historic home. "Shall we?"

Philip watched the two women as they left the room, one tall, willowy, gliding, the other short, stout, waddling. When they were gone, he brought the Scotch glass to his nose and sniffed at the smokey bite of the peat. He took a sip and wondered what tales Genevieve would have when she returned.

Mrs. Baker led the way down the hall to a double doorway. She flipped a light switch and the ash-paneling of the study glowed with lamp light.

"What a wonderful room," Genevieve said. Looking at the double-sided partners desk and floor-to-ceiling bookcases, it was easy to conclude this was the 12TH Earl's sanctuary.

"It is special, isn't it?" Mrs. Baker's eyes misted. "His last few years, Lord Crosswick spent most of his time here or in his bedroom. It's dark now so you can't see it, but there's a lovely view of the garden."

"You were with him for a long time, weren't you?"

"Thirty-seven years, my lady, every year a pleasure."

As they spoke, Genevieve wandered around the 12TH Earl's study. She stopped in front of a full-length painting, hanging above the green marble fireplace. A stunning young matron beamed from the canvas, surrounded by three children: a solemn boy with his hand protectively on his mother's shoulder and two girls, both with their mother's smile and mischief in their eyes. "Oh my," Genevieve was struck by the woman's radiance. "Who is this beauty?"

"Ah." Mrs. Baker's wistful smile promised a tender story. "This is the spectacular Charlotte Camille Chaubert, Countess of Crosswick, wife of Philip George Winston Laney, the 9TH Earl of Crosswick. She was French and brought a great deal of style to this house and Wilmingrove Hall, as you will see when you're there. She and the Earl were the forces behind the Laney Museum of Fine Arts here in London. Charlotte was also an animal lover; she and

Lord Crosswick were major donors to many animal rights groups."

"If she was half as magical as she looks, she must have been spectacular. Look how radiant she is. Please tell me she and the Earl were mad about each other?"

"They adored each other, and London adored them." Mrs. Baker pulled a tissue from her cardigan pocket and blew her nose. Her eyes clouded with tears.

"What is it, Mrs. Baker? Have I said something to upset you?"

"Indeed not, my lady." Mrs. Baker sniffed and dabbed at her eyes. "I'm so sorry, but their story ends so tragically. It always makes me sad."

"What do you mean? What happened? Tell me, please." Holding Mrs. Baker's gaze, Genevieve sat on the corner of the desk.

"On the evening of the Earl and Countess' fortieth wedding anniversary, they invited thirty friends for dinner, men in white tie and women in satin and feathers and jewels. The guests gathered in the foyer with Champagne, waiting to toast the countess when she made her grand entrance."

Genevieve leaned forward, not wanting to miss a word.

"When Charlotte appeared, beaming at the top of the stairs in a silver gown, all the guests fell silent. She was still breathtaking at sixty-four, with her hair piled high and diamonds flashing at her ears. The gown's train swept to her side. At the foot of the stairs, the Earl raised his glass to toast her, and said," Mrs. Baker cleared her throat before she said in a tearful voice, "'To my magnificent bride of forty years. No one else has ever walked the earth, whom I could love as I love you.'"

"What a romantic toast. I can see why you get a bit misty when you tell this story." With the back of her hand, Genevieve wiped a tear from her cheek.

"At the end of the toast, the band struck up Charlotte's favorite song 'Oh You Beautiful Doll' and Charlotte blew a kiss to the Earl. When she started down the stairs, the toe of her shoe hooked on her gown's silver train. She tried to grab the banister, but missed and tumbled head over heels, smashing her head over and over on the stairs. By the time she reached the bottom, her neck had snapped." Mrs. Baker's voice broke as she finished the story. "To this day, we feel her presence. We smell her perfume wafting through the house."

The blood drained from Genevieve's face. For an instant she felt an icy hand on her shoulder then it was gone. Eyes wide, breath shallow, Genevieve asked, "Was her fragrance a rose scent?" She held her breath waiting for the answer.

Mrs. Baker's eyebrows shot up and her mouth formed a perfect 'O.' "How did you guess? She wore Otto of Roses, an elegant scent made from a very special Bulgarian rose."

"Mrs. Baker." Genevieve felt faint.

"What is it, my lady? Are you all right?" The housekeeper took Genevieve by the arm and helped her to a chair next to the desk. She handed Genevieve the Port. "Drink this," she ordered.

The heat of the wine slid down her throat as Genevieve drained the glass. Looking into the face of the woman who had cared for this house for nearly four decades, her eyes burned with tears. "Mrs. Baker, Charlotte came to my bedroom tonight."

EIGHT

EYES WILD, ROBE flapping, Genevieve burst into the living room. "Philip, come with me!"

Philip saw the sweat on Genevieve's brow as she tugged him to stand. "What's going on? Did something happen?"

She pulled Philip toward the door. "It did, but it was more than a hundred years ago." A hand on each shoulder, Genevieve pushed Philip in front of the painting of Charlotte Chaubert.

He threw a concerned glance at Mrs. Baker.

"It wasn't the furnace that opened the bedroom door, and it wasn't furniture polish I smelled," Genevieve said, defiance emphasizing each word. "You see the woman in this painting?"

"I do," Philip said, caution edging his voice. "She's beautiful. Who is she?"

"Mrs. Baker, please tell Philip, er, Lord Crosswick, the story you told me."

Mrs. Baker shared the tale again while Genevieve sniffed and whimpered until Mrs. Baker finished.

From her place on the loveseat next to the fireplace, Genevieve said, "That's who came into the bedroom tonight. That's whose perfume I smelled."

Philip rubbed his face with both hands, before looking at Mrs. Baker and then Genevieve, his brows arched. "Mrs. Baker, do you think that's the case?"

Mrs. Baker twisted the tissue in her hand, her voice quivering. "Well, people have spoken for a century of the countess having a presence in Margrave House. I never met Charlotte directly, but I did witness an event. In fact, a young woman who was here for about a year helping the Earl, had several encounters with Lady Charlotte. It was in this very room they met for the first time."

The hall clock bonged, and Philip jumped, hairs prickling on the back of his neck. "Wow, that startled me," he laughed.

"Spooky, isn't it?" Genevieve met his laughter with hers.

Humoring Genevieve, Philip said, "Sure, G. Maybe just a little. But what about this girl who encountered Charlotte? How was she helping my cousin?"

"Do you mean professionally or personally?" Posing the question as delicately as she could, the color rose in Mrs. Baker's cheeks.

"I'm not sure how to answer that." Philip shrugged. "Uh, both I guess."

"The young lady was here from America for a year on a Laney Museum of Art Fellowship. Lord Crosswick was cataloging his collection at Margrave House and requested an intern from the LMFA program to help him."

"And this young American showed up at the door?" Philip asked.

"Lord Crosswick seems to have been drawn to American women," Genevieve said, a note of pride in her voice.

"He was. American women have a lively spirit. I think he was drawn to that. Though he was in his seventies and bound to his wheelchair, Lord Crosswick was handsome, charming, and filled with youthful energy." The housekeeper's eyes sparkled as she talked. "I must admit, even I had a bit of a crush on him." Smiling sweetly, she looked up at Philip and Genevieve through her lashes, seeming much younger than her fifty-seven years. "The young lady, Revy Harris was her name, came three afternoons a week and sometimes on Saturday as well. She and the Earl quickly formed a good working relationship. Midway through the summer, she started staying for dinner, then after a while, she would linger late into the evening. When I served dinner, I began to notice flirtatious glances between the two of them."

"Of course!" With a flash of recognition, Genevieve realized Mrs. Baker had been a witness to history. "You were here at that time!"

"Yes, I was, and, though the Earl and Revy were discrete during their time together, I knew Lord Crosswick was smitten and the relationship was developing into something more than work. My first thought was that she would break his heart. She was very young and seemed... I don't know. She seemed very aggressive. I guess she frightened me a little. But it was wonderful to see Lord Crosswick greet each day with an enthusiasm I'd not seen before. He was always kind and such a gentleman, but after Ms. Harris started coming to the house, he was full of joy."

"Were you jealous at all?" Genevieve surprised herself. Though she had been wondering how Mrs. Baker felt about a young woman sparking life into Jonathon, she hadn't intended to ask the question so directly.

"Oh, my lady." Ms. Baker's laughter filled the room. "You must remember I have been in service since I was eighteen and, except for my first two years as a housemaid in a country house near Woburn, I've been here at Margrave House. I know my place and my feelings for Lord Crosswick were not passion, but admiration."

Genevieve felt heat in the tops of her ears. "Mrs. Baker, I'm so sorry. I didn't mean to insult you."

"You just have to chalk it up to us being spirited Americans," Philip said, his comment bringing smiles all around. "Please tell us about Ms. Harris' encounter with Charlotte. Why in the world would she be the one to cross paths with this aristocratic ghost?"

"Aah. That's a good story, indeed," Mrs. Baker regained her rhythm. "During her first week here, I helped her find records to do her research on the works of art. Those first few days, she would come to the kitchen at teatime, and we'd have a cuppa. I got to know her a bit and found her interesting. Though they had different coloring, she reminded me of pictures I'd seen of Katherine Robeson, the Earl's fiancée. Revy was fair and Katherine had dark hair and olive skin. Maybe it was their eyes. But, as I said, there was something unsettling about her."

Genevieve tucked her legs under her and pulled the edge of her robe over her bare feet. "Can you describe what was unsettling?"

"I've thought a lot about it, but I've never been able to pinpoint why she made me uncomfortable. One day we were looking for a file in the Earl's study and Revy asked about Charlotte's painting. I told her Lady Crosswick's fatal story and the rumors of her lingering presence at Margrave."

"Did that make her run screaming from the house?" Genevieve was only half kidding.

"Quite the contrary, my lady. Revy got very excited. She said she was born en caul, that's when a baby is born with the amniotic sac intact. But that's all I knew."

"We're familiar with a caulbearer." Philip had been sitting in an overstuffed chair for the last few minutes, fatigue overtaking him, but the conversation was so compelling, he didn't want to interrupt it. Stifling a yawn, he said, "Our granddaughter Ella was born en caul. It's very rare and, if Ella is any indication, everything they say about these special babies is true."

"Do you know that people born en caul can be clairvoyant and sensitive to spirts?" Genevieve chimed in.

"Yes, I do now." Eager to share the rest of the tale, Mrs. Baker picked up the pace. "Revy said from the time she was a child, she was able to feel the presence of spirits and she often knew something was about to happen before it did."

"So, she thought she might be able to communicate with Lady Crosswick?" Genevieve asked.

"She did. She was certain of it. And she proved to be right."

"Really?" Philip and Genevieve said in unison.

"How so?" Philip was anxious for facts.

Mrs. Baker walked to the garden window and looked out into the night. The black panes reflected the warmth of the glowing room behind her. Mrs. Baker's husky voice was barely audible as she began. "The first night Revy stayed for dinner, she and the Earl were working here in the study. For the previous two days they had been cataloging the works in this room. That particular day, they spent the afternoon confirming the provenance of Charlotte's portrait."

Genevieve pulled a thick throw from the back of the loveseat and dragged it across her lap.

"When I came into the room to announce dinner, Revy asked if Lord Crosswick and I smelled roses. I smelled nothing. She said the fragrance was overwhelming. As I was about to leave the room a cold wind swirled around Revy, like a tiny tornado. Her long hair stood straight up in the column of wind. Nothing outside of the funnel moved. It only lasted a matter of seconds. The wind stopped as abruptly as it started, leaving no evidence that it had ever happened. If all three of us hadn't witnessed it, we wouldn't have believed that it happened."

Eyes wide, Genevieve was rigid in her chair.

"This really happened?" Philip said. "Right here in this room?"

"Right here where I'm standing." Mrs. Baker pointed at her feet. "It happened right here."

Philip blew out a puff of air, shook his head and said, "Wow. Just wow." He shook his head, then asked, "After that first incident, there were more?"

"Yes, several." Mrs. Baker's eyes danced. "Nothing as dramatic as that first encounter, but small things: a cold hand on Revy's shoulder, a page magically turned in a research book she was using, papers moved on the desk. All things that could be explained away or brushed off. But just before Revy walked out of the door for the last time, she said she felt a frigid kiss on her cheek."

Genevieve walked across the room to the gas logs burning on the hearth. She shivered and tugged the throw around her shoulders. "Why did she leave?"

"Ah, like so many things concerning the 12TH Earl, the parting was sad, and it broke his heart to insist she go."

Genevieve pulled a tissue from her pocket, prepared to dab her tears again.

"Revy was young and beautiful and had her entire life ahead of her. Lord Crosswick didn't want her to wither, spending her years caring for an invalid. I overheard their arguments. She pleaded her love, she begged him to let her stay. He insisted she could not. In the end, he told her she was no longer welcome at Margrave House. And she left, apparently with Charlotte's blessing. I can attest to the fact that was the last romance Lord Crosswick had in his life and he lived many years after that. "He was too beautiful a man to have suffered such tragedy in his life." Mrs. Baker wept quietly for a moment, then dabbed her eyes, sniffed, and walked to the desk. She picked up a small photograph of Revy and handed it to Genevieve. Staring at her was an enchanting sprite, her violet eyes filled with love. Her chin rested on her right hand and on her finger was a massive square ruby surrounded by diamonds.

"What a beauty," Genevieve said. "And what a stunning ruby."

Philip joined her in front of the fire and took the photograph Genevieve handed him. "I see why Jonathon fell in love. I can't imagine how difficult it was to let her go."

"I assure you, he was devastated." The energy had drained from the room. "My lord, my lady, if there's nothing else, I believe I'll retire."

"I think that's a very good idea." Philip's shoulders slumped. "I'm desperate to go to bed, but, Mrs. Baker, this evening has been worth missing a lot of sleep."

Rather than fatigued, Genevieve was energized. Her earlier encounter with Charlotte promised future contact with the spectacular spirit. "I think it's exciting. Thank you, Mrs. Baker for sharing this with us. I look forward to lots of exchanges with the magnificent Charlotte Chaubert."

"Come on, G. Let's go to bed. This is just the beginning of our new life. I have a feeling we're going to need all the rest we can get if we're going to keep up with our adventure." Genevieve massaged the back of her neck as Philip led her out into the hall. "Good night, Mrs. Baker. Sleep well"

"And you, my lord. You don't need to stop and smell the roses tonight." Mrs. Baker chuckled at her joke. She flipped the light switch off and pulled the double doors closed. As she walked away from the study, an icy tingle slid down her spine and she wondered if Charlotte had been watching them.

NINE

To Genevieve, few adventures were more exhilarating than flying in a helicopter. The physics of going straight up and down was more than a little mystifying. It was better than a rollercoaster and harrowing enough to send a shock of excitement through her. She and Philip had taken a helicopter to a glacier in Alaska once, where they were the middle craft in a parade of three. Following the lead chopper through an icy canyon at high speeds was thrilling. That was twenty years ago and now, here they were in an AgustaWestland AS609, an aircraft with the speed, range and altitude of a fixed-wing turboprop airplane and the vertical take-off and landing versatility of a helicopter—and it belonged to them. On opposite sides of the cabin, Philip and Genevieve had their noses pressed against the window, watching the London Heliport on the south bank of the River Thames as it diminished in size. They shot to a thousand feet.

Their pilot, Captain Bruni, greeted them over the intercom. In a lilting Italian accent, he described the sites. "If you look down, you'll see we're following the Thames past Westminster and Big Ben, past St. Paul's. Just after the Tower Bridge we'll turn north and head across the Yorkshire moors to Wilmingrove Hall."

"I assume the coffee I smell brewing is coming our way soon." Philip's arms were folded over his chest and his voice was curt.

"What's the matter with you?" Genevieve pulled her attention from the view to her sulking husband.

"Honestly, G, I'm exhausted. After days of monumental changes in our lives, and last night's ghost fest, I just need time to process everything. Don't you?"

"I think we're looking at this from two very different perspectives." Genevieve changed seats so she faced Philip. "I've gone full circle. I was beyond excited when we heard you inherited your title and all that comes with it." Genevieve leaned forward, her elbows on her knees. "Then, when Mrs. Proctor told me her concerns about Wilmingrove Hall, I was sure the law firm was using the estate as a cash machine. But after you pointed out that Mrs. Proctor was probably just gossiping to ingratiate herself, I decided to stop seeing problems around every corner. I decided to just enjoy our good fortune." She sat back and folded her hands in her lap. "And, as for Charlotte, our beautiful ghost, I'm thrilled. Never in my life did I think we'd own a house with a ghost as a resident. I love it!"

Philip couldn't help smiling at Genevieve's wide eyes and flushed cheeks. He cradled her hands in his and brought them to his lips. His smile faded as he said, "I hate to burst your bubble, but last night when I finished going over the stock portfolios, I studied some of the other files."

"From the look on your face, I assume whatever you found wasn't good."

"Well, for one thing, there have been a lot of huge expenditures over the last eighteen months, one of which is this helicopter. Why do we own a twenty-five-million-dollar helicopter?" In response to Genevieve's look of surprise, Philip said, "That's what was expensed. I mean, don't you think it's unlikely Jonathon, the recluse, bought a helicopter on his deathbed? This fabulous aircraft isn't more than a couple of years old! Who bought it?"

"That's a good question." Genevieve leaned forward again, scooting to the edge of her seat.

Philip continued, "The last two years, while Jonathon was in failing health, Holmes Fitch Smythson Morrow, as trustees, have had free rein over the estate. If they chose to—" Philip stopped mid-sentence.

An enthusiastic young steward brought a tray of coffee and chocolate-covered biscuits through to the passenger cabin. "Excuse me, my lord. May I serve coffee?"

Genevieve looked at the young man's name badge. "Thank you, William." She smiled up at him as he stooped to avoid the cabin's low ceiling. "My husband was just saying he would kill for a cup of coffee, so you may have saved both our lives."

"My pleasure, my lady." William grinned, showing a gap in his front teeth.

"So, William, do you always crew this craft?" Philip was anxious to know more about their pricey asset.

"Yes, until recently, my lord. But I'm about to join your Bombardier crew. I also staff at Wilmingrove Hall when they need me." William's face radiated the enthusiasm of a young man on the brink of a big adventure.

Genevieve couldn't help but smile. "Well, we're delighted you're with us. There are a lot of exciting things ahead for all of us."

"How often does this helicopter fly?" asked Philip, still wanting to know more about the chopper.

"A couple of times a month. A few of the partners from the law firm go between Wilmingrove Hall and London pretty often." Eager to endear himself to his new employer, William continued. "They do know how to enjoy themselves." As the words came out of his mouth, William seemed to know he had overstepped his bounds. "I beg your pardon. That was most inappropriate," he back peddled. "I look forward to serving you any way I can, my lady, my lord. Please never hesitate to call on me, even for the smallest thing."

Amused by his embarrassment, Philip said, "Thank you, William. I hope you don't live to regret that!"

William offered an uncomfortable nod as he poured coffee from the Laney-crested china pot into mugs.

"Will there be anything else, my lord?"

"I think we're good for now. Thank you, William," Philip said.

"My lord." Nodding, William backed out of the cabin.

Genevieve waited for William to exit. As soon as he was back in his forward seat, she turned to Philip, sloshing her coffee, a few drops landing on her jeans.

"Well!" She said in a loud whisper as she set her mug on the console beside her. "How about that? If you need one, you have a spy already in place! You two can play sleuth and I'll just enjoy myself. How's that for a plan?" Genevieve vibrated with excitement and Philip couldn't help chuckling, captivated by his bride of many years. Though Genevieve was a beauty in jeans or a ball gown, working at her computer or pulling weeds in the garden, at this moment, she was breathtaking. Philip reached out and pulled her head towards him until her face was within inches of his. Staring deep into her green eyes he said, "You're a mad woman and I love you for it!" He kissed her lightly on her lips then deepened the kiss until there was heat. "If we had any privacy, I would be on top of you right now."

"Coward," Genevieve said. "Where's your sense of adventure?" She unlatched her seatbelt. Before he realized what she was doing, Genevieve had straddled him and was returning his kiss, hers even more urgent than his. Philip grabbed Genevieve's bottom, a cheek in each hand and squeezed. Pulling back, she said, "The minute we're alone, you're on!"

"Oh, you think? I'm not sure I can wait that long. I may jump you when you least expect it!"

"Jump me?" Genevieve laughed, sitting back in her seat, and refastening her seatbelt. "I don't think I've ever heard you use that phrase before."

Philip laughed, "I've never been an outrageously wealthy nobleman before."

Before Genevieve could reply, the intercom crackled. "Lord and Lady Crosswick, this is Captain Bruni. We are twenty-five miles from Wilmingrove Hall and have begun our decent so please make certain your seatbelts are secure. We'll be on the ground in about ten minutes."

Genevieve leaned toward the window, her knees pressed

against Philip's. They looked at each other, linked fingers, then looked back at the view below. Dotted with curly-horned sheep, rolling hills rose and fell. Then, on the horizon, they saw the hazy outline of a huge building nestled in the mist. Second by second the Laney family seat came into sharper focus until Genevieve gasped.

"Are you kidding me?" Philip couldn't believe his eyes.

The Warwicks had seen hundreds of photographs of Wilmingrove Hall and had viewed a drone video of the property. They had read an article in *Britain Magazine* from years ago, featuring Wilmingrove Hall as a "Jacobean Treasure." People repeatedly told them how magnificent the Hall was, but nothing had prepared them for what was coming into focus. Buff-colored Yorkshire stone glowed in the light of the afternoon sun. The helicopter followed the long lane, which was flanked on either side by silver birch and ended with a circular driveway at the front façade. The chopper swooped to the left of the vast building, hovered above the helipad, then set down gently.

Genevieve squeezed Philip's hand. "Oh my," she said. "Just, oh my."

"Here we go." Philip handed Genevieve her sweater.

William came from the galley to open the door. "Lord and Lady Crosswick, welcome home."

The Warwicks ducked through the helicopter door and down the steps. Before them was an imposing sight. Wilmingrove Hall sat on the edge of a manicured bluff overlooking the river. From the front, there was no hint of the exquisite terracing in the back or the acres of parterres.

A fireplug of a woman stood just off the edge of the landing pad, dressed in a tartan skirt, starched white shirt and sensible cordovan oxfords. Her ramrod posture made the most of her stocky five feet. There was no question, this was Bertie MacIntosh, the Scottish head housekeeper.

Though there was plenty of room between the chopper blades and their heads, Philip and Genevieve bent over as they walked toward Mrs. MacIntosh.

"Mrs. MacIntosh?" Philip said holding out his right hand in greeting. "I'm Lord Crosswick and this is, as you may have guessed, Lady Crosswick.

She ignored Philip's hand, which he yanked back. "My lord, my lady, I'm pleased to meet you both and relieved you're here. We've been without a lord of the manor for much too long." Mrs. MacIntosh's sober expression softened only slightly as she offered a small curtsy.

"We're anxious to learn everything about being a proper earl and countess. I'm sure you have a manual that can tell us all we need to know, and we'll be up to speed in no time." Oozing charm, Philip smiled and chuckled, but Mrs. MacIntosh was unamused.

Genevieve gave Philip a discrete elbow in the side and stepped in to smooth things over. "Mrs. MacIntosh, Lord Crosswick and I are grateful for your loyalty to the Laney family and for your years of service here at Wilmingrove Hall. From everything we've been told, you've been an excellent captain on a rudderless ship. We look forward to learning about the estate from you.

As custodians, we'll work to preserve and protect this historic property."

Philip couldn't help but roll his eyes while Genevieve waxed a bit too rhapsodic trying to win over the somber Scot. But it worked.

At Genevieve's words of appreciation and praise, Mrs. MacIntosh's face eased into a soft smile. "Lady Crosswick, I vow to do my best for you and Lord Crosswick. There are many things I know you'll wish to address, and I am at the ready. Shall we go to the Hall? Tea will be served, and the staff is anxious to meet the new Earl and Countess. Wallace had to go to Glasgow yesterday, but he'll be back late this afternoon. He asked me to express his apologies, but it was unavoidable. His sister had to go into hospital, and he is her only sibling."

"I'm sure we should know, but who is Wallace, Mrs. MacIntosh?" Philip asked.

Mrs. MacIntosh looked up at Philip, rolled her eyes and said, "My lord, Wallace has been the butler of Wilmingrove Hall for the last thirty-five years." With that, they got into a stretch golf cart and began the short journey from the landing pad up the hill to embark on the most revealing part of their adventure yet.

TEN

M RS. MACINTOSH SLOWED the golf cart to a stop in front of the Hall's massive front door. Above the oak portal, set into Yorkshire stone, was a weathered Laney crest with its family motto, "Garde Le Roi."

Mrs. MacIntosh smiled with pride as she explained, "The motto, 'Guard the King,' comes from the Laney family's role saving King Charles II. Your ancestor, Colonel John Laney, was a supporter of the king. After the Battle of Worcester, where Cromwell's army defeated the Royalists, Charles fled for his life. Colonel Laney hid the future king at his mansion in Staffordshire. From there the fugitive prince was taken, in disguise, by the Colonel's eldest sister, Jane, to her cousin's residence in Bristol."

"It sounds dangerous." Genevieve was riveted.

"It was. If it had been discovered they were helping Charles, they could have lost everything, including their lives." Mrs. MacIntosh's admiration was obvious. "After the restoration of Charles to the throne," Mrs. MacIntosh continued, "the Crown demonstrated its gratitude to the Laney family. Jane received an annual Royal pension of £1,000 for life. Her brother, John, was granted the Arms of England, the three lions on a red field and the Royal Crown. As you can see," Mrs. MacIntosh pointed to the crest, "the Arms of England were combined with the motto, 'Garde Le Roi,' to create the Laney coat of arms."

Looking up at the crest, Philip was overcome with the reality that he was the next link in an unbroken chain of rich, important history. His eyes stung. He cleared his throat. "I, um, I'm a bit overwhelmed," he said. "I didn't expect this to be such an emotional experience. Being here at Wilmingrove Hall makes it all real. Until now, it's been about balance sheets, big numbers, and a lot of fun, but being here, where my ancestors built a legacy over hundreds of years...well, I feel it. It hadn't occurred to me that I would experience such a connection."

Genevieve squeezed Philip's hand.

Mrs. MacIntosh smiled, pleased. "It doesn't surprise me, my lord. It doesn't surprise me at all. The Laneys are a compelling family with great strengths passed from generation to generation. It's no wonder you are beginning to feel the Laney blood coursing through your veins. And I would venture to say this is only the beginning. You and Lady Crosswick are going to be glorious standard bearers."

Philip tucked Genevieve's hand under his arm. "I'm going to need all the encouragement I can get," he said, offering the two women a sheepish smile.

"I will be your biggest cheerleader," Mrs. MacIntosh said. "Now, would you like to see where your cousin lived as a child?"

"Yes, please," Philip answered.

Mrs. MacIntosh stood aside for Philip and Genevieve to

precede her through the door, but Philip motioned her to go ahead. "Please, Mrs. MacIntosh, lead the way."

"As you wish, my lord." She stepped through the door and into the grand salon.

Walking into the imposing hall, Genevieve was assaulted by the strong fragrance of roses pouring from a large blue and white ginger jar sitting on a sideboard. She inhaled recalling Charlotte Chaubert's perfume and shivered.

"Are you chilly, Lady Crosswick?" Mrs. MacIntosh was quick to ask.

"Oh, no. I'm fine," Genevieve said. "But I do have a crazy question. Do you know about Charlotte Camille Chaubert, the 9TH Earl of Crosswicks' wife?"

"Oh, the beautiful Charlotte." Mrs. MacIntosh raised her clasped hands to her chin. "Isn't the Countess's story tragic? I spoke to Mrs. Baker this morning and she told me you met Charlotte last night, in a manner of speaking."

Genevieve opened her mouth, closed it, opened it again before she spoke. "Well, I, um," Genevieve stammered. "Um, as you said, what a tragedy. I cried when Mrs. Baker told me how she died."

"Yes, Mrs. Baker said you were moved to tears."

Genevieve shouldn't have been uncomfortable that the two housekeepers had been gossiping about their new lord and lady, but she was.

"So, what did you think of our resident ghost?" Mrs. MacIntosh asked.

"When you say resident ghost, do you mean the ghost who lives at Margrave House?"

Mrs. MacIntosh leaned close to Genevieve and dropped her voice to a whisper. "Occasionally, she spends time here, at Wilmingrove Hall."

"Are you serious?"

"I'm quite serious, my lady. For the last few years, she's been coming once or twice a year. Usually around the holidays or during an event. She was last here in the winter when Sir Mark brought clients for a shoot."

"How did you know she was here?" Genevieve realized she had lowered her voice to meet the housekeeper's whisper and bent over so she and Mrs. MacIntosh almost touched foreheads.

"The shotgun shells are kept in the estate office under lock and key. On the morning of the shoot, every single shell had been replaced with a rose. The shooting party couldn't find a shell anywhere." Mrs. MacIntosh beamed. It was obvious she loved telling this story. She raised her hand before Genevieve could comment. "I know. You're going to say anyone could have been playing a prank. But the stable girl, Missy Overton, swears she saw a woman in a shimmery, silver dress sweep through the barn the night before, carrying a basket. When Harrington checked the security cameras, he saw what looked like whisps of smoke wafting through the stable hall. The next day, he found the basket in the tack room. Full of shells."

Genevieve said nothing for a moment, then she threw back her head, howling with laughter. Still giggling, she said, "This is great. I guess our ghost has quite a sense of humor. She's going to be a lot of fun to have around. Mrs. Baker mentioned Charlotte was quite an animal activist. Think of all the pheasants who lived another day thanks to Charlotte exchanging roses for shells."

Wandering from room to room, engrossed in one spectacular painting after another, Philip heard Genevieve's roar of laughter. "What's going on? What did I miss?" he said as he returned to the grand salon.

"Mrs. MacIntosh just told me that Charlotte is in residence with us from time to time here, at the Hall."

"Oh, is she?" Philip's eyes sparkled. "Well, that's exciting. Another beautiful woman at the Hall! Is she here now?" Philip smirked.

"Scoff if you will." Mrs. MacIntosh looked at him over the wire rims of her glasses. "When you're awakened by an icy touch on your cheek and the smell of Otto Rose perfume in your room, don't expect me to come running," she said, with surprising cheek.

"Mrs. MacIntosh," Genevieve soothed. "As I told Philip this morning, I love Charlotte's presence. What could be better than her enchanting spirit hovering around us? If she's a kind ghost, that is."

"She has always been funny and charming, and she loves playing tricks. So be on your toes. Especially you, Lord Crosswick. She adores handsome men."

Philip blushed.

"I see no reason for her to change," Mrs. MacIntosh said. "Lady Crosswick, what made you think about Charlotte?"

"A few minutes ago, when we walked into the foyer, I smelled roses. The fragrance reminded me of my encounter with Charlotte yesterday, and I did wonder if she ever comes here. Apparently, the answer is yes. Where do you get these gorgeous blossoms?" Genevieve asked, burying her nose in a fuchsia floret.

"They're grown right here. Your gardens and greenhouse are designed for year-round blossoms, herbs, cold-weather vegetables and, of course, we have our own chickens, eggs, lambs and plenty of fish and game. Do you shoot, my lord?"

"Not yet," Philip said. "But I could be persuaded to learn. I like the clothes."

Philip's infectious grin coaxed a giggle from Mrs. MacIntosh and the color rose in her cheeks.

"You would cut a fine figure in a tweed shooting jacket and breeks, my lord," she gushed.

Genevieve leaned into Philip and whispered in his ear. "I believe Mrs. MacIntosh just batted her eyelashes at you."

Mrs. MacIntosh scurried ahead of the Warwicks. "Come, let me show you to your room. You can freshen up before tea." She led Philip and Genevieve through the grand salon to the grand staircase.

Looking up to the landing, Genevieve struggled for words. At last she said, "This is like something from a movie set. It's stunning. And everything is perfect. I don't see any cracks in the plaster, any peeling paint. It must take a lot to keep everything so beautifully preserved."

"I'm glad you're pleased, my lady." Mrs. MacIntosh fidgeted. "Sir Mark is fastidious about the maintenance of the Hall. He spares…" Mrs. MacIntosh caught herself. "He's a fine custodian of the estate," she finished.

Climbing the stairs, Philip stopped midway. He looked up twenty feet at the paneled walls covered with portraits painted over several centuries. "Mrs. MacIntosh, are all these portraits my ancestors?"

"They are." Mrs. MacIntosh paused on the landing at the top of the stairs. "There is a book in the library by Kenneth Baron. I'm sure you'll find it interesting. It chronicles all the artwork in the Hall. Not just the paintings, but every piece of art including bronzes, fountains, and any historic architectural elements of note. It's a comprehensive reference work and will be helpful when you have questions about any of the works: their history, their provenance, the artist… anything, really. I'll make certain it's on the library table for you."

"Sorry, I got sidetracked by this stunning landscape," Genevieve called from the bottom of the stairs. "The signature looks like it says 'Gainsborough'."

"It does," said Mrs. MacIntosh. "It was one of his last landscapes."

"I see." Genevieve started up the stairs, shaking her head in disbelief. "So, the Hall has quite a collection?"

"Yes, my lady. You and Lord Crosswick have quite a collection, as you will see when you look at Kenneth Baron's book."

Following Mrs. MacIntosh down the broad hall, Philip and Genevieve glanced at each other, silently making faces of awe, surprise and disbelief. They walked by several closed doors until they saw light spilling from an open doorway ahead on the left.

"Lord and Lady Crosswick, I chose the Green and Gold Room

for you because it has a lovely south-facing view of the gardens and river," said Mrs. MacIntosh as they arrived at the bedroom. She stepped aside and ushered the Warwicks into an emerald jewel box.

Genevieve gasped as her eyes swept around the room. Walls covered in jade leather and striped with burnished-gold molding served as the backdrop to a massive four-poster bed. Each fluted bedpost was brushed in gold leaf and pushed ten feet towards a coffered ceiling. A pale green silk duvet covered the bed. Pillows of gold and verdant hues were layered several deep, obscuring the headboard.

Polished mahogany floors peeked out from under the edge of a massive green needlepoint Aubusson rug, which stretched the width and breath of the room. Though the bedroom was large and the ceilings high, the colors and textures created a cozy chamber. An overstuffed sofa sat in front of a fireplace ready and waiting for the first chilly night.

"Mrs. MacIntosh, I'm speechless," said Genevieve. "I've never seen such a beautiful room." Genevieve walked around the chamber, trailing a finger over smooth silks and running her palm over woodwork gilded with gold leaf. She breathed in the sweet fragrance of lilies and daphne, which rested in a green and white Wedgewood vase.

Her circuit around the bedroom ended at the green-veined marble fireplace.

Hanging above the mantle was a portrait of an elegant young woman with dark hair and porcelain skin. She leaned forward, as if listening to an unseen companion. Her cornflower blue dress matched her eyes. Velvet sleeves slid off pale shoulders, just enough to offer a glimpse of delicate bones. Her left hand lay in her lap while the right cradled her heart-shaped face, her elbow resting on the arm of the tapestry-covered chair. Genevieve moved closer to the painting, then closer still. She blinked. She rubbed her eyes.

Philip and Mrs. MacIntosh had been talking about the history of the Green and Gold Room while Genevieve moved from piece to piece, appreciating each treasure. Now she froze in front of this exquisite portrait, eyes riveted on the woman's right hand. Her long, slender finger was encircled by a wide gold band on which perched a stupendous, square-cut ruby, surrounded by two rows of diamonds. A magnificent ring, and one Genevieve had seen before, just last night. Her heart pounded in her ears as she realized this priceless family heirloom had been stolen.

ELEVEN

THE THREE OF them sat together on the down-stuffed sofa opposite the fireplace, looking at the portrait hanging over the mantle. Wedged between Philip and Genevieve, Mrs. MacIntosh balanced Kenneth Baron's book about the treasures of Wilmingrove Hall on her knees. It was opened to page seventy-four where a reproduction of the painting filled the glossy sheet. Mrs. MacIntosh read the description aloud.

> "Victoria Catherine Winston Laney, only daughter of James and Imogene Gilcrest, the Duke and Duchess of Wallingford and wife of James Charles Philip Laney, the 8TH Earl of Crosswick.
>
> The portrait was painted by Andres Gilbert in 1849 and given by Lady Crosswick to the Earl on their first anniversary. The ruby and diamond ring worn by Lady Crosswick was a gift from Lord Crosswick to his wife on the birth of their first son. Gilbert added the ring a year after the painting was completed.
>
> Andres Gilbert became a favorite of Lady Crosswick, and subsequently painted each of the Laney's four children. It was widely rumored that Lady Crosswick admired more than Gilbert's skills on canvas. In correspondence

found after her death, one of Lady Crosswick's closest friends commented that William, the Countess's youngest son, had black hair and brown eyes so similar to the coloring of Gilbert rather than the fair hair and blue eyes of his father. The confident also wrote that the 8TH Earl was, perhaps, too busy securing the financial future of the Laney dynasty to notice his wife's new-found passion for art and artists."

As she finished reading, Mrs. MacIntosh closed the book and looked up at the likeness of Victoria Catherine Winston Laney. "It's been years since I read about Lady Crosswick's portrait. She was certainly bonnie and a most interesting woman."

"She was beautiful, I have to agree. And a bit of a vixen, it would seem." Genevieve eyed the countess with a wry smile. "Can you tell us anything else about the ruby ring? Does it show up in any other portraits of the Laney ladies?"

"We can look through the book. Or better yet, let's walk around and look at the original works." Philip rose to his feet, took the book from Mrs. MacIntosh and put it on the coffee table then helped her off the sofa.

"Before you do anything else, I must insist you meet the staff and have tea." Mrs. MacIntosh spoke with surprising authority. "You have to be starving."

"What a good idea, Mrs. MacIntosh." Taking her elbow, Philip guided Mrs. MacIntosh toward the door. "There will be plenty of time to investigate the mystery of the ruby ring," he chuckled. "That sounds like a Poirot title. Mrs. MacIntosh, give us ten minutes and we'll be downstairs."

"Of course, my lord. The staff will be waiting in the grand salon," Mrs. MacIntosh said over her shoulder as she walked out of the room.

Half an hour later, Philip and Genevieve had met their twenty-person staff. Their head cook was jolly, round Elsie Lomax, and their estate manager, Sean Harrington, exuded presence and natural authority, qualities perfect for his role. They also met Andrew Frazier, windswept from the Scottish Highlands where he learned his skills as a falconer.

Now they sat at a round table in the charming, cozy conservatory. French doors stood wide, allowing the balmy afternoon air to waft in. Blue and yellow jacquard linens covered the table ladened with a bowl of perfect, red strawberries, and tiered trays of tea sandwiches, petit fours, and scones. Everywhere she looked, Genevieve marveled how meticulously everything at Wilmingrove Hall was appointed and preserved. In an age when venerable estates scrambled to keep the rain from pouring through the roof and stately homes had turned shabby chic into an art form, no cost had been spared to maintain the Hall to a high standard.

"Philip, don't you love that everything at Wilmingrove hall is perfect? Nothing is run down or fraying or tired," she said, shoving a rather-too-large bite of scone, clotted cream, and jam into her mouth.

Philip looked up from spreading preserves on his scone. "I'm not surprised you're falling in love with this place. It's wonderful we haven't inherited a big house with termites and a sieve for a roof, but I keep wondering who's writing the checks to maintain everything? If there's anything unscrupulous going on, we'll figure it out, but in the meantime…" Philip reached across the table to catch a jammy crumb at the corner of Genevieve's mouth. "I think my favorite thing about being an earl other than having a billion pounds and owning this grand estate is that I can have scones, clotted cream and jam anytime I want."

"You know, Philip, you don't need all this to have scones, right?" Genevieve gestured to their surroundings. "Even commoners can get a scone whenever they want, anywhere they are," Genevieve said.

"I know, but somehow, they're so much better when you're very, very, very wealthy. He took a bite, closed his eyes, and sighed a blissful sigh. At last, he opened his eyes. "Okay. Let's talk about the estate. I've been thinking a lot about what might be going on here and I'm sorry to say, my list of concerns is piling up."

"So, you've been making a list of your suspicions? What a sleuth!" Genevieve teased. "Don't forget David will be here tomorrow with issues to talk about. Can we wait until he gets here? Oh, did you remember to send the chopper back for him?"

"Of course, I did," Philip shot back, his cheerful mood replaced by exasperation.

Genevieve's eyebrows arched.

"I don't want to wait until tomorrow. I've been hinting at this since we left New York and you keep putting me off. I want to talk now, so we're both on the same page when David comes," Philip finished with a barbed tone.

"Okay," Genevieve snapped. "But I don't know if that's going to happen, Philip."

"Why not?"

"I'm so excited about sharing our good fortune with the kids that I don't want to imagine there are any problems. You, on the other hand, seem to see bad omens everywhere you look." She ran her hands through her hair and puffed air from her cheeks. "Why can't we just enjoy this moment? Everything in life has ups and downs." Her eyes softened. "Look, Philip, I'm sure there are going to be challenges ahead. But for now, let's enjoy our extraordinary fortune."

"That's how people get conned. It's how people lose money. We can't both be Pollyannas unless we want to lose everything as quickly as we gained it."

"I'm not being a Pollyanna." Genevieve leaned forward. "I just want a moment to enjoy myself. Shame on me." Sarcasm dripped from each word.

"G, I understand. I do." Philip's voice softened and he reached across the table for Genevieve's hand. "You know misery loves company. I don't want to be the only one with reservations. Will you at least listen to my worries?"

Genevieve kissed Philip's knuckles, one at a time. "I'll promise to start looking around every corner for bad guys if you'll promise to enjoy our windfall just a little bit."

Philip turned his hand palm to palm in Genevieve's and shook it. "It's a deal," he said.

"I'll go first." Philip pulled a small notebook out of the pocket of his sweater and flipped it open.

"You're kidding me," Genevieve said, barking a laugh. "You really have written a list?"

"I didn't want to forget anything, so I made a few notes." Philip leafed through several pages. "Okay. The first thing was the law firm using Wilmingrove Hall as a corporate retreat."

Genevieve shrugged. "I'm sure they were here often enough, keeping an eye on things. It's logical that Jonathon would have said, 'Use the Hall, guys.'"

Philip looked up from his notebook. "That's reasonable. But why didn't they mention it? We've spent a lot of time with the senior partners this week. They could have filled us in on their side deals."

"I'll give you that." Genevieve played with a sandwich on her plate. "What's next?"

"Why do we have a Bombardier jet? Why do we have an AugustWest 604, the newest of the new, twenty-five million pound, very fancy helicopter?"

"It's actually an AgustaWestland."

"Whatever," he snapped." Very strange for a man who was a recluse for more than sixty years." Philip began to tick off entries as he spoke. "Who's responsible for all of Jonathon's properties, well, now *our* properties, being maintained to an impeccable standard? Who authorizes all these expenditures? And one last, but very big revelation."

Genevieve sat a bit straighter waiting for the reveal.

Philip pulled the Kenneth Baron book of Laney art from

under his chair and plopped it on the table. He flipped to page eleven then swirled the book toward Genevieve. "Does that look familiar?" He challenged.

Genevieve's forehead furrowed. "I don't understand. What am I looking at?'

"That painting you're looking at is attributed to the Laney collection, but we saw it hanging in the New York City law offices of Holmes Fitch Smythson Morrow, our illustrious team of attorneys."

"When...wha...I...uh...I don't even know what to ask."

"Leaf through the book. You'll find the other paintings we saw in the offices. Looks to me like they've, uh, *borrowed* a few of our priceless works of art. Odd David didn't mention the paintings were ours when we asked who the collector was."

'Oh, Philip." Genevieve wrung her hands. "You don't think David knows about this do you?"

"I have no idea, but remember, he did say he has concerns about his firm's relationship to our estate. When he gets here, we'll see what he has to say. I wouldn't be surprised if this is just the tip of the iceberg." Philip slapped his notebook closed and pointed his finger at Genevieve. "What do you say to that, Watson?"

She puffed out a noisy breath and slumped back in her chair. "You're way ahead of me in 'the game is afoot' department. I'll give you one thing, Sherlock: we need to find out who has access to the Laney money. In all our meetings we have never discussed the mechanics of how money flows in and out of the estate. Who has access to our accounts? What checks and balances are in place? Other than the various brokerages and investment banks where a substantial part of the estate is managed, how and where is money invested? We've spent most of our time getting through the legalities of transferring the holdings from your cousin to you. Gosh, I hope David turns out to be one of the good guys.

"I'm counting on it," Philip said. "It's going to be an interesting visit."

"Yup." Genevieve stared at her plate. "Worrying about David is going to keep me up tonight, but I guess there's nothing we can do about it until he gets here." She looked back at Philip. "What are you up to this afternoon?

Leaning back in his chair, Philip scratched his chin. "I'm going to spend time with Sean Harrington." Philip glanced at his watch. "In fact, I need to get a move on. Harrington and I have an appointment with the police."

"The police?" Genevieve's eyebrows shot up. "You've already broken the law?"

"Very funny, G. They're coming to interview me."

"As the new lord of the manor? Ooo." She fluttered her eyelashes and patted her heart. "Will there be TV cameras and a dashing reporter?"

"Don't get excited. It's one cop coming to make sure I'm not a crazy person so they can transfer the gun licenses to me. Apparently we have a sizable collection. Then Harrington's going to show me around the estate. Can you come, or do you have something better to do?"

"I'd love to join you." Genevieve thrust her lower lip into a pout. "That would be such fun, but I'm going to spend the rest of the afternoon with Mrs. MacIntosh and Wallace, who should be back from Glasgow by now. We're going to tour the house from top to bottom, go over household budgets, and discuss events on the calendar. You know, all the usual things one does as lady of the manor." Genevieve offered a dismissive wave of her hand.

"Can you get through the entire house in one afternoon? That's a lot of ground to cover." Philip looked at his watch. "It's 4:30 already."

"We'll get started today." Genevieve stifled a yawn. "I'm sure it will take a week or so to get a feel for how all of this works. I want to learn as much as possible before David comes tomorrow. The more we know, the more he can help."

"That's exactly why I want to spend time with Harrington," Philip said. "He's going to be a wealth of information and, you know, everybody loves to gossip. I bet I come away with a lot more than just facts about annual yields and forest management."

"I also need to choose bedrooms for the kids for next week." As she mentioned the children, Genevieve's face glowed. "I'm so excited they'll be here soon. FaceTime doesn't do justice to the reality of what's happened over the last couple of weeks. Even Julia will be blown away!"

"I think you're right. Even she might be the tiniest bit dazzled. It's going to be fun doing a big show and tell. Alex will love the horses and Andrew Frazier can put on quite a falcon show for the kids. He's impressive, isn't he?"

"He's drop-dead gorgeous and seriously charming, that's what he is!"

"I thought you'd say that." Philip looked amused. "Ella will think she's a princess, Wilmingrove Hall's her castle, and Andrew Frazier is her Prince Charming."

"If I don't call dibs on him first. You know, I outrank our granddaughter." Genevieve picked up the last strawberry and brought it to her lips.

"I'd say you outrank everyone in the county. Except for me, of course." Philip crossed his arms, jutted out his chin, and pursed his lips. "Please do remember your place, my dear woman."

"You arrogant aristocrat!" Genevieve giggled. Instead of popping the juicy berry into her mouth, she tossed it, hitting Philip on his chest, leaving a red stain on his pullover. He looked down at his lap where the berry landed.

Eyes wide, Genevieve gasped. "Oh my God, Philip! I'm so sorry. I shouldn't have done that! I was just kidding around."

Philip plucked the piece of fruit clinging to his sweater and tossed the strawberry into his mouth. Leaning on the table and trying to keep a smile from his eyes, he loomed over her. "Madam, when you least expect it, I shall exact my revenge," he said, with as much ice in his voice as he could muster.

Genevieve stood and walked around the table. She looked into Philip's handsome face, slipped her hands around his waist, and drew him close. "Lord Crosswick, I hope your revenge is as exhilarating as everything else in our lives." Her lips brushed his. "I'm having the most exciting adventure. When we made our wedding vows, you promised our marriage would never be dull and by God, you've kept your word."

Philip kissed her. He could feel her smile beneath his lips. He pulled back just enough to say, "Upstairs?"

"I'll race you."

TWELVE

ALF AN HOUR later, Genevieve descended the grand
staircase, buttoning the cuffs of her blouse and running
her fingers through her hair.

Mrs. MacIntosh was waiting in her small office near the
kitchen.

"I hope I haven't delayed us too long," Genevieve said. "Philip
and I, uh… had to take care of something." To her surprise, heat
flushed her cheeks.

Mrs. MacIntosh rose from her chair, seemingly unaware of
Genevieve's embarrassment. "My lady, your timing is perfect.
Wallace is waiting for us in the cellars. We thought we'd start
at the bottom and carry on upward floor by floor. There are one
hundred and thirty-seven rooms in the Hall, so we'll get our
steps in today. She smiled and tapped her Fitbit, then gestured
for Genevieve to precede her through the door.

They passed the servants' dining room and the kitchen, then
headed down a small passageway and through a large wooden
door.

"Be careful, please," Mrs. MacIntosh cautioned as they started down a curved stone staircase. The temperature dropped with each tread until they stepped off the last stair into a cool, stone room lined with racks of bottles. The overhead lighting was soft and indirect.

In the middle of the room, a man of about sixty sat in front of a laptop, with a green-shaded lamp casting a circle of light across the small desk.

When he saw Genevieve, the butler popped to his feet. Wallace was exactly as Genevieve had pictured him. A fastidious fringe circled the bald crown of his head, and his black suit and starched white shirt were immaculate.

"My lady, welcome to your wine cellar. What a pleasure to meet you at last." Wallace gave a quick bow of his head. "We are thrilled that you and the Earl have arrived."

Genevieve offered a warm smile. "The Earl and I are excited to be here, Wallace. I trust your sister is better?"

"Very kind of you to ask, my lady. She is. She's well on the mend."

Genevieve turned slowly where she stood. "Wow," she whispered under her breath. "Wallace, I have to say, I didn't expect this. I anticipated a nice collection, but this! There must be several thousand bottles here."

Wallace gestured around the cavernous space. "Actually, my lady, there are eight thousand and fifty-four reds, seven thousand and twelve whites, three hundred and twenty-two bottles of Champagne and two hundred and four bottles of Port. Would you like a tour?"

Genevieve clapped her hands at the prospect of wandering through the cellar. "Oh, yes, please."

The three of them sauntered down an aisle stocked with high-shouldered, straight-sided bottles filled with Bordeaux wines. "What a stupefying collection! We're going to have to drink frequently and heavily, Wallace."

"My lady, you'll be interested to know, this row in particular has many bottles from your vineyard in St. Emilion. I have no doubt you will fall in love with Chateau Beaulieu. It's a beautiful property producing exceptional wines; one of the best boutique vineyards in Bordeaux.

Genevieve couldn't stop grinning.

"In addition to Chateau Beaulieu bottles, we cellar fine wines from other regions of France, many from Spain, Italy, and the U.S," the butler paused to wipe dust from a bottle's edge with his cuff then continued, "some from Germany, South Africa, Australia, New Zealand, and, of course, Argentina is well represented."

"It sounds as if no self-respecting wine producing country has been left out."

"Indeed, my lady." Wallace's chest swelled.

"And what are we doing with all these wines? It's been years since Wilmingrove Hall hosted grand parties that would warrant such a lavish wine collection. Talk to me, Wallace. Who's drinking all this fine grape?"

Though the cellar was cool, tiny beads of perspiration popped out on the butler's forehead. He glanced at Mrs. MacIntosh, whose nod was almost imperceptible, gulped then looked back at Genevieve. "As you know, my lady, we here at Wilmingrove

Hall have been fulfilling our duties at the direction of the trustees of the estate, Holmes Fitch Smythson Morrow. Everything at Wilmingrove Hall is directed by Sir Mark Holmes."

Genevieve nodded, encouraging Wallace to continue.

"Often, he emails a list of wines to be sent to various locations, including his London residence and to the homes of the other partners. I always include a shipping copy in the case, so Sir Mark knows I keep track of every bottle that leaves the wine cellar. I don't know if he reimburses the estate…" Wallace paused, "… but I rather doubt it."

Mrs. MacIntosh pulled the corners of her mouth down and gave Wallace a subtle shake of her head.

Ignoring Mrs. MacIntosh's look of caution, Wallace went on. "Of course, my lady, I have maintained scrupulous records of every bottle that has come in to or gone out of this cellar for the last forty years."

Genevieve was not shocked at Wallace's revelations. The firm's free-wheeling access to the Hall's wine collection was in keeping with Philip's suspicions. "I have no doubt you could tell us where every drop has gone, Wallace," Genevieve reassured him. "Sixteen thousand bottles of top-quality wines and spirits… hmm…Wallace, what's the value of the collection?"

"The market price of the cellar fluctuates, but it's safe to say that the average value is around three."

"Three hundred thousand pounds?" Genevieve gulped.

"No, my lady. That's three *million* pounds. The collection is insured for three and a half million, which allows for substantial additions without increasing the insurance."

"I see," Genevieve said, but she didn't. She couldn't imagine anyone owning three million pounds of wine. Yet another surprise to share with Philip. The hits just kept on coming.

Wallace invited them to sit at the table in the tasting room.

Mrs. MacIntosh pulled a lace-edged handkerchief from her sleeve. "My lady, it is a great relief to have you and the Earl here."

Genevieve smiled at the compliment.

Mrs. MacIntosh looked down at her fidgeting hands, avoiding Genevieve's gaze.

Wallace nodded his encouragement.

Mrs. MacIntosh cleared her throat. "For some time, Wallace and I have shared misgivings with some heads of your other households. We all feel uncomfortable with some things that have occurred at Wilmingrove Hall, Chateau Beaulieu and your horse farm in Kentucky.

Genevieve's smile faded. "What do you mean, uncomfortable?"

Mrs. MacIntosh faltered. "It's not really my place…"

Genevieve touched the housekeeper's sleeve. "Mrs. MacIntosh, you can tell me anything. You already had the courage to tell me we have a ghost at Wilmingrove Hall. After that, anything else should be easy," Genevieve teased.

Mrs. MacIntosh couldn't help but smile. "You make a fair point," she chuckled. "Lady Crosswick, you have wonderful people running your properties, but we are subject to the directions and whims of the trustees. We're not always confident their actions are in the best interest of the estate, but it's not our place to question them. It's a great relief to be able to share our concerns with you."

Much to Mrs. Macintosh's surprise, Genevieve squeezed her hand.

"Our loyalty has always been to the Earl and the estate rather than to the trustees."

Genevieve rose from her chair, put both hands on the burnished oak table and leaned forward. She looked into the earnest faces of the two long-serving loyalists. "I promise I'll share everything you've told me today with Lord Crosswick. The Earl already has suspicions about the law firm's ethics, and I promise, this is not our last conversation about the questionable practices of Holmes Fitch Smythson Morrow." She stepped away from the table. "But for now, let's get three glasses, open a bottle of Chateau Margaux, which I'm sure we have, and continue our tour."

With their burden shed, Mrs. MacIntosh had a spring in her step and Wallace actually smiled. Glasses in hand, the three climbed the stone staircase from the cellar to the lower-level floor. Their first stop was the servants' dining room, which, though renovated to a modern standard, retained the aura of another century. A long, oak table was alive with the spirit of years of below-stairs life.

Genevieve pulled out a wooden chair and sat. "I can just imagine the servants gathering around the table, with the butler at the head, of course," she nodded at Wallace. "Taking their meals, darning socks, gossiping about the gentry upstairs and sharing the daily trials of their lives. Lives devoted to providing comfort to those in the grand rooms above."

Mrs. MacIntosh and Wallace exchanged smiles.

Genevieve rose and moved on to the kitchen. "This space is massive," she said, awe in her voice.

"It has been refitted with a number of upgrades in the last two years. The old icebox was replaced with large stainless-steel refrigerators, including a walk-in freezer." Mrs. MacIntosh walked to the back wall of the kitchen and heaved open a thick door.

Genevieve's breath formed little puffs as she stepped into the freezing room. Bundles were stacked on wire stainless steel racks five feet high, running the length and width of the room. The contents of each package was handwritten in black marker on the white butcher's paper. "What in the world are we doing with all this meat?" Before Wallace or Mrs. MacIntosh could speak, she said, "Don't tell me…the partners."

Wallace nodded. "The partners like to have certain cuts of meat when they come to the Hall." Wallace looked at Mrs. MacIntosh for support.

"They like to live well," she confirmed.

Genevieve shivered from the cold and hugged herself as she left the freezer. "Another arrow in Philip's quiver," she muttered. "Or another 'steak' through the partners' hearts." She chuckled at her joke. "Brrrrr. Remind me to put on a winter coat before I go in there again."

Mrs. MacIntosh opened a cupboard and pulled out a square linen tablecloth the yellow of the kitchen walls. Folding it into a triangle, she draped it across Genevieve's shoulders. "There, my lady. This should warm you."

"Why, thank you. That's very sweet."

"We can't have the lady of the manor catching cold." Wallace handed her a refilled glass of wine.

'Ooo, thank you, Wallace." Genevieve cradled the glass between her hands as if it were warm. "Now, tell me more. What other improvements have there been in the last few months?"

Under the fourteen-foot trough sink was a bank of four commercial dishwashers. "The sink has been here for years, but the dishwashers are new." Mrs. MacIntosh confirmed.

"I love the blue and white Delft tiles. They're so cheerful with the yellow walls."

"The paint is new, but the tiles are original to the house." Mrs. MacIntosh took a sip of her wine.

"That is without a doubt the largest Aga I have ever seen," Genevieve exclaimed. "And right next to a twelve-burner La Cornue, my dream stove! Are these both new?"

"Yes, my lady."

Genevieve scratched her forehead. "This is confusing. Why are the partners spending all this money to upgrade the kitchen? When was the last big party at the Hall?"

Mrs. MacIntosh's face clouded. "I wouldn't call it a party, but there was a large gathering after the Earl's funeral at the local church. At least five hundred people came to pay their respects over the course of three hours. That was the last time there were so many people to feed."

"But what about—," Wallace froze, silenced by a steely glance from Mrs. MacIntosh. "But, Bertie," he insisted, "Lady Crosswick wants us to tell her anything we think is dubious. I think feeding thousands of visitors every year falls into that category."

Genevieve's jaw dropped. "What do you mean, '*thousands of visitors?*'"

"Two years ago, Sir Mark told us the house would open to visitors to supplement the income of the estate." Wallace looked skeptical. "I'm sure you know that many stately homes have opened to the public to defray some of the maintenance costs."

Genevieve nodded. "The Earl and I have visited numerous great houses that welcome visitors. But I thought Wilmingrove Hall, and the estate are on solid financial ground." Genevieve closed her eyes and shook her head. She felt more confused with every revelation.

Wallace scowled. "Mrs. MacIntosh and I were most concerned with the arrangements. People toured the main floor and the ballroom on the first floor before they went through the stable and the gardens for one ticket price. For an additional fee, they could have tea at the stable cafe and see Andrew Frazier's falconry show."

"I think Philip's meeting with Andrew this afternoon." Warmer now, Genevieve pulled the makeshift shawl from her shoulders and put it on the counter.

"Lord Crosswick will love seeing our birds of prey in action. It's a magnificent sight," said Wallace.

"I can't wait to see the falcons and hawks, too. Working birds are so exciting. I love that the public can see the birds in action, but I'm not wild about them coming into the house. Are we still doing tours?"

"We are not," said Mrs. MacIntosh. "Sir Mark announced we would no longer open the house a couple of months after Lord Crosswick died."

"Hmmm." Genevieve chewed her lip. "Was that around the time they tracked down Philip—uh, Lord Crosswick?"

"It seems a bit too coincidental, don't you think, my lady?" Disdain dripped from Wallace's words.

"Mrs. MacIntosh, do you have any idea how many people toured the Hall? Are we talking about a few tourists, or a lot?" Genevieve pressed.

"Over the course of the two years, I believe we had about sixty thousand people visit the Hall. I can check my records for an exact number."

"Good lord! Sixty thousand people!" Genevieve was stunned.

"That's how many people who paid an average of fifty-four pounds per ticket. Then there were additional sales from high tea in the stable cafe."

"Good lord," Genevieve said again. "That's over three million pounds. Where did that money go?"

Wallace shrugged his shoulders and looked at Mrs. MacIntosh, who shook her head.

Genevieve tugged a heavy stool from under the kitchen's center island and sat on the edge. She drained her wineglass. It tinkled as she put it down on the marble counter. "My head is spinning from all this information." Genevieve put her elbows on the counter and rested her chin on her clasped hands. For a moment, silence filled the room, then she said, "I have a huge question for both of you. Do you think Sir Mark has managed the estate well or has he taken advantage of having no earl heading the family fortunes?"

Mrs. MacIntosh and Wallace looked at each other.

Wallace studied his black wool jacket and picked invisible lint from his lapel. Looking back at Genevieve, he said, "My lady, there is no question in our minds that Holmes Fitch Smythson Morrow, and in particular Sir Mark Holmes, took liberties as trustees of the Laney estate." Relieved of the burden of carrying this dark secret for years, Wallace let out a mighty sigh.

"You two!" Moved by a rush of fondness for her housekeeper and butler, Genevieve blinked back tears. "Lord Crosswick and I owe you both an enormous debt of gratitude for your years of stewardship under the most challenging circumstances. You two are spectacular. Wallace, why don't you open another bottle of this Chateau Margaux? Catch up to Mrs. MacIntosh and me in the...where are we going next, Mrs. MacIntosh?"

"The grand salon, then the music room."

"Onward and upward. Wallace, we'll see you upstairs."

Genevieve didn't know if it was the wine or the adrenaline rush from being an amateur sleuth, but she felt a distinct buzz of exhilaration. She set a brisk pace up the back staircase to the main floor. Mrs. MacIntosh followed behind, keeping up as best she could, huffing her way up the stairs.

They popped out into a small stairwell brightened by yellow plaster walls, hung with photographs of Wilmingrove Hall over the years. "Aren't these wonderful?" Genevieve thrilled at the history in front of her. "Look at this picture of all the staff. There must be almost a hundred servants in this photograph!"

Mrs. MacIntosh tilted her head. "Actually, there were one hundred seven people in service at the Hall in 1884 when this was taken. In its heyday, this house required a huge staff to maintain the lifestyle of a landed family."

"Hard to imagine. This aristocracy thing was big business, wasn't it?" Genevieve stopped in front of a picture of elegant people. "The upstairs crowd," she said under her breath. She leaned forward until her nose was six inches from the photograph. She squinted, trying to bring the image into sharper focus. "Is this Charlotte?" Genevieve pressed her finger on the glass. Pointing to a beautiful woman of about forty.

"It is, my lady."

"She looks so much like the portrait I saw at Margrave House. The artist was very good." Genevieve's breath coated the glass. She pulled back a few inches and ran her sleeve over the fog, leaving little damp streaks.

Moving to Genevieve's side, Mrs. MacIntosh stood on her toes to get a closer look at the family gathering. "You're looking at three generations of Laneys. This was taken two years after Wilmingrove Hall was completed. You can see how vivid the coat of arms is. This is James Charles Philip Laney, the 8TH Earl." She pointed to a man with a gray moustache trailing down his cheeks into mutton chops. His top hat shaded his eyes so only the bottom of his face was visible. "He's the earl who secured the Laney fortunes."

"Who is this?" Genevieve pointed to a clean-shaven man.

"That, my lady, is Philip George Winston Laney, the 9TH Earl and Charlotte's husband." Mrs. MacIntosh pointed to a lanky blond boy with regal bearing. "This is George William Morris Laney, the 10TH Earl."

"I don't know how you keep all the earls and their names straight," Genevieve said with admiration.

"I've lived with them for a long time. You'll get the hang of it. Shall we continue?"

"I guess we should. We have a lot of ground to cover, don't we?"

"We do, my lady, and I plan to give you the full fifty-four-pound tour." She gave Genevieve a sly smile. "So, we'd better get on our way." Mrs. MacIntosh moved ahead and began her docent tour in the salon.

In her poshest Yorkshire accent, the housekeeper began her lecture. "Wilmingrove Hall was built as a country retreat by the 8TH Earl of Crosswick. By the mid-1850s, many great British family fortunes were on the wane. But the 8TH Earl was a clever man. Through several decades of shrewd business moves, the generations of earls significantly altered the Laney fortunes and ensured the family would remain financially sound well into the future." She cleared her throat and went on. "With that sense of security, the 8TH Earl felt comfortable spending thirty-four million pounds to create Wilmingrove Hall for his family and future heirs. He began constructing Wilmingrove Hall in 1874. After numerous delays, the Hall was completed in 1882."

Genevieve suppressed a smile, both impressed and amused by Mrs. MacIntosh's formal presentation.

Mrs. MacIntosh reached into her skirt pocket. To Genevieve's surprise, she pulled out a laser pointer and flicked on the light. She pointed toward the ornamental moldings twenty feet above.

"Though premade crown molding and cornices were available, the 8ᵀᴴ Earl insisted all decorative elements for the Hall be hand crafted. No expense was spared. The estimated value of the Hall in today's currency is two hundred and fifty million pounds." Mrs. MacIntosh walked regally to the center of the salon. It was obvious she took great pride in Wilmingrove Hall and its illustrious history.

"Very impressive, Mrs. MacIntosh. You should be giving tours at The Tate."

Mrs. MacIntosh surprised Genevieve with a wink. "They couldn't afford me, my lady,"

Genevieve's jeans pocket vibrated. She pulled out her phone to see Philip's face fill the screen. She held up one finger. "Mrs. MacIntosh, just a moment, please."

"Hi, cute boy," she answered with a smile.

His voice business-like, Philip got straight to the point. "G, I know you're in the middle of your tour, but we need you here for a few minutes."

Genevieve looked up at the ceiling, impatient to get back to Mrs. MacIntosh. "Why?"

"The policewoman is here to interview us for the gun license transfer. I didn't know she'd want you here, too, but she does."

"I don't want to interrupt my time with Mrs. MacIntosh and Wallace. I'm learning a lot. You really need me?

"Kafritz, the police officer, wants you here."

"All right." Genevieve blew out an annoyed huff. "I'll be right there." Turning to her tour guide she asked, "Which way is the estate office?"

THIRTEEN

G ENEVIEVE HIKED DOWN the terraced hill and arrived at the estate office ten minutes later. The small room had floor-to-ceiling pine shelves fitted on two walls, each packed with binders. A boot jack caked with mud sat just inside the door, and a Labrador Retriever lay dozing by a wood-burning stove, which warmed the room.

Sean Harrington sat at his desk with Philip looking over his shoulder at a computer screen. Across the desk, a policewoman faced them with her back to the door, her uniform a bit too large for her small frame.

As Genevieve walked in, Philip looked up and smiled.

The chocolate Lab raised his head to see who was disturbing his nap. Finding Genevieve of little interest, he rolled onto his side, stretched his legs in front of him and was softly snoring again within seconds.

Harrington stood up. "Lady Crosswick, thank you for coming. I know you were in the middle of something, but Sergeant Kafritz wanted to meet you and explain the importance of transferring the ownership of the gun collection."

The officer stood and turned.

Genevieve blinked, trying not to show her surprise. She couldn't remember ever seeing anyone quite so homely. It was hard to tell her age. She could be in her twenties; she could be close to forty. Her mousy brown hair was parted in the middle and pulled back into a severe bun, which accentuated her coarse features. Her eyes, magnified behind thick rimless glasses, had no distinguishable color and her nose was too large for her face. The whole image made Genevieve think of the funny nose and glasses she loved to wear as a child. The officer's complexion was pasty, but her mouth was startling. Her lower lip was as full and ripe as a cherry, and her upper lip was a perfect cupid's bow. It was a beautiful, perfect mouth on an achingly plain face.

Genevieve pulled her attention from the sergeant's appearance. She started to extend her hand then, remembering herself, dropped it back at her side. "Sergeant Kafritz. Thank you for including me. It might be hard for you to imagine because we're Americans, but Philip and I are not used to owning guns. This is all new to us."

"Lady Crosswick." The sergeant gave a deferential nod. "I'm glad you joined us. I was just about to do an inventory of the gun safe and cross reference the paperwork." Kafritz had a lisp and a Yorkshire accent. "But before I do that, why don't I give you an overview of the procedure." She looked around at her audience of three. "Then you can all get back to what you were doing. I'll take the inventory and leave the keys wherever you like."

For fifteen minutes, Sergeant Kafritz rambled on about the UK's strict gun laws until Genevieve was numb with boredom.

When at last the sergeant finished her lecture, Genevieve couldn't leave fast enough. She loped from the estate office up the path and the stairs, until she stood in the doorway of the housekeeper's office, panting, her face glistening with sweat.

Looking up from her paperwork, Mrs. MacIntosh chuckled. "Ran all the way, did you?"

Genevieve smiled. "I think we're becoming friends," she said to herself. And they resumed the tour.

FOURTEEN

THE MUSIC ROOM was one of Genevieve's favorite spaces. Tucked into the southwest corner of the house, it had a beautiful afternoon glow. Fourteen-foot windows offered stunning views over the gardens and out to the river. Genevieve, a life-long pianist, couldn't resist sitting at the Bosendorfer grand, running scales up and down the keyboard. It was one of the most elegant pianos she had ever played; it was in perfect tune and the action of the keys was agile and responsive.

"Oh, my lady, you play the piano." Mrs. MacIntosh clapped her hands with delight. "How wonderful it will be to hear music in the house!"

"I've played since I was a child, but like most kids, I hated practicing. I just started playing again a few years ago. And I've never played a Bosendorfer! I'm sure all of this is a dream and I'll wake up any moment." Surveying the room, everywhere she looked was perfection. British elm paneling and floors gave the room a magical radiance. As she sat on the toile-covered piano bench, she could almost hear string quartets, piano recitals, operatic concerts, and jazz combos.

"Was the music room used a lot?" she asked.

"Before his accident, the 12ᵀᴴ Earl was in residence at the Hall for months at a time. He loved music, all kinds. According to our Wilmingrove Hall historian…"

"We have an historian?" Genevieve interrupted.

"Yes, my lady. His name is Fenton Morrissey. I've asked him to join us." Mrs. MacIntosh shoved her sleeve past her Fitbit to glance at the time. "He should be here any minute."

As if on cue, an Ichabod Crane-lookalike bumbled through the door and across the room, juggling a stack of thick volumes in his skinny arms. His mop of ginger hair bounced with every step he took. He failed to watch where he was going, tripped over a small footstool, and staggered to keep upright.

"Lady Crosswick!" A tome toppled from his tower of books, crashing to the floor.

Genevieve stooped to pick up the volume as another book fell, thumping her on the head. She smashed to the floor, thunking her nose on the hardwood.

"What's going on here?" Wallace bellowed as he strode through the door, a bottle of Chateau Margaux in each hand. Then he saw his mistress lying face down on the floor. "What's happened? Lady Crosswick, are you all right?"

Mrs. Macintosh squatted beside Genevieve as she pushed herself to her knees and twisted to sit on her bottom. She wiggled her nose to assure it wasn't broken, then touched her fingers to her nostrils. No blood. She began to giggle. The giggle rolled from her throat, exploding into a belly laugh.

Mrs. MacIntosh stared open-mouthed while Wallace grabbed Genevieve's arm and tugged. "Let me help you up, my lady," Wallace said.

The more Genevieve tried to stop laughing, the more she gasped for air.

Fenton Morrissey had not moved, still clutching his books. He was frozen in place, eyes popping out of his head, his face the color of his starched, white shirt.

Genevieve remained sitting on the floor, resisting Wallace's efforts to pull her to her feet. At last, her laughter subsided. She gazed up at the trio towering over her. "Please don't look so worried. That was hilarious. I'm sorry we don't have a video of the fiasco!" Finally, she stuck out her hand and allowed Wallace to help her up.

Without ceremony, Genevieve rearranged her sweater and pulled her jeans up by the belt loops. "So, Mr. Morrissey, this has been quite an auspicious introduction."

Her genuine smile was such a relief to Morrissey that his breath, which he'd been holding for the last minute, whooshed out.

"Wallace, shall we open those bottles and find another glass for Fenton?" She pointed to the wine Wallace had plunked on the piano.

Turning back to the historian, Genevieve pointed to a sideboard. "Mr. Morrissey, why don't you put your books over there."

Grateful for the suggestion, he laid the pile on the dark-green marble top.

"I was just asking Mrs. MacIntosh to tell me about the history of the music room. She said you are the authority." Genevieve touched Morrissey on the arm, hoping to put him at ease.

As he began sharing the room's history, a transition came over the gawky man and he began to sparkle. "Oh, my lady, we have historic confirmation that many notable musicians graced Wilmingrove Hall: Billie Holiday, Ella Fitzgerald, and Aaron Copeland." He moved to the curve in the piano, struck the pose of a model and clasped his hands at his chest. "Photos show Leontyne Price standing right here on this spot singing arias." He headed back to the credenza. "I brought several books from the library, one of which I used to bludgeon you." He smiled sheepishly, hoping Genevieve would enjoy the joke. "I know you're in a bit of a hurry this afternoon, so I'll put them on the library table for you and Lord Crosswick."

"Please do! And I'd love to spend time with you next week familiarizing myself with the library. But I want to get a helmet and pads before we meet again." Genevieve returned his joke.

"Just one last thing. I did want to ask if by any chance you put this on the library table?" Morrissey handed Genevieve a book with a glossy, black dust cover, bright red ink splashed across the front. In jagged letters it said *How I Killed My Daddy,* a novel by Olivia H. Conway. "It appeared this morning. I thought perhaps you brought it with you."

"No, Fenton. I haven't seen this before. Interesting title." The hall clock chimed five, and Genevieve turned to Mrs. MacIntosh. "I suppose we should pick up the pace or we'll still be touring the house at midnight. Fenton, I look forward to spending time together soon." She put her hand on his tweedy shoulder. "And thank you for today."

"It's been my pleasure, Lady Crosswick."

"I thought we would just cover the main floor this afternoon. We can resume the tour at your convenience." Mrs. MacIntosh led the way to their next stop. "I know Sir David is coming tomorrow, so you will be busy while he's here. Perhaps early next week would be a good time to carry on."

"That sounds like a good plan, Mrs. MacIntosh. I'll count on you to organize it. Where to next?" Not used to drinking wine in the afternoon, Genevieve felt a bit woozy. She would have loved a nap before dinner but didn't have the heart to cut the exploration short. Mrs. MacIntosh and Wallace were anxious to share the glories of the Hall, and perhaps they would tell her more about Sir Mark's shenanigans. She also didn't want to break the spell of new camaraderie developing between them, so on they pressed into the drawing room.

The moment they entered the grand chamber, Genevieve was enveloped in a sweet, delicate fragrance. She looked around the room searching for bouquets of cut flowers. She saw none.

"Mrs. MacIntosh, I smell roses."

"Do you? It's Charlotte, I suppose." The housekeeper sniffed the air. "I don't smell a thing, but that's not unusual. Often Charlotte reveals herself to just one person in the room."

"Charlotte? Are you serious?" Genevieve rolled her eyes. "Well, I smell roses, so I guess I should feel honored. But why me?"

"Perhaps she's reaching out to you because you are now the matriarch of the Laney clan, and she wants you to know you have her support. This was always her favorite room, so it makes sense she would greet you here. She finished redecorating it just before her accident."

A warmth spread through Genevieve at the suggestion that Charlotte had chosen to embrace her. She did a slow turn, admiring the soft colors and light playing off polished wood and faceted chandeliers. She could imagine elegant Edwardian women draped across the chase lounges and divans, laughter and chatter filling the room. "She did a splendid job," Genevieve said.

"Shall we, my lady?" Wallace motioned for Genevieve to go through to the next room.

The thirty-six-foot-long dining room was grand and opulent, with one wall lined with the same soaring French doors found in the music and drawing rooms. Cherry floors gleamed, and imposing sideboards anchored each end of the room. Eager to miss no detail, Genevieve took in color and texture, fabric, wood, and metal until her gaze stopped on a painting above the fireplace.

"Wallace, Mrs. MacIntosh, who is that?" Genevieve pointed to a modern portrait of a very handsome man in formal attire.

"That, my lady, is the 12TH Earl of Crosswick, the current Earl's cousin. He was quite a figure, wasn't he? Do you see the resemblance to the current Earl?"

"Oh, my. I do." There was no question. Philip was Jonathon's doppelganger. "He's magnificent. He looks exactly like Philip twenty years ago. How old was the Earl when this was painted?"

"The portrait was painted when he was thirty-six, six months before his skiing accident. He had just become engaged to

Katherine Robeson, the daughter of an American media mogul."

"Lord Crosswick and I learned the story when we were in London. It's tragic. He gave up the love of his life because he was paralyzed, and then he met Revy Harris and it happened all over again." A tear slipped down Genevieve's cheek and she swiped it away with her knuckle. "There's no end to sad Laney family stories, is there?"

The tour had lost its energetic sparkle. Maybe it was the sobering story about the Earl's sad love affairs or perhaps the giddy effect of the Chateau Margaux was fading. It was hard to tell.

Genevieve looked away from the 12TH Earl's portrait and refocused her attention on the enormous dining table. "How many can we seat around the table when it's fully extended?"

"Forty with the table as-is and fifty-two with all the leaves in place," Mrs. MacIntosh said. "When the table is formally set and the dining room is ready for a dinner party, it's quite grand!"

Genevieve stood with her hands on her hips, imagining the beautiful room filled with women in stylish gowns and men in black tie, glasses clinking, candles flickering, the sound of music wafting in the air. "I have an idea," she said, her energy sparking again. "Don't you think we should plan a big dinner party, or at least a whopper of a cocktail party? I don't know who we would invite, but I'm sure with some thought we could come up with a wonderful group."

"Oh, yes!" Mrs. MacIntosh grinned.

"We could celebrate the new Earl and Countess of Crosswick taking their place at the helm of Wilmingrove Hall." Genevieve leaned close to Mrs. MacIntosh and Wallace. "And maybe we could set a trap for our crafty Sir Mark. What do you two think?"

"That's a wonderful idea, my lady," Mrs. MacIntosh agreed.

Wallace's smile nearly gave him away, but he mustered his composure just in time. "Splendid. Simply splendid, my lady. Wilmingrove Hall will be radiant. You and the Earl will bring this grand house back to life! Mrs. MacIntosh and I will be proud to be a part of it. An elegant party is the perfect trap to ensnare Sir Mark. But, perhaps more important, you need fine cheese to catch a posh rat."

"To the beginning of a new era," Genevieve raised her goblet and with only a splash of wine left, she clinked glasses with her co-conspirators.

Philip and Genevieve shared a cozy table in the study by a crackling fire, dining on salmon from their own river, late-season tomatoes, and home-grown brussels sprouts.

"Charlotte's here," said Genevieve, before sipping a soft white Bordeaux from their St. Emilion vineyard.

Philip stopped, his fork midway to his mouth. "You're kidding!" he said, eyes crinkling from his broad smile. "How do you know?"

"I smelled her." Genevieve tilted her chin and blinked. "Mrs. MacIntosh says I'm special."

"I wouldn't argue with that." Philip gathered more food on his fork.

"I'll let you know the next time Charlotte and I get together." She laughed. "Thanks for stealing half an hour of my time with that gun transfer business. I certainly didn't need to be there. Sergeant Kafritz is unusual, wouldn't you say?

"She was. She was extremely…" Philip paused, searching for the right word. "…competent."

Genevieve held her breath and stared at her plate. She knew if she looked at Philip, she would burst out laughing. "Competent. That's the right word." She giggled.

"Can you believe this?" Philip closed his lips around a forkful of salmon. Butter oozed from the corner of his mouth and a groan of pleasure hummed in his throat.

Genevieve sat back in her chair, amused as she watched her husband wallow in the pleasure of his meal. "You're hilarious. You'd think you'd never had a good meal before."

"Maybe everything is so delicious because it all came from our estate." His smile reached his eyes. "Those are words I never thought I'd say."

Genevieve nodded. "All day I've felt I'm in a fairytale. Everything is perfect… maybe too perfect." Small lines of concern feathered the corners of her eyes.

"I didn't expect to hear that. At lunch you were falling in love with the house and thrilled that it's not shabby." Philip crossed his eyes. "I'm getting whiplash. You're like a yoyo. 'I'm happy. I'm worried. I'm happy. I'm worried.'"

"Really, Philip, it's hard for a yoyo to give you whiplash." Genevieve put her elbows on the table and rested her chin on her fisted hands. "You're right. I changed my mind after my tour with Mrs. MacIntosh, but for good reason. But first, I want to hear about your tour. Do you like Mr. Harrington?" Genevieve asked.

"A better question is, does Mr. Harrington like *me*," Philip said.

Genevieve looked puzzled.

"We met at the stables before Sargent Kafritz arrived and, as I walked through the door, Harrington started bombarding me with complaints about Sir Mark."

Philip went on, corroborating everything Mrs. MacIntosh and Wallace had told Genevieve earlier that day. "Get this: there was even a visitor who took cuttings of several types of ivy and snipped a huge bouquet from the rose garden. Harrington said she thought the price of the tour entitled her to flowers and ivy! He was steaming, but once he realized I was not in favor of Wilmingrove Hall functioning as an amusement park, we became mates pretty fast."

Genevieve leaned back in her chair. She grinned, enjoying Philip's rendition of similar stories she had heard earlier from their housekeeper and butler. She took a slow drink of her wine and nodded at her husband. "Go on."

"That's just the beginning." Philip emptied his glass and refilled Genevieve's goblet then his own. "Harrington told me during the past two years, Mark Holmes has run at least fifty thousand people through our home."

Genevieve enjoyed Philip's use of our home.

"And Mrs. MacIntosh has been serving as docent for the tours."

Genevieve nodded, the faintest smile on her lips. "I had Mrs. MacIntosh's tour today. She's very good."

"So, you know all of this?"

"I do."

"Okay, Miss Smarty Pants. Did you know Sir Mark ran high ticket events here during shooting season?"

"I did not."

"Groups from all over the world have been paying thousands of pounds to shoot pheasant and grouse. When I asked where the money goes—and it's a hell of a lot of money—Harrington said he hasn't seen…." Philip paused as Lottie, a petite young lady from the kitchen staff, appeared in the doorway.

"My lord, may I serve the pudding?" she asked.

"That would be great." He waited until she retreated, then leaned on his forearms across the table. "Should we worry about any of the staff spying on us for Sir Mark?" he whispered.

Genevieve grinned at him, thinking he was joking. But his brow furrowed, and a genuine look of concern clouded his eyes.

She snorted a laugh. "You're serious," she said with disbelief.

Philip sat back in his chair as the door opened again.

Lottie entered, carrying two raspberry souffles puffed two inches above the ramekin rims. She poured steaming coffee into their Limoges cups.

Philip watched her every move until she disappeared through the door when he spoke again. "I don't know. It just occurred to me when Lottie came in. But you don't think it's something we need to worry about, so never mind. Anyway, it's your turn. How did your day go and what do you think about my revelations? Inquiring minds want to know."

Genevieve took a luxurious bite of her warm raspberry souffle. The tartness of the berries played perfectly with the sweetness of the fluffy egg cloud. She sighed a note of pleasure. "Philip, you and I have spent the day getting the same information from three reliable sources. I think it's safe to say, we have a trap to set and a rat to catch."

FIFTEEN

YESTERDAY'S BEAUTIFUL DAY had turned chilly and wet, and the rain sheeted down. Though it was midday, lamps lit every corner of the house. As he descended the stairs, Philip couldn't help wondering what their electric bill must be. He often found himself turning off lights he felt were unnecessary, although he knew Genevieve would roll her eyes and call him ridiculous if she saw him.

Just as Philip passed through the foyer, the front door burst open. "David!" Philip said. "I didn't realize you had arrived. Whoa, are you drenched!"

David stood dripping on the marble floor, wet hair plastered to his head. "Rather! It's bucketing down out there, and the flight wasn't brilliant, I can tell you."

With perfect timing, Wallace appeared, towel in hand. "Sir David, may I take your coat?"

"Wallace, how wonderful to see you! It's been ages. I don't think I've seen you since the last Pony Club gymkhana here at the Hall. Remember? The Duchess of Margress was so squiffy she drove the pony trap into the reservoir. Wasn't Sir Henry with her when they went in? God, they were a funny sight."

"I'm sure I don't know to what you refer, Sir David." Wallace took David's coat, handed him the fluffy white towel and winked at him. "Drinks will be served in the library when you're ready, my lord."

"Wallace, could you please tell Lady Crosswick Sir David is here? I'm not sure where she is," Philip said.

"Of course, my lord," Wallace said over his shoulder. He left with the dripping coat and damp towel.

Philip and David moved into the library, where a fire threw welcoming warmth into the room.

"Have a seat, David," Philip said, motioning to over-stuffed chairs near the hearth. "Man, am I glad you're here. We've only been here twenty-four hours, and we have mysteries popping up everywhere. I'm sure you can shed light on most of them."

"Your lordship, I—"

Philip cut him off. "Will you stop with the 'lordship' crap! This is starting to get on my nerves."

David grinned. "In the twenty-first century it really is absolute bollocks, isn't it?"

"God, yes! As an American, I've always been seduced by your class system. I thought it would be great fun to be a peer, but after a couple of weeks in the thick of it, it's rubbish, as you say."

Philip pulled a chunky log from the wood box and tossed it into the fireplace. Flames snapped, gobbling the dry timber. "David, wouldn't you say the important thing about having wealth and privilege is noblesse oblige? Genevieve and I've been talking a lot about this. Both of us want to do extraordinary work with the massive inheritance that's fallen into our laps. We're going to need your help to figure out how to do the greatest good with what we have." Philip ran his hands over his face, then blew air from his puffed-out cheeks. "God, David, I'm sorry. I should at least wait until you have a drink in your hand before I start bombarding you!"

"David!" Genevieve's warm greeting reached across the library as she entered the room.

Both men smiled, watching her stride to where they were seated.

"Please don't get up! You two look very cozy sitting here." She flashed a grin, looking every inch the part of a lady to the manor born. A short, purple cashmere sweater hit just at the waistband of a purple, green, and black wool tartan skirt that swished around the tops of Genevieve's cordovan ankle boots. She had pulled her hair up and clipped it into a messy bun with a silver fastener.

With his butler's intuition, Wallace was at her side. "My lady, what would you like to drink?"

"Wallace. I think a glass of the Margaux we had yesterday would hit the spot," Genevieve leaned into Wallace and dropped her voice, "or did we drink it all?"

"I'm sure I can find a drop for you, my lady."

"Ooo, super. Thank you. You know, Wallace, I think of all the marvelous things about being the Countess of Crosswick, you are one of my favorites. If you're not already, you should be a national treasure."

As color rose in Wallace's cheeks, the butler offered Genevieve a silver tray with delicious-looking morsels. "My lady, it is a genuine pleasure to be in your service. Will there be anything else?"

"Thank you, Wallace. I think we have everything we need at the moment. Lunch in about an hour will be perfect," Genevieve said.

"As you wish, my lady." Wallace retreated and the threesome was alone.

Genevieve scooched forward in her chair. "Okay, boys. What did I miss?"

"Lord Cr…"

Philip shot David a sharp look. David raised both hands, palms out. "All right, all right."

'What's that about?" Genevieve screwed up her face.

"I've insisted David ditch our titles and call us by our first names, but it may take a while before he gets the hang of it. Feel free to wrap his knuckles until he gets it right, G."

Genevieve threw David a wicked look. "It will be my pleasure," she said, rubbing her hands together.

The threesome spent the next hour talking about the various characters at Holmes Fitch Smythson Morrow.

"I've been with HFSM for twenty years. I've always been proud to be part of a firm that had the highest standards, but in the past four or five years, things have changed." David rolled his wine glass between his palms then took a long, slow swallow. "As long as I have been with the firm, the partners have used Wilmingrove Hall as a retreat, but I believed it was with the full knowledge of Lord Crosswick. They were respectful and, as far as I know, never abused the privilege of being here. But a while ago, even before Lord Crosswick began his decline, it seemed the partners began to take advantage of the Earl's generosity. I'd say it started when they brought the art into their offices."

"We were going to ask you about that." Philip's eyebrows arched, waiting for further explanation.

"I didn't want to tell you when we were in the New York office. I was hoping Sir Mark would explain why they have millions of pounds of your art collection on the firm's walls. But he didn't. When did you figure it out?"

"We saw the works in a book by Kenneth Baron that lists all our art and antiques." Philip's mouth tightened to a thin line."

"Please believe me. I intended to tell you from the beginning." Little beads of perspiration dotted David's upper lip.

Genevieve and Philip looked at each other then back at David. "If you say that's one of the things you're concerned about, we believe you. What else do you have to tell us?"

David's right knee pistoned up and down. "Well, Sir Mark began the tours, and the shoots, and then they bought the jet and the helicopter. And there was some scuttlebutt about Sir Mark freely availing himself of the offerings of the wine cellar." As David spoke, Philip and Genevieve exchanged knowing glances. "It seemed to start slowly then accelerate to warp speed." As David spoke, it was clear his concerns were the same as the Warwick's.

"Do you know anything about Revy Harris and a ruby ring?" Genevieve walked to the fireplace, pulled a small log from the wood holder, and tossed it onto the pile glowing on the hearth. It caught, crackling, and spitting sparks.

"Revy Harris?" David's face was blank.

"Yes. When we were at Margrave House, we saw a photograph of a beautiful young woman named Revy Harris, on the Earl's desk." Genevieve wielded an iron poker, pushing the logs further back into the firebox. "I guess you'd have no reason to know who she is. Over twenty years ago, she was a Fellow with the Laney Museum of Fine Arts. As part of her internship, she helped the 12TH Earl catalogue the Margrave House collection." Genevieve replaced the poker and turned away from the fireplace, flushed from the heat. "According to Mrs. Baker, she went from intern to inamorata in just a few short months. But, David, the reason I'm interested in her is not because of that salacious story. It's because I was dazzled by the ruby ring she was wearing in the photo."

Philip, who had been absorbed answering a text, glanced up from his phone. "Don't let her kid you, David. She wants all the details about the hot sex between the cute American and my cousin."

"Okay, you got me. I probably wouldn't cover my ears if you have any of those tidbits." Genevieve wiggled her eyebrows up and down and twisted her lips to a lascivious smile. "But seriously, boys," she said tapping a fake cigar, "I want to know about the ring."

Vibrating with excitement, Genevieve told David of seeing the same ring on Revy's finger in the photograph that she later saw in the portrait of Victoria Catherine Winston Laney, the 8TH Earl's wife. "I want to know how this pipsqueak American wedeled her way into Jonathon Laney's life and ended up with an extraordinary Crosswick treasure."

"You believe this girl has illegal possession of a Laney family heirloom?" David looked skeptical.

"Yes, but she's not a girl anymore. She'd have to be about your age, or maybe a bit younger. You know, quite long in the tooth." Genevieve slapped her thigh, cackling.

David ignored her joke. "Genevieve, if Lord Crosswick was having an affair with this beauty, he might well have given her a piece of jewelry." He shrugged his shoulders. "An old, crippled man may need more than charm to keep a beautiful young lover. I've never had to use it myself, but I understand jewelry is a hell of an aphrodisiac."

Genevieve rolled her eyes. "I suppose you're right. I just thought she might have conned him out of it. That's a lot more interesting than Jonathon giving it to her in exchange for, you know…" she hugged herself, pooched her lips out and made kissing sounds. She glanced at Philip, who was punching send on his phone. "Philip what are you doing on your phone?" she asked, annoyed.

Philip put his phone back in his pants pocket. "I was just answering a text from Sir Mark."

Genevieve leaned forward on high alert. "What did he want?"

"He asked if David got here all right." He threw David a questioning look. "Is he always so concerned about your whereabouts and wellbeing?"

"Absolutely not. That's strange." David bit his lower lip. "I didn't realize he even knew I was coming to Wilmingrove Hall."

"Reeeally?" Genevieve stretched out the word. "Do you think he's worried you'll tell us things he doesn't want you to share?"

"Hmmm." The corners of David's mouth drew down. "There's a chance he's wondering why I'm here. But as far as I know, he doesn't suspect I think he's a miscreant."

"If indeed he's been dipping his toes into the Laney Pond, 'miscreant' is a much-too-elegant name to call him." Philip's eyes were flinty, and his voice edged with steel. "I can forgive a lot of things, but I pity anyone who exploits my family. If we confirm Sir Mark has misused his position as my cousins' trusted guardian, I don't envy him."

The smoldering logs hissed in the fireplace. Genevieve sat still as a mannequin, eyes wide, lips taut. There was no question in her mind that with every new revelation about the House of Crosswick, Philip felt more a part of the illustrious bloodline and more protective of his ancestry.

After several minutes, David broke the heavy silence. "I guess this is as good a time as any," he said looking solemn. "I have something to tell you."

"Oh boy," Genevieve said and bit her lower lip. "This can't be good."

David set his wine glass on the table beside him and folded his hands in his lap. He felt his heart accelerate and took a deep breath to calm himself. "One of the reasons I wanted to come to the Hall this weekend, in addition to talking to you about these fiduciary concerns, was to let you know that I've decided to leave the firm. Of course, that means I will no longer be your solicitor."

"No, it doesn't," Philip said immediately. "You can be our attorney and we will be your sole client. Genevieve and I have talked about this, and we're convinced Sir Mark is an embezzler." He spat out the word. "His behavior's blatant. He's arrogant, and he thinks I'm too naïve to see what he's doing. Hubris will bite him in the ass every time." Philip rose and walked to the sideboard.

"David, we're about to do battle with Sir Mark and his mighty law firm," Genevieve said. "We need you for that. After we destroy them, there's plenty of work with the Laney estate, the museums, and the Foundation.

"You know we can afford to pay you what you're worth. Well, we'll need to pay you *more* than you're worth. You couldn't possibly live on what you're worth." Philip grinned as he refilled David's glass.

David returned the smile with a rude gesture. "You can stop beating me up anytime."

Genevieve held out her glass for Philip and piled on. "David, we need a brilliant legal mind to help us, but in this case, we'll settle for yours." She threw her head back in mock hilarity.

"Whoa! I'm being brutalized here!" David held up both hands. He looked at Philip and Genevieve, his gaze shifting from one to the other. "Are you serious? Work for the Laney Estate as my sole client? I swear, I'm not here to solicit your employment."

"Don't be absurd," Genevieve said. "You can't leave us in the lurch. We might be on the verge of taking down Holmes Fitch Smythson Morrow." Genevieve pumped her fist. "You don't want to miss that!

David looked at Genevieve, then Philip, then back at Genevieve. "Listen, you two. I've been a slave to the firm since my wife died four years ago. An extremely well-paid slave, but a slave, nonetheless. The idea of working with you is very appealing, even though you're Yanks."

"Good. I'm glad you won't let the fact that we're ugly Americans get in the way. For some crazy reason, David, Genevieve and I trust you. We need you. Don't we, G? Bring on some smart, young talent if you need help; it would be a wonderful opportunity for any newly minted lawyer to work with you. We'll hammer out a compensation package. We're paying the law firm a fortune so whatever we work out, we'll most likely save money."

"I don't have to think about it. There's nothing I'd like better than working with you. I can't think of a more interesting way to spend my time. All that is to say, I accept your proposal, but with a slight alteration." He leaned forward, a grave look on his face. "Having said all this, I think for the time being, I need to stay at the firm."

Genevieve looked crestfallen. "Why is that? I want you away from those horrible people immediately. If Sir Mark is suspicious of you, could he do you harm?"

David almost sprayed wine from his nose. He swallowed and spat out a harsh laugh. "My God, Genevieve! In the twenty years I've known Sir Mark, I've never seen him do anything more violent than dress down the club steward for skimping on the olives in his martini. Mark's a pompous old man, but he wouldn't harm a fly. I'm sure he thinks anything he's taken from your estate is deserved and complimentary"

Genevieve let out a sigh of relief.

"They might fire my arse." David made a gravely sound in the back of his throat. "But they won't cross the street to punch my lights out."

"I'll ask you again. Why can't you leave them right now, today?"

"I like our plan. And I need to stay at the firm to gather forensic evidence. Because I'm one of the partners assigned to the Laney Estate, I can access more than two hundred years of information without arousing suspicion."

"Is there a confidentiality issue or conflict of interest here? Would you be in trouble if you're caught sharing information that will incriminate the firm?"

"I could, but if I uncover evidence of his wrongdoing, Sir Mark certainly isn't going to press charges. If this doesn't go our way, however, I could be disbarred. I'll be useless to you then. But I've always wanted to attend clown college."

"Well then," Philip raised his glass. "Here's to having our very own jester."

<hr />

With her ear pressed to the slim crack in the paneling, she could hear their every word. The secret passageway was narrow, but she was a sylph and able to float easily through the corridor. She couldn't believe her luck. The people she had targeted for over a year were beginning to gather under one roof. How very convenient. She felt a tickle in her nostrils from the dust in the hidden hall and brought her rose-scented handkerchief to her nose. Scrunching her face, she willed the sneeze to evaporate.

SIXTEEN

S UNDAY MORNING AFTER breakfast, the threesome set out to explore the estate before David returned to London. They drove down lanes, bumped through fields and across streams. The old Land Rover Defender had seen many years of service and had the nicks and dents to prove it. Philip loved its worn, rugged appearance: a vehicle born to work and happy to do so.

Philip lumbered across a rutted field, which merged into a stand of trees. He eased the Defender to a stop. "Look over there," he whispered, pointing.

In the back, Genevieve squinted and leaned forward through the seats. "What are we looking for?"

"There's a deer in that stand of birch," Philip said.

"That's a red deer." David pulled his sunglasses to the bridge of his nose and looked over the top of them. "You often see them in the Highlands."

"Wow!" Philip grabbed his phone and snapped several pictures. "That's quite a pair of antlers."

"He's magnificent." Genevieve gaped in awe.

They watched in silence until the buck wandered deeper into the trees, then the Defender lumbered back across the field until they reached the lane.

"I have no idea where we are." Philip looked at David for an indication of which way to go.

David looked at his GPS. "I think you need to turn around to return to the Hall. It looks like we're four or five miles west of the manor."

Philip looped back into the field. As he drove back onto the narrow gravel road, a loud explosion pierced the air, and the glass shattered on the passenger's side.

Philip slammed the car to a stop. "What the fuck!"

David slumped forward, held in place only by his seat belt.

"David! David!" Genevieve shrieked. Blood streamed down the left side of David's head. Stunned, she reached forward to touch the sticky warmth oozing from a five-inch-long rut across his skull. "Philip, David's bleeding!

Philip pivoted in his seat toward his limp friend. "David." He shook the lifeless body. "David!" he yelled again, pulling up one of David's eyelids. To his relief, David's pupil reacted to the light.

Genevieve yanked the cardigan from her shoulders, wrapped it around her hand and pressed hard against David's wound. Philip punched the screen on his phone. Almost instantly they heard Mrs. MacIntosh's voice on the speaker. "Mrs. Mac, call 999. David's been shot and we need an ambulance. We'll be back to the Hall as fast as we can get there."

Philip gunned the engine, gravel spraying. He accelerated on the winding lane, taking the turns at breakneck speed. Genevieve swayed drunkenly in the back, trying to keep pressure on David's wound.

Eight minutes later the Defender screeched to a stop in front of Wilmingrove Hall. Harrington and Wallace stood at the ready. Harrington held a shotgun, Wallace a decanter of brandy. Sirens wailed in the distance, quickly gaining volume.

Mrs. MacIntosh flew out of the front door, waving her cell phone. "The ambulance is on its way," she cried.

The terrified group huddled in the driveway, watching with relief as a police car and a lemon-yellow ambulance screamed toward them along the allee with a "nee-naw, nee-naw". Moments later the cavalcade arrived in a flurry of noise and flashing lights. Three paramedics jumped out of the transport almost before it stopped.

"He's over here!" Philip stood next to the open passenger door, his eyes on David's lifeless body.

"Excuse me, sir. Please step back." Carrying an oxygen tank the paramedic stepped in front of Philip. He put two fingers on the inside of David's wrist. "Faint pulse," He said to his partners.

Afraid to let go, Genevieve was still applying pressure to David's skull. The EMT put his hand over Genevieve's and gently pulled it away from the wound. "Thank you, Ma'am. I'll take over from here." He probed David's bleeding skull. "No entry wound," he said. "A bullet appears to have grazed his skull. The wound looks shallow." He put the oxygen mask over David's mouth and nose, securing the elastic behind his head. Two medics eased him from the car and onto a stretcher.

"Where are you taking him?" Philip began focusing on next steps.

"We'll take him to LGI. Leeds General," said the red-haired paramedic with 'P. Jamison' embroidered on his jacket. "That's the nearest trauma center."

Two paramedics were already in the back of the ambulance with David. They inserted an IV and attached electrodes to David's chest, all while talking through their wireless earbuds to the LGI trauma surgeons. The third tech slammed the rear double doors, sprinted to the driver's side, hopped in, and gunned the engine. The ambulance retreated until it turned onto the main road, when the siren split the air once more.

Unable to move, everyone watched until the ambulance was out of sight. Twenty-four minutes had elapsed since the crack of the gun shot. It seemed like a nanosecond. It seemed like forever.

"Philip, I'm going to the hospital while you deal with the police." Genevieve turned to the house to get her purse.

Philip grabbed her arm. "Harrington should take you. You don't know the roads and it will be faster if he drives. And, G." Philip lifted Genevieve's hands in his. "You'll want to wash your hands and change." They looked down to see the brown stains on her wool skirt and palms, all smeared with David's blood.

Genevieve's pulse quickened. Tears stung her eyes. "Oh, Philip." Her voice was raspy. "What if..."

"Don't." Philip put a finger on her mouth and stopped her before she could finish her thought. He kissed her forehead, then her lips. "Go get changed. Harrington and I will have things ready for you to leave when you come back."

Genevieve kissed Philip on the cheek then raced into the Hall, still clutching her bloody sweater.

"Actually, my lord, it would be faster to take the helicopter." Harrington was standing at Philip's side. "Captain Bruni was waiting to take Sir David back to London this morning. He's in the chopper, ready to go. I'll go tell him they're flying to the hospital rather than London."

When Genevieve returned twenty minutes later, Mrs. MacIntosh was waiting with the golf cart. The chopper blades were already circling in a rhythmic slap, slap, slap by the time they reached the helipad. Genevieve ducked to climb the helicopter's stairs, walked to the back, and took her seat.

"My Lady. May I get you anything?" asked William.

"Thank you, but no, William." She pulled a tissue from her pocket to dab her eyes and blow her nose. She snapped her seatbelt. The door closed with a "thunk," and they were ready for takeoff.

On the ground, Philip saw the chopper rise, pause, then shoot forward. He watched until it disappeared over the horizon, and willed everything to be all right.

"Excuse me, Lord Crosswick." Buried in his thoughts, Philip was startled by a husky voice. "Sorry. Thought you heard me come up. I'm DCI Fields." The rumpled man scratched his head, tousling his thinning hair, leaving several strands sticking straight up. "We have an interesting situation here, don't we?" Cigarette smoke escaped from the policeman's mouth with each word. He took a last drag, flicked his cigarette butt to the ground, and toed it into the gravel driveway.

Philip gave Fields a withering look and pointed to the stub. "Do you mind?"

Confused, the copper gazed at his shoe before realizing Philip's meaning. He squatted with a grunt, picked up the butt and put it into his pocket with no apology.

"Shall we go into the Hall, Lord Crosswick? Somewhere we can talk."

"Follow me," Philip snarled, and headed toward the main house.

The detective tried to keep up with Philip's long strides, wheezing with each step. Just inside the Hall, Fields stopped. He bent over, his hands on his knees to catch his breath.

"Are you all right, Detective?" Philip turned to see Fields's bright-red face.

The policeman held up one hand and said nothing for a moment. "I'm fine," he gasped. "Just a bit winded. You're a fast walker." At last, he stood, his breath less labored. "Where to?"

"We'll go to my office." Philip led the way through the grand salon, where several uniformed men and women milled around, some on phones, some waiting to be given a task.

"You might want to give up those cigarettes. And more fruits and vegetables wouldn't hurt you." Philip couldn't resist chiding this tubby, frowsy man.

Arriving at his study, Philip motioned for Fields to sit in a green leather wing-back chair.

Mrs. MacIntosh was right behind them, carrying a tray with coffee service. Without asking, she poured Philip's coffee then handed a cup to Fields. She placed a plate of chocolate biscuits on Philip's desk in front of the detective and scurried out, closing the door behind her.

DCI Fields leaned forward, eyeing the wafers, a drop of saliva at the corner of his mouth. "These are my favorite fruits and vegetables." A chuckle rolled from the back of his throat, and he plucked two biscuits from the plate. He took a gulp of his coffee then a bite of cookie. Crumbs sprayed the front of his shirt and the lapels of his rumpled suit.

Philip walked to the study windows, needing a moment to tamp down his disgust for this man. He was stunned at the number of officers already outside combing every inch of the terrace, each wearing latex gloves and blue paper booties. A policewoman picked up a cigarette butt, no doubt another one of Fields's, and placed it in an evidence bag.

"What's going on out there?" Philip turned back to the detective. "Why are there cops all over the terrace? Why aren't they in the field where David was shot?" Philip grew angrier with each question he asked. He stood in front of Fields, menacing the detective "Do your people know what the hell they're doing?"

"I assure you they do, my lord," Fields shot back, all of a sudden looking less like a fool, more like a detective. "We have police everywhere, including the field and woods near the shooting. They are combing the area for shells, footprints, fibers, anything that will shed light on who tried to kill Sir David, you, and your wife."

"Me? My wife?" The blood drained from Philip's face. He

froze, his eyes locked with the detectives. He paced back to the window, looked out, and then strode back across the room to stand in front of Fields.

"Lord Crosswick please sit down," Fields directed. "Please, my lord, sit."

"Tried to kill…" Philip half sat against the edge of his desk, his arms stiff at his sides, his knuckles white, gripping the curved, mahogany top. His armpits felt clammy. "Wasn't it an accident? Someone hunting. Maybe a couple of guys were drunk and thought…."

"My forensics team dug four bullets out of the car. Two embedded in the back seat, two in the passenger door. This rules out hunters accidently firing at your vehicle."

"Tell me, Fields, who would want me dead?" His voice cracked as he asked the unthinkable.

"You tell me." Fields turned the question back to Philip. "Has anything out of the ordinary happened to you in the last few months that would make you a target?"

"I barely know anyone in this country. That makes no sense." Philip ran his hands through his hair then rubbed his face with his palms. He studied his shoes and chewed his lower lip. "You're talking about the inheritance."

"Money is a powerful motivator." Fields's gaze lasered into Philip.

"So, you're suggesting David wasn't the target." The silence in the room waited for someone to speak. "Only my family stands to gain by my death. That's my wife, son, daughter-in-law and their two young children."

"Have you already altered your will to reflect the inheritance?"

"It's in the works, but no. The estate is complicated. As you might imagine, it will take some time to complete the will and make all the transfers."

"Is there somebody who would benefit if the will *isn't* changed?"

For the first time, Philip noticed the keen intelligence in the detective's eyes. He shoved himself to stand and walked back to the window. Deep in thought, he stared out at the terrace without seeing. The entertaining mystery of whether Sir Mark was embezzling or not had turned into a potentially deadly whodunit. If he was in danger, Genevieve and the rest of his family would be targets as well, wouldn't they? With that jarring thought, Philip spun away from the window.

"Fields!" His eyes were wild. "Genevieve needs protection. You need to make a call and get somebody to the hospital."

The detective tilted his head and stopped his fingers from drumming on the arm of his chair. "A security team has already been dispatched."

Philip looked at him, with relief and new admiration. "I guess this isn't your first rodeo," he said with a sheepish smile.

"Or as we Brits would say, 'I didn't come down with the last shower.'" Fields looked at Philip with genuine sympathy. "I don't suppose this is what you expected when you learned you'd just inherited a title and a fortune, is it?"

"It is not. Quite the contrary."

Fields didn't hear the vibrating hum, but Philip lunged to grab his phone from where it sat on his desk, knocking over a small vase. Genevieve's grinning photo filled his screen as he jabbed 'accept' and looked around for a cloth to sop up the water trickling its way across the desktop.

"G," he shouted into the phone. "I've been waiting for you to call. How is David?" Philip held his breath, waiting for Genevieve to answer.

"I don't know," she sobbed into the phone. "They won't tell me how he is. They won't tell me anything, not even if he is still alive."

DCI Fields righted the vase, plopped the flowers back in haphazardly, and dabbed up the little bit of water with a linen napkin. He leaned towards Philip, straining to hear Genevieve's words. "Put her on speaker," he whispered.

Philip laid the phone on the desk and the detective bent forward, aiming his voice at the speaker. "Lady Crosswick, this is Detective Chief Inspector Fields. I'm here with the investigative team. I'm not surprised the hospital staff won't release Sir David's information to you. Our Data Protection Act safeguards the privacy of patients. While you're talking to your husband, I'll phone and find out Sir David's status. I'll be right back."

"Thank you, DCI Fields. I knew someone could help."

Philip could hear Genevieve's annoyance. He waited until Fields was well out of earshot. "G, are you okay? I'm so sorry I'm not there with you."

"You're right where you should be. Sorry about the tears. They're frustration more than anything else. I was about to pop somebody in the nose, I was so exasperated. Does DCI Fields know what he's doing?"

"An hour ago, I would have said he's a joke, but I stand

corrected." Philip sat in his leather desk chair and leaned back. His temples throbbed with tension. He rolled his head in slow circles hoping to relieve the ache in his neck.

"What made you change your mind?" Genevieve's voice was full of warmth.

Philip relaxed, comforted hearing his wife. The throbbing in his head begin to ease.

Just as he was about to respond, Fields walked back in. His chubby cheeks bloomed at each side of his smile. "Put me on speaker. Lady Crosswick, I just had a word with Michael Murton, the hospital head."

"Believe me, I know who he is. I had *several* words with him just a few minutes ago, none of them pleasant," Genevieve's voice dripped sarcasm. "I'm sorry, DCI Fields. What did you find out? Is David all right? My fingers are crossed."

"Uncross your fingers, my lady. Has Mr. Singh joined you in the lounge? He is Sir David's surgeon."

Philip and Fields could hear Genevieve talking to someone at her end of the phone. Introductions were exchanged and Mr. Singh began. "When he arrived, though Sir David was conscious and stable, it appeared he had lost a great deal of blood. Head injuries generally bleed profusely. Until they are thoroughly assessed, it is difficult to determine their severity.

"Sir David was most lucky. The bullet grazed the left side of the skull, creating a shallow, ten-centimeter channel from the left temple to just above the ear, more like an abrasion, really. The incident was sufficient to make him lose consciousness, due more to shock than injury. Blood loss was not as substantial as originally thought, so it was not necessary to transfuse the patient. Sir David is alive because of a matter of millimeters. A few millimeters to the right and you would be planning a funeral. As it turns out, he didn't even need sutures, just a bandage. We don't often see such good fortune."

At one end of the phone Genevieve couldn't breathe. At the other, Philip had no words.

DCI Fields broke the silence. "How is Sir David now?"

"Aided by the morphine, he has been sleeping, but he was waking just before I came to the lounge. Lady Crosswick, anytime you want to see him, you may. I'd like to keep him here a day or two to insure we have missed nothing. If he progresses as I expect, we will discharge him on Tuesday. He should rest for about a week, resuming his usual activities after that. As I said, he was extremely lucky. Now, if you'll excuse me, I'll get back to my other patients."

"DCI Fields, give me a few minutes to talk to my wife, then we can resume our conversation. Why don't you go to the kitchen and have Mrs. Lomax get you a sandwich or something?" The detective's eyes lit up at the mention of food and he went off in search of the kitchen.

"Tell me what's happening there," Genevieve said. Philip could hear the longing in her voice to be at Wilmingrove Hall and with him.

"Police are swarming everywhere and they're interrogating every person on our staff. They dug two bullets out of the back seat of the Defender, where you were sitting. They believe one was the bullet that grazed David." Philip went silent.

"Philip, did I lose you?"

"No, no. I'm still here." His voice was husky. "The bullet missed you by inches." He cleared his throat. Cleared it again. "G, I can't stand to think about what might have happened."

"Philip, nothing happened to me." The terrifying implications of Philip's words didn't immediately register. "I'm here, safe and sound. It's David we have to worry about."

"Nonetheless, the York police are sending two plainclothes officers to the hospital. They'll be with you until you come back to the Hall. Then we'll figure out what we should do going forward. I guess we should have done something about security when David suggested it in New York."

"Do you really think I need protection here at the hospital?"

"I do." Philip left no room for argument. "DCI Fields believes this was attempted murder. He also believes David may not have been the target." His voice cracked. Silence reclaimed the air between them.

Blood rushed to Genevieve's head. "Do you think they're right?"

"I have no idea, but I can't think of any other reason our car would be peppered with bullets, can you?"

Genevieve tried to hold on to her thread of calm, but it was quickly dissolving.

A firm knock at the door startled her.

"I heard a knock. Is that the security detail?" Philip snapped.

She looked up as a man pushed open the door just enough to stick his head in. "Lady Crosswick?"

"Philip, hold on. I think the police are here."

"I'm going nowhere," Philip said at the other end of the line.

The men moved into the lounge, scanning the room as they walked toward her.

"Lady Crosswick, I'm DCI Marcum and this is DS Cromwell. Did anyone inform you that you would be assigned a protection detail?"

"My husband and I were just talking about that. Is it absolutely necessary?"

DCI Marcum shifted from one foot to the other and cleared his throat. "Given the circumstances, it seems prudent to take such precautions until we have determined what's going on here."

Genevieve put the phone back to her ear. "Did you hear that, Philip?"

"I did and I agree. As soon as you've seen David, get into the chopper, and get home. Until then, do exactly as the police advise. Please, G. You have two jobs: see David, then get back here safely. I love you."

Tears sprang to Genevieve's eyes. Philip's love was always evident, but he seldom said the words. He preferred to tell Genevieve in deeds: a pat on the bottom, a kiss on the back of the neck, a cup of coffee delivered to her in bed. Hearing the words out loud pricked her emotions, which were already raw.

"Philip, I love you, too.

She couldn't keep the smile from her face. What a bunch of fools. She was throwing them into chaos, and it was so easy. This was going to be fun. A lot of fun.

She waited until the mighty Lord Crosswick and the buffoon detective left the study before drifting back through the dark corridor, careful to move silently, until at last, she came to the stairs that took her to just behind the wine cellar, then out the door near the stables. She had to get back before she was missed.

SEVENTEEN

A FEW DAYS AFTER David was shot, the police swarmed the estate, finding a lead, tracking it to a dead end, finding another lead, tracking it to another dead end. There was a frenzy of activity when forensics experts confirmed the bullets came from a 1994 Purdey rifle, which was part of the Laney gun collection. The rifle was always kept under lock and key in the gun safe in the estate manager's office. The only people with keys to the safe were Sean Harrington, the estate manager, and Andrew Frazier, the estate falconer. All guns were accounted for when Sergeant Kafritz took inventory the Friday before the shooting.

The morning of the shooting, Harrington had taken a shotgun into the woods to check a fox trap. When he returned, he replaced the shotgun and noted all the guns were in the safe. He insisted to the police the keys were in the lockbox. When the police retrieved the Purdey rifle from the safe, it was wiped to a spectacular sheen, just like the other forty-seven guns in the collection.

DCI Fields was convinced either Harrington or Frazier was the culprit. He couldn't imagine how anyone else could have accessed the Purdey rifle. However, after hours of interviews, Fields confirmed alibis for both men: when David was shot, Frazier was forty miles away in York meeting with a conservation specialist, and security footage confirmed Harrington was working in the stables.

When that lead fizzled, all the coppers agreed the whole thing was a hell of a magic trick. What the police couldn't agree on was how this magic trick was done, who did it, and what the motive was.

It was four weeks since the shooting and still little was resolved. During David's recuperation at the Hall, he, Philip, and Genevieve spent endless hours reviewing, hypothesizing, and speculating.

"The only thing that makes sense is that Charlotte's ghost took the rifle, floated out into the field and shot at David," Philip offered one rainy afternoon as they threw around ideas.

"And why would she want to shoot me?" David asked.

Proud of his theory, Philip grinned. "Because, of course, you don't believe in ghosts and that pisses her off!"

They debunked each other's theories. They went down one rabbit hole after another, each one more preposterous than the previous.

One evening after dinner, the three sat in the library before a crackling fire. After several glasses of wine, Genevieve was sure she had the answer. "I've got it! I've got it!' She bounced on the edge of the love seat where she sat with Philip.

"Oh, do tell," David said with an overly posh accent.

"Remember Revy Harris, the American girl Jonathon Laney fell in love with, then sent away?

"No." David shook his head. "But go on."

Genevieve stopped bouncing and sat still on the edge of her cushion, eyes wide and intense. "I bet Revy Harris heard about Philip's inheritance and went berserk, thinking it should be hers, since Jonathon had been her lover. She came here intending to kill Philip so she could get her hands on the estate, but she wasn't a very good shot and hit David instead. What do you think of that?"

The room was dead silent for a moment, then David threw a toss pillow at her. "Hisssss! Boooooo!"

The men rained down a chorus of jeers until she put her palms up in surrender. "No, huh?"

"Of all the crazy theories we've conjured, that's maybe the craziest. But you're still pretty cute." Philip leaned forward and planted a kiss on her cheek.

With each deflated speculation, they returned to the facts they knew, facts that pointed to Sir Mark Holmes: Sir Mark had created numerous revenue streams at the Hall, extracting large sums of money from the estate, and he had used the Laney wine collection as his personal never-ending cellar. And then there was the recent, extravagant upgrade of the kitchen, and the flawless maintenance of the Hall—though those were hardly capital offenses.

In the end, David suggested that when Philip became the heir to the Laney fortune, Sir Mark feared his schemes would soon be discovered. Genevieve believed that Sir Mark panicked at being found out and hired someone to shoot at the Defender, thinking this would frighten the Warwicks back to the States. There were many holes in their plotline, and they had not addressed the mystery of the Purdey, but the three amateur sleuths bolstered each other with high fives as they advanced their scheme to ensnare their villain.

"So, we're all in agreement: we'll host a fabulous party. We'll invite the partners from Holmes Fitch Smythson Morrow, some of the peers we've met, people from our museum and the Foundation, our neighbors, and any other fancy people who come to mind." Genevieve gathered steam as she talked about the gala that she'd already planned in her head.

"David, your job is to spend the evening with Sir Mark. Ply him with alcohol and draw him out about how he used the estate to line his pockets."

"Yes, ma'am. Whatever you say, ma'am." David gave a smart salute.

"Philip, your job is to charm the other partners into telling you anything that might support our theory that Sir Mark is the villain in all of this."

Philip narrowed his eyes and raked his hands through his thick hair. "I'm sure they'll spill their guts the moment I spin my web of charisma. They won't be able to resist my suavity."

"Suavity?" Genevieve and David said together.

"Ha! Where did you get that word?" David scoffed.

"I think it's a word. But if it's not, it should be." Philip's grin lit his eyes. "Either way, it describes me to a tee, don't you think?"

"Sure, Philip." Genevieve gave him a sidelong stare then looked back at David, who shrugged his shoulders. She raised her goblet and they all stood to toast for good luck.

"I guess we're ready, then!" she said, and drained her glass.

EIGHTEEN

I T H A D B E E N years since the Hall felt so vibrant. Mrs. MacIntosh and Wallace were in their full glory supervising, arranging, rearranging. Genevieve directed caterers to the kitchen, musicians to the landing on the grand staircase and the last of the flowers to the bar. Wilmingrove Hall pulsed with energy. Staff bustled. Florists had filled every room with aroma and brilliant color. Extended to its full length, the dining table glittered with silver, crystal, china—all polished to a spectacular sheen. Six towering candelabras adorned the center of the table, swathed in coral roses. On every hearth, fires awaited a match.

"Tutu!" Cheeks pink from the chilly wind, nine-year-old Alex rushed into the great hall, anxious to tell his grandmother about the morning's explorations. Hot on his heels, seven-year-old Ella clutched a bag of oats with a hole in it, leaking its treasure onto the sparkling marble floor.

Much to Philip and Genevieve's delight, their son, daughter-in-law and grandchildren had arrived two days before. Because of the unresolved shooting, Philip suggested the family remain within the estate: the house, stables, gardens, and the mews.

Happy to oblige, they had spent every moment exploring the many nooks and crannies of Wilmingrove Hall, still overwhelmed by the grandeur.

"Yes, my darlings!" Genevieve beamed. "What exciting adventure have you been on?" For Philip and Genevieve, the joy of having their family with them was overwhelming. Genevieve had not stopped smiling since they arrived. The couple loved watching their family discover excitement and delight at every turn. Alexander and Ella had already experienced a falconry lesson. Alex was in love with the Harris hawk he had flown. Ella was in love with dashing "Hawk Man," as the children were now calling Andrew Frazier. For Alex and Ella, this was their own personal fairytale.

"We fed the horses!" Ella flaunted her punctured sack. "Uh-oh," she said, watching the oats stream to the floor.

Swooping in, Mrs. MacIntosh snatched the bag and closed her hand around the hole.

"Never mind, Lady Ella. It's nothing. We'll take care of this quick as a flash and everything will be tickety-boo. Come on, you two. Let's go to the conservatory and have a tea party." Mrs. MacIntosh turned to Julia, raised an eyebrow to ask permission.

"Have fun!" said Julia.

And off they went.

Genevieve gathered her clipboard, cell phone, sweater, and glasses. "Are you two ready for some lunch?" she asked Duncan and Julia. "Your dad and David are meeting us in the conservatory."

"What's he been doing?" Duncan asked. Since Philip was confirmed heir to the Laney title and fortune two months ago, he and Duncan had talked often about the vastness of the estate, but Duncan couldn't fully appreciate what it all meant until he experienced it in person. The magnitude of wealth and responsibility was hard to comprehend. As his parents had told him, it was life changing for all of them. There were many decisions to be made, but none that had to be made today. So, for the moment, he and Julia would enjoy the pleasure of this unfolding adventure.

"He's been supervising the caterers. You know your dad. Any chance to hang out with people who know what they're doing in the kitchen is too tempting. Duncan, it's your responsibility tonight to make sure he stays where the party is, not where the party is being prepared." Philip loved all things culinary. He loved learning about food. He loved experimenting with food. He loved the process as much as the product. Perhaps in another life, he would have been a master chef, but at this point, dabbling was satisfying enough.

Though a lavish evening was mere hours away, Elsie Lomax had crafted a picture-perfect luncheon for the four Warwicks and Sir David.

"I could get used to this," Julia said.

Genevieve motioned for her daughter-in-law to take a seat next to David, looking out over the vast gardens. Duncan held the chair opposite for his mother.

"Look at that, G. We did something right! What a gentleman." Philip loved having their son with them.

"Do you need help with your chair, old man?" Duncan grinned at his dad.

"Be careful, little boy." Philip looked up at his handsome six-foot-three son. "You're not a spring chicken anymore, you know. It won't be long before we're the same age."

Duncan straightened, adding another quarter inch to his frame. Looking down at his father, he said, "No matter how old we are, neither one of us will ever dunk a basketball!"

"Yup, one of our great failures, for sure," Philip agreed. The banter continued as they ate and drank their way through a jolly lunch until Philip raised the subject of the evening's event. "This party we're throwing tonight, we need to tell you about some of the people. Most of the partners from the law firm will be here tonight, including Sir Mark Holmes."

Julia's dark curls bounced as she looked from Philip to David then back to Philip. "Does this have anything to do with David being shot?"

"Sir Mark was in London at the time, but he could have an accomplice or have hired someone to do his dirty work. The police aren't keen on us investigating on our own."

"Mom, Dad, I think I have to be the voice of reason here," said Duncan. "Don't you think the intelligent thing to do is to come home with us after the party?"

"What?" Genevieve's response was more forceful than she had intended. "Why would we do that?"

Duncan looked at David. "David, help me out here. Hell, you're the one who was shot. Don't you think it's too dangerous for my parents to stay here? And what about you? You could come back to the States with them until the police figure out what's going on here."

David rolled his dessert fork between his fingers. "I, um…" he began, unsure what to say. He placed the fork back by his plate.

"Duncan, don't drag David into this." Philip's heart warmed at his son's concerns. "I can't say the idea hasn't occurred to me, but your mother and I think we should stay and help the police."

"We just don't want anything to happen to you," Julia chimed in.

"Okay, everybody." Genevieve stood, ready to get back to work. "Let's see what happens tonight. Maybe Sir Mark will stand at the top of the grand staircase, make a dramatic confession then throw himself on our mercy."

"Any bets?" Duncan said.

NINETEEN

AT THE STROKE of half six, the parade began. Rolls after Jag after Bentley after Porsche rolled down the long driveway to Wilmingrove Hall, depositing their tony passengers at the stately home's grand entrance. Lights blazed in every window, spilling onto lawns and terraces. Furs, that hadn't seen an outing for years, draped over bare shoulders.

◆ ❍ ◆

She was lying on her stomach in a grove of silver birch, fifty yards from the manor's façade. Looking through high-powered night vision binoculars, she could see diamonds glittering on ears and sparkling around necks as guests moved into the great hall. The chill of the ground crept its way through her black, lycra bodysuit until it reached the flesh of her prone torso. It was time to steal into Wilmingrove Hall and melt into the bustle of the party.

It was time to let them know she meant business. She felt her excitement rise and willed her breathing to slow.

⋯ ∷ ⇥●◗◇◖●⇤ ∷ ⋯

Philip and Genevieve greeted their guests in the grand hall alongside Duncan and Julia, introducing the future Earl and Countess of Crosswick. Philip and Duncan made a handsome father and son duo, resembling a Ralph Lauren advertisement in their classic tuxedos, pleated-front shirts, and black hand tied bowties.

Standing between them, Genevieve was the picture of easy grace in a long-sleeved gown with a burgundy velvet off-the-shoulder top and full tapestry floor-length skirt, her waist cinched by a wide burgundy belt. Her radiant smile greeted each guest.

To Duncan's left, Julia completed the elegant family picture in a flesh-colored figure-hugging gown with a black lace overlay. It was easy to see she was a runner. A mass of curly mahogany hair sat loosely piled on her head, tendrils dancing around her cheeks. She grasped each person's hand as they made their way down the line to her and welcomed them with her warm smile.

Next to Julia at the end of the receiving line, a liveried server offered each guest a glass of Champagne, at which point everyone could move into the party.

Most of the invitees hadn't entered Wilmingrove Hall for years, if ever. If they had attended a town or county event—a fete, a town celebration, perhaps sheep dog trials—they would only have roamed the grounds. The house would have been off-limits. But now, invited by Lord and Lady Crosswick, guests moved through the grand hall, eyes wide with awe. They drifted into the drawing room, dining room and music room, drawn by the sound of a jazz pianist at the Bosendorfer. Wilmingrove Hall was dressed to dazzle.

By ten minutes of seven, the contingent from Holmes Fitch Smythson Morrow began to arrive. First through the door was the youngest partner, Henry Fitch and his wife, Gillian. Henry looked less disheveled than when Genevieve met him in New York at the law offices. Perhaps he had shed a couple of pounds, was sporting a fresh haircut, or maybe it was his well-cut tuxedo. Whatever it was, Genevieve thought he looked quite sweet. At the other end of the spectrum, his wife Gillian was breathtaking, her wippet-thin frame draped in layers of flowing crimson silk, each tier edged in fuchsia. She had pulled her blond hair into a severe chignon, which gave her a slightly feral look.

"Who's that?" Philip said under his breath.

"I think it's Henry Fitch's wife, Gillian. Brace yourself."

Genevieve felt Philip tense. "She looks scary."

"Lord Crosswick, Philip! I'm Gillian Fitch," she gushed, rushing toward Philip, hands outstretched. "How marvelous to meet you at last." She kissed Philip on both cheeks, leaving a streak of red lipstick. She wiped his cheek with her thumb as she held his gaze.

"Gillian," Genevieve cut in. "We're delighted you and Henry could join us this evening. And Henry." Genevieve thrust her hand across Philip to grab Henry's hand, breaking Gillian's hold on Philip. "We couldn't be happier to see you!"

Philip threw Genevieve an amused sidelong glance. Duncan looked down at his mother, tickled at how she was protecting her territory.

To Genevieve's relief, other partygoers from the firm began to pour through the door, prompting the Fitches to move down the line.

And so it went for the next half hour until most guests had arrived.

"Why don't you two go have some fun," Philip said, relieving Duncan and Julia of their co-hosting duties. "That was quite a maneuver, my beautiful little blocker," Philip chuckled into Genevieve's ear.

Genevieve gave him a kiss on the cheek. "A girl's gotta do what a girl's gotta do to protect her husband from vultures in evening gowns!" She winked and floated off into the boisterous crowd.

TWENTY

FOR THE LAST hour, Philip had been holding court in the music room, talking to a group of foundation staff and Lillie Langdon, the Executive Director of the Laney Museum of Fine Arts Foundation. They were young, creative, energetic, and full of fun. The pianist was playing Miles Davis, the mood in the music room was full of life, and Philip was having a wonderful time.

He saw Genevieve across the salon, caught her eye, and waved her over. It took her several minutes to make her way through the crowd. Everyone wanted a piece of Lady Crosswick, the Lady of the manor and architect of this dazzling evening. At last, she reached Philip's side and slid her hand into his, squeezing it. The exuberant cluster of artsy guests greeted her with toasts and *la bise*, the French double-cheek kiss. It always amused Philip and Genevieve how the English loved everything *from* France but loathed the French.

Genevieve whispered in Philip's ear. "Have you seen David? Do you have any idea how he's doing?"

"When I saw him last, he was in the library with Mark. I've been shirking my hosting duties far too long, talking to this group, but I've been having a terrific time. These kids are brimming with ideas for the Foundation, and I've picked up some interesting tidbits that might explain where some of the money from the Hall has gone."

"That's exciting and more than you bargained for. I can't wait to hear. Have you seen Duncan and Julia? I hope they're having a good time."

"They always do," Philip said. "I'm sure they're busy charming all our guests."

"Of course, they are. It's impossible not to be charmed by those two. Why don't you go find David and Mark while I spend some time with the Foundation crew? You're well on your way to establishing a good relationship with these youngsters, old man. I'd like to do the same." Genevieve threw Philip a wicked grin.

He returned the favor by squeezing her bottom and hoping no one had noticed.

She watched as he wove his way through the crowd, navigating the flood of merrymakers. She felt a little giddy and couldn't help but smile as he turned from the far side of the room to look at her, and she threw him a kiss. "Lucky girl," she thought, then turned back to the energetic, young group.

Philip made his way through the grand salon where a noisy group crowded around the bar. Cheers and claps erupted every few seconds. As he watched, a bottle flew up high above the heads of the crowd, followed by a roar of appreciation.

"What's going on?" he asked a guest as another whoop exploded from the crowd.

"The barmaid's putting on quite a show."

Philip edged into the middle of the swarm of guests until he could see the main attraction, a young, sprite of a girl. Black, spikey hair surrounded a heart-shaped face, highlighted by enormous brown eyes and a full crimson mouth. Her clever banter accompanied the deft preparation of drink after drink. She was a circus act with a stand-up comic's patter. Philip marveled at her skill and antics, wondering if she worked for the caterer.

He finally backed out of the crowd and continued his search for David and Sir Mark. He found them in the library in front of the fireplace, which sparked and crackled with new logs. Compared to the other rooms, the library was an oasis of calm.

Deep in conversation, the two men didn't notice Philip until he was directly in front of them. The moment they felt his presence, they stopped speaking and looked up.

"So, what am I missing?"

Sir Mark motioned to the chair across from him. "Lord Crosswick, please join us,"

"Thank you, Sir Mark. But please call me Philip."

"If you call me Mark."

"I can do that, Mark. I hope you both have been having a good time. Have you had anything to eat? And where are your drinks?"

"We have drinks coming." said David. "Philip, the food is scrummy. Were you in the kitchen all day cooking?" David teased.

"Of course, I did it all. Not bad, eh?"

"Not bad at all. Ah, great. Drinks." David rubbed his hands as a server arrived carrying a silver tray with two tumblers, one with two fingers of what appeared to be whisky, the other filled close to the brim with a golden liquid, a wisp of warmth rising from the glass.

David looked at the server apologetically. "I know I asked for a mead, but I changed my mind. Would you please bring me a whisky, neat?"

"But, sir, the barmaid told me to be sure I gave you the mead."

"And so you have." David plucked the glass from the tray. "Now, would you please bring me a tumbler of scotch?"

"David, take my whisky," Sir Mark said. "I quite fancy a mead."

The two exchanged glasses and Mark took a sip. "This is brilliant." He inhaled the honeyed aroma. "Philip, is this made on the estate?" He took a longer draw this time. "If it is, you should bottle it. It would be a spectacular revenue stream."

"I have no idea where the mead is from." Philip raised an eyebrow at Sir Mark's candor about creating cashflow from the Hall but decided not to comment. "What have I missed? Have you two solved the world's problems?"

"Not all of them. I've been telling David about opening Wilmingrove Hall to the public the last couple of years and how much revenue it generated for the Foundation."

Surprised at Mark's openness, Philip leaned forward.

Sir Mark continued, "In, oh, probably the last five years of his life, Lord Crosswick became concerned about the financial security of the estate. He wanted to insure the properties and the Foundation were sufficiently endowed. No matter how much I assured him of their fiscal health, the older he got, the more he worried. This is not unusual. Often aging brings on irrational financial fears. I've seen it over and over." Mark spoke with ease with no indication that he might be lying.

For the first time, Philip wondered if their conjecture about Sir Mark being the villain was unfounded.

Sir Mark took a long, slow drink of mead, closing his eyes in enjoyment. He licked the residue from his lips. "Delicious."

"I'm so glad you like it." Philip had not seen Sir Mark in a relaxed setting before and he liked this charming version.

Mark set his glass on his side table and went on. "It would be an understatement to say Jonathon Laney was in command of his empire until the end. Three years ago, he charged us with two massive projects. The first was to update all his transportation. He wanted a new plane, new helicopter, new cars. He intended to visit his holdings in France, America, and, of course, Wilmingrove Hall. To do that, he would need transportation that could accommodate his needs."

"This is fascinating." Philip thought Mark Holmes was either a masterful liar or he was telling the truth.

"The second was to make certain all his properties were in excellent repair and self-sustaining. His intention was to divest himself of any property that wasn't financially autonomous. He gave Winston Fitch and me eighteen months to accomplish the task, with instructions for strict confidentiality." Mark picked up his glass and the last of the golden mead was gone.

David's curiosity was piqued. "Why did he want it to be confidential? Why was that important?"

"The markets, David. The markets. He didn't want anyone to get wind of his plan to dump his unproductive holdings. He feared the markets would interpret that as financial vulnerability. At ninety-five, the old man was still sharp as a needle. Winston and I worked like demons, creating revenue streams, eking out every pound we could from the properties."

As Mark spoke, Genevieve wandered in and perched on the arm of Philip's chair. She and Mark exchanged smiles, and he continued.

"We could do nothing to create revenue with the apartments in Paris and New York. They were, however, appreciating at a fast clip. The vineyard in St. Emilion and horse farm in Kentucky had always done well, but Wilmingrove Hall was all outgo, no income, so that was the big challenge. And I just told you what plans we implemented here to correct that. Successfully, I might add."

Perhaps it was fatigue, perhaps an excess of drink, but Sir Mark began to slur his words, and his eyes glazed. But he carried on speaking:

"The properties were always maintained to a high standard, so needed no major upgrades, though we did refurbish the main kitchen here. And we quietly auctioned off some wine. I think Wallace was quite suspicious of that. By the time the eighteen months was up, and everything was in place, the Earl's health had declined, and he was unable to travel."

At the far end of the library, a regal case clock announced the time in bass chimes. Genevieve was stunned. "My goodness. I can't believe it's midnight."

"I dare say your guests are beginning to overstay their welcome. Me included." Sir Mark stood, weaving as he did so. "My goodness, I feel a bit dizzy. Good mead, I suppose." A sheepish smile fluttered across his face, and he steadied himself, putting his hand on David's shoulder.

Philip stood up as well and gripped Mark's elbow. "Are you okay? You look pale. Genevieve, why don't you go find Margot? David and I will stay with Mark."

"Of course. I'll be right back." Concern for Mark churned her stomach as she walked into the grand salon. Her eyes searched for a squat, gray-haired matron. Though Lady Margot Holmes lived on the frumpy side of sixty-five, she was a bundle of energy with a lusty wit. Genevieve heard the peal of her raucous laugh before she saw her.

"Lady Margot." Genevieve strode across the marble tiles, waving her hand.

Margot was chattering and giggling with a clutch of partner's wives. When she saw Genevieve, her grin widened. "We were just saying what a brilliant evening this has been. You are wonderful for having all of us."

The women talked over each other, thanking Genevieve, cooing about the fabulous food, and marveling about the beauty of Wilmingrove Hall.

"And the barmaid! Wherever did you find her?" asked Elizabeth Smythson. "She was simply fabulous!"

"It's been such fun for us to have all of you here." Genevieve hooked her arm into the crook of Margot's elbow, anxious to pull her away, but not wanting to alarm her. "We want to do it again very soon, maybe during the holidays. But for now, I'm going to have to borrow Margot," Genevieve said, finessing Lady Margot away from the cheery klatch. As they moved toward the library,

Genevieve's voice was gentle. "Margot, Mark doesn't seem to be feeling very well. He's in the Library with Sir David."

Margot looked up at her host, her eyes filed with alarm. "Oh, my lord, Genevieve, Mark has a serious heart condition. Just last week, his cardiologist warned him to be careful." Her short legs lengthened their stride.

When they walked into the library, Julia was holding Mark's wrist, looking at her watch as she took his pulse. Mark's head tilted back against the sofa cushion, his pale face bathed in sweat.

"Mark!" Margot's hands flew to her face, her eyes huge with fear. She bolted to Mark's side, plopping on the sofa. "Julia, what's wrong with him? Is it his heart?"

As she stroked her husband's damp forehead, he opened his eyes, peering through narrow slits. Attempting a reassuring grin, he croaked, "Maybe I had a bit too much mead. I feel terrible." He closed his eyes again.

Margot leaned over to kiss his cheek, startled at how cold his skin felt.

Julia opened her medical bag, which Duncan had collected from their room. Her stethoscope in her ears, she listened to the erratic rhythm of Mark's heart, checked his blood pressure, his pupils, his temperature.

"Genevieve," Julia nodded toward the door. The two women rose, and Genevieve slipped her arm around Margot's shoulders, pulling her with them. When the three were just outside the library, Julia took Margot by the arms. "Margot, I don't believe Mark had too much mead. His blood pressure is very low, and I'm not sure what the problem is but Philip has called an ambulance. I want him to go to the hospital immediately."

Margot's breathing turned jagged. She blinked hard, tears squeezing onto her lashes. "He looks like a ghost." Little choking noises stuck in her throat before a sob burst out.

"Margo, I've got to get back to Mark," Julia said as Genevieve gathered Margot into her arms. They stood hugging each other and weeping for several minutes until Genevieve saw her daughter-in-law standing in the doorway. Instinctively she tightened her arms around the weeping woman. In the distance, Genevieve heard the faint wail of a siren gaining volume as it approach.

Julia stood as still as a statue, clutching her hands in front of her. Her face was shattered with sadness and tears streamed down her cheeks, dripping off her chin onto her collarbone. Holding Genevieve's gaze, Julia bit hard on her lower lip and shook her head almost imperceptibly. "Mark is dead," she mouthed.

TWENTY-ONE

TWELVE HOURS EARLIER, Wilmingrove Hall had throbbed with energy, music, laughter. Now, it was like a tomb, ticking clocks haunting the main floor and a steady drizzle sheeting the windows. The gloom throughout the Hall was as thick as fog. Not even lamps glowing in every room could cheer the house.

Usually full of fun and life, Philip and Genevieve sat deflated, their mood at odds with the cheerful yellow and blue breakfast room. Philip drank his third cup of coffee while Genevieve nibbled at a piece of toast, dabbing her red eyes now and then. They looked up as David entered without a word and walked to the sideboard. He stared at the pastry offerings for several minutes without making a choice. At last, he poured a cup of coffee and dragged himself to the table, shoulders drooping.

"I can't believe it. I just can't believe it," he moaned.

Genevieve squeezed his shoulder. "They think it's a heart attack. Did you know Mark had heart issues?"

David gave her a wan smile. "I did. He had a pretty serious

heart attack about three years ago. My God. Poor Margot."
Looking down at the table, he held his head in his hands
and shaded his eyes. Droplets hit the linen tablecloth. Tears,
Genevieve assumed.

"I was sure Mark was an embezzler. And probably behind the
shooting." Philip stared into his coffee cup. "Boy, do I feel guilty."

Genevieve blew her nose, then sniffed. "I'd say there's plenty of
guilt to go around. We all thought Mark was a bad guy, including
Wallace and Mrs. MacIntosh. And all the time he was carrying
out Jonathon's directives. We got it so wrong." She inhaled a
shaky breath. "Now we're back to who shot at David. Or you,
Philip."

David raised his head. His eyes were red-rimmed and
glistening. "The shooting seems a thousand years ago, doesn't it?"

"Lord Crosswick." Wallace had slipped unnoticed into
the breakfast room and stood near the door. All eyes turned
to the butler. "I'm sorry, my lord, but Penelope Ballard, the
Commissioner of Scotland Yard, is on the phone for you. She
insists she must speak to you."

"The head of Scotland Yard? Why in the world is she calling
me?" Philip strode to the sideboard and picked up the phone.
"Philip Warwick here." He locked his gaze on David and
Genevieve. "Yes, Commissioner Ballard. How can I help you?"

He took a sharp intake of air and his face paled. "When did
you get the report?"

David and Genevieve could hear the caller's voice but couldn't
make out the words.

Philip hesitated then asked, "Do you know what kind of
poison?"

"What? Poison?" Genevieve whispered. She looked at David, whose eyebrows arched into the furrows on his forehead, his eyes as round as marbles. She shook her head in disbelief and mouthed "poison" again.

"Yes, Commissioner, I understand. Our son and his wife return with their children to the states in the morning and Sir David Weatherington was going back to London tomorrow. Do they need to change their plans?" Philip looked at his wife and friend.

They strained forward, trying to hear more.

"Of course, of course. We'll expect them." Philip was ready to end the conversation. "Yes, you're right, we have a helipad. Of course, we'll make sure it's available for your team. Ten o'clock. Yes, yes. I appreciate you making the call yourself. Goodbye, Commissioner."

As Philip hung up, he met David and Genevieve's fearful gazes with tears in his eyes. "Mark had a heart attack all right, but it was caused by poison. Poison in his mead."

TWENTY-TWO

"**A**AAllllleeeexxxx, EEEllllllaaa."

Engrossed in a cutthroat game of checkers, Alex and Ella didn't hear their whispered names.

"Ella! You can't move that way." Alex snatched her red piece off the board, closing it in his fist.

Incensed, Ella screamed, "Stop it, Alex! Put my checker man back on the board!" She grabbed his fist and pulled on it with both hands.

Scrunching his face and gritting his teeth, he held fast.

"Give it back! Give it back." She sobbed angry tears.

"Myyyyy daaarliiiings." Louder this time, the ethereal voice floated between the screeching of the children locked in sibling combat.

They stopped, mid-tug.

Alex looked at Ella. "Did you hear that?"

Ella waited, listening.

Again, the breathy voice purred, "AAAlllleeeexxxx, EEEllllllaaa."

"Who's that?" Alex looked right, then left.

"Where are you?" Still holding Alex's fist, Ella searched the room with suspicious eyes. "Where is she, Alex?"

"I'm here, children. I'm here in the wall."

Alex and Ella's fear mirrored each other, eyes wide, mouths agape.

"Don't be frightened. Come play with me. We can have so much fun."

Alex released his fist and the checker dropped to the floor.

"Alex, Ella," Julia called.

The children heard their mother's footsteps approaching.

"Lady, are you still there?" Alex asked the voice in the wall.

No response.

Julia stood in the doorway, an unnaturally bright smile lighting her face. She and Duncan intended to hide Mark's tragic death from their young children as best they could. There was no need to share the harsh realities of life with them yet. It would all come soon enough.

"What have you two been doing?" She kissed the top of Alex's head, scooped Ella onto her hip and squeezed her.

"Mommy, not so tight," Ella squealed.

"We were playing checkers until Ella cheated…"

"I did not!"

"You did, too!"

"Please stop, you two. You need to stop arguing over every little thing."

"And we were talking to a woman in the wall." Alex said, matter-of-factly.

"Oh, were you, indeed? What fun." Julia ruffled Alex's hair and tickled his neck. "How about some lunch?"

'I'm starving," they sang in unison.

She heard their steps retreat. What an unexpected gift. Two innocent children to play with. Things just kept getting better and better, except for Mark. Poor Mark… that was unfortunate. She hated it when things didn't go as planned.

TWENTY-THREE

"**M**OM, HAVE YOU seen my wax jacket?" Duncan called.

Genevieve was standing on the landing talking to Ms. MacIntosh. A sense of déjà vu welled in her. She rolled her eyes and chuckled. "As I've told you for forty years, it's exactly where you left it."

Duncan heaved an exhausted sigh.

She took pity on him. "Have you looked in the mud room? That's the logical place."

"I know. I was on my way. Just thought I'd ask."

Genevieve descended the stairs, keeping her eyes on her son. She knew him better than anyone and could tell by his slumped shoulders and worried eyes, that something was amiss. "What's wrong, darling boy?"

"What could possibly be wrong?" Sarcasm dripped off each word. "Since you've been here, someone shot at Dad, and now someone poisoned your attorney."

"Ah, yes, I see your point." A tender smile raised the corners of Genevieve's mouth. "Hardly a time to celebrate, is it?" She put her arms around Duncan and hugged the man she still thought of as her little boy.

Duncan's tone softened as his arms tightened around his mother. "Aren't you afraid someone tried to kill Dad? They could be trying to kill you as well. It makes a hell of a lot more sense they're after you two, rather than David. You have a lot more money than he does. When Julia, the kids and I leave tomorrow, I want you to come with us."

Genevieve gave Duncan a final squeeze. "Let's see what these people from Scotland Yard have to say. Then we can decide. Is that fair?"

"I can live with that. Let's hope we'll *all* live with that," he said, smiling down at her. "Now, I need to find my jacket. Harrington is taking Alex and Ella to an Angus farm. Another adventure with their pal and we won't have to worry about little ears hearing gruesome stories." Duncan headed to the mud room at the back of the house.

By ten thirty, eight people sat in the drawing room anxious to explore the details of Sir Mark Holmes' poisoning. The salon smelled of steaming coffee and pastries, fresh from the oven. The five civilians had no appetite. The three police officers ate heartily.

"Good morning," Chief Superintendent Francis Darlington commanded the room from his wingback chair. With his salt-and-pepper hair, Harris Tweed jacket, and polished brogues, the Chief Superintendent looked the part of a fictional Victorian detective. The two deep furrows etched between his eyes enhanced his ruggedness.

He began. "My team and I have assumed responsibility for this investigation. So far there has been an attempted murder," he nodded at David, "and as of Friday, the murder of one peer in the residence of another. As such, this case has been elevated to Scotland Yard. Though DCI Fields has done a fine job, the Met feels it necessary to bring greater resources to this investigation."

Darlington addressed Morris MacTavish, his subordinate. "Chief Inspector, the report," he said, his voice oozing authority.

Genevieve and Philip exchanged an impressed glance.

MacTavish placed a slim file in his superior's waiting hand and addressed the room. "Please be advised these proceedings are being recorded." His professional obligation completed, he resumed his position at the table in the corner.

Chief Superintendent Darlington sat with his elbows on the chair arms, hands tented. He looked around the room, his gaze lingering on each person. "I must say, this is a fascinating case," he said. "Very Agatha Christie. It appears that Sir Mark was murdered by poison in his mead." Darlington leaned forward. "We bagged Sir Mark's glass from Friday night at your party. There was a residue of mead left, enough to analyze, and that's where we found the poison. I understand, Sir David, you were with Sir Mark when he drank the mead."

"Yes, I was with Mark most of the evening." David stopped to clear his throat. "About an hour before everyone began to leave, one of the young servers asked me if I would like a mead. He said the barmaid had been told it's my favorite drink, and the caterers brought a special Polish mead just for me." David told the officers the story of switching drinks with Mark. As he finished, the blood drained from his face. "That means the poisoned mead was meant for me, doesn't it?"

Silence blanketed the room, all eyes riveted on Darlington.

The Chief Superintendent picked up his coffee cup and drained it. "Looks that way." He walked to the sideboard and refilled his cup. "Whoever did this went to a great deal of trouble and risk, and they had little control over the outcome. Here's something interesting. This mead was poisoned naturally. It was made from honey produced from rhododendron nectar. Most of the time this kind of honey wouldn't kill anyone. It would only make a person feel a bit ropey."

"I don't know what ropey is," Julia said, puzzled.

"Sorry, ma'am. It means unwell. I think you Americans might say 'sick.'" Darlington looked in his file folder, flipping through the pages. "The medical examiner said it can cause nausea, drooling, vomiting, slow pulse, low blood pressure, diarrhea, seizures, and coma. Sir Mark had a heart condition— arrhythmia—that made his ingestion of the poisoned mead fatal."

"I'm sure you know Sir David had an attempt on his life last month." Julia said. "You realize David may be a target of some crazed murderer?"

Darlington snorted his response. "Of course, we're aware of that. The confusion with the drinks makes sense when you consider the previous attempt on your life, Sir David. Sir Mark as the unfortunate bystander seems plausible."

"This means the person who's trying to kill me was here, in Wilmingrove Hall." David still looked stunned. "Have you talked to the barmaid?"

Darlington bit his bottom lip. "That's a bit of a problem. The caterer claims the barmaid was hired by Wilmingrove Hall. Your housekeeper insists she came with the caterers."

"This is crazy," Duncan said. "Is it even safe to be in this house, Chief Superintendent? Is it safe for our family and for David to be at the Hall?" Duncan paced the room, his anger on full display. "That's twice someone has attempted to kill David on my family's property. As far as we can tell, the local police aren't close to discovering who shot David last month and now that person seems to be moving freely around the estate. Officers from York and the National Crime Agency were here Friday night and still Sir Mark Holmes was served a drink that poisoned him. How in the hell did that happen?"

"Duncan, please." Genevieve was touched by her son's protective instincts. "This news is frightening, but we need to be calm and help the authorities. Perhaps now they'll approach this situation with more urgency. We certainly will."

"I appreciate your voice of reason, Lady Crosswick." Darlington nodded his thanks. "I understand how distressing this news is, and how it emphasizes the fact that Sir David's life is in danger."

"If I may interrupt," Philip's annoyance had built to near eruption. "David was shot in the head almost two months ago. That was a pretty good indication his life is in danger, don't you think?" Philip glared at Darlington, his nostrils flaring.

"I understand your frustration, Lord Crosswick."

"I don't think you do," Philip said, still seething.

Darlington continued as if Philip hadn't spoken. "I must say, however, in both attempts on your life, Sir David, perhaps the goal of the assailant was not to kill you, but to frighten you and Lord and Lady Crosswick. Think about it. When you were shot, it wasn't a fatal wound—"

"But it could have been," David interrupted.

"Yes, but it wasn't," Darlington acknowledged. "And Friday night if you had drunk the mead, you would have been wretched, but you would not have died... probably."

"Very comforting," David scoffed.

"Excuse me, my lord." Wallace stood at the door, holding a gold box tied with a navy-blue ribbon. "A courier just delivered this and said it was urgent that Chief Superintendent Darlington receive it immediately. I thought I should bring it right in."

"Of course, Wallace. Thank you." Philip motioned for Wallace to give the box to the Chief Superintendent.

"Put it over on that table." Darlington jerked his head towards an inlaid mahogany antique.

"You mean the Hepplewhite sideboard, sir?" The arrogance in Wallace's voice was hard to miss.

Darlington nodded, Wallace's disdain lost on him. "Franklin, put your gloves on. Assuming it's not a bomb, open it."

The lowest ranked of the three Scotland Yard officers opened his satchel, pulled on latex gloves and approached the package. "There's a card, sir."

"And?" Darlington barked.

Franklin eased the card from under the ribbon and read out loud:

> *Chief Superintendent Darlington,*
> *Please share this lovely mead with Sir David.*
> *I made it especially for him.*
> *I was pretty annoyed the drinks got all mixed-up*
> *Friday night.*
> *Do tell Margot I'm sorry about Mark...oops.*

"Open the box, Franklin."

Gingerly, Franklin tugged the end of the ribbon, pulling the bow loose.

"Step it up, man!" Darlington snapped.

Franklin lifted the box lid and peered inside.

"Well, what is it?" Darlington was out of his chair and striding towards the sideboard.

Cradled in a velvet nest was a small, lidded pewter tankard. Red sealing wax oozed from around the rim, keeping the lid secure.

"Lord Crosswick. Call your butler back in here," Darlington ordered.

"I'm still here, sir."

Surprised, the Chief spun around. "Tell me everything you can about the courier."

Wallace drew himself up to his full height. "The courier was a woman, about five feet, six inches and maybe eight and a half stone, very lean. She was dressed head to toe in black, wearing a Shoei helmet. The visor was down, and, I believe, she spoke with a slight accent, though it was difficult to hear her because of the visor. The motorcycle was a Ducati Superleggera V4, red with black trim. The reg was MI99 DVD."

Everyone in the room stared at Wallace with surprise and admiration.

"Wallace! Impressive, very impressive." Philip smiled at his butler.

"In my youth, I raced motorcycles, my lord. I never got over my love for a fast, open ride."

"You're an onion, Wallace." Genevieve grinned and shook her head. "We keep peeling you and finding new layers."

"Could we get back to the courier?" Chief Superintendent Darlington pressed the group to stay on topic. "Can you tell me anything else?"

"One other thing. As she handed me the package, she laughed."

Darlington rubbed his late-afternoon stubble. "Arrogant. Pretty damn arrogant. Assuming the assailant is the same person who dropped off the package, we know several things. We know that person is a woman, five feet, six inches tall, lean, a motorbike rider, egotistical, self-assured, no doubt a thrill seeker. If she is the same person who shot at you, Sir David, we know she is an expert marksman. If she was the barmaid, we know she is a chameleon easily changing her appearance to suit the role. And if she made the mead, she is someone who knows about brewing. And, as I said, she's arrogant. That could be her Achilles heel. I'd say we know quite a lot if we make a few assumptions."

Philip said. "That's a lot of information from a brief encounter."

Darlington relaxed into his chair and chuckled. "I dare say, she wanted us to know everything I just told you. She's a clever little minx. We're going to have to be at the top of our game to stay ahead of this one."

TWENTY-FOUR

ACH NURSING A glass of scotch, Philip, David, and
Duncan recapped the day's events in Philip's study. It had
been a long, brutal day.

On both sides, questions had been asked and answered.
Tempers had flared, accusations had flown, competence had been
challenged. The bartender was a key suspect and was nowhere to
be found, with little prospect of tracking her down. Tomorrow
promised to be another grueling session.

David looked at Philip and Duncan with exhausted eyes.
"Before Mark died, it never occurred to me that this mystery
might not be solved. Now I think it will be a miracle if it is, and
maybe even more of a miracle if I live through it."

Philip took a swig of his drink then set his glass on his desk.
"I know what you mean. As naive as it sounds, before last Friday,
I kept thinking the police had it wrong and it was hunter's shots
gone awry. But now..."

"I'm glad at last you both realize how serious this is." Lines
etched their way between Duncan's eyebrows.

Philip's computer tweeted. He glanced at his screen and saw their London housekeeper, Anna Baker, was calling him on Messenger.

"Oh crap! What now?" Philip muttered to himself as he hit 'Accept'.

Mrs. Baker popped onto the screen.

"Mrs. Baker. Is everything okay at Margrave House?" Philip tried to keep any trace of concern out of his voice.

"Everything is fine, Lord Crosswick. I just have a question for you."

Philip noticed she was in the study. His mind flashed to the night she told them about Charlotte's tumble down the stairs to her death, becoming the Laney family ghost. "How's Charlotte doing?" he smiled.

Mrs. Baker gave a robust laugh. "Our favorite ghost mentioned she would be at Wilmingrove Hall with the family. Have you seen her?"

"Genevieve smelled her in the drawing room when we first got here, but I don't think she's made herself known since then." They smiled at each other.

Philip motioned to David to come to his side of the desk. "Mrs. Baker, I don't think you've met Sir David Weatherington, have you?"

"No, we've never met, though I certainly know you by repute, Sir David. You did a smashing job tracking down Lord and Lady Crosswick and we thank you for that. Though with all that's gone on at Wilmingrove Hall, I wonder if Lord Crosswick is happy he was found." Mrs. Baker's dimples pierced her cheeks as she grinned.

"I can't say it's been dull, that's for sure." Philip relaxed at the sight of Mrs. Baker's cheerful face.

"Lord Crosswick, the reason I called is that you and Lady Crosswick are receiving quite a few invitations. Would you like me to forward them or respond on your behalf?"

"We won't be back in London for some time. If you could send our regrets, I'm sure Lady Crosswick would appreciate it."

"Consider it done."

Philip could feel David hanging over his shoulder, leaning closer and closer. When he turned his head, his lips were almost on David's. Startled, Philip sat back, and David moved even closer to the monitor. "Mrs. Baker, that picture on the desk, could you please bring it closer to the screen so I can see it?"

"This photo?" Mrs. Baker turned the silver frame toward the computer.

"Who is she?"

Mrs. Baker blinked at David's sharp tone. "Why, she was a very close friend of the 12TH Earl. Her name was Revy Harris."

"When were she and the Earl, um, close?" David was hardly breathing.

Mrs. Baker ran her sleeve over the glass of the frame, wiping off non-existent dust. "It was twenty-one, maybe twenty-two years ago, after a brief affair, that Lord Crosswick insisted she return to America."

"She's American," David voice was flat.

Philip gripped David's arm. "Do you know her, David?"

"I do." In an instant, loathing, lust, and panic he hadn't felt for years raged through him. "I know her, and I now know who's trying to kill me."

TWENTY-FIVE

AFTER A SLEEPLESS night, of pacing, thinking, rethinking, and doubting, David gazed out the windows at the terrace, where huge pots overflowed with fall flowers of blues, reds, and oranges, still drenched from yesterday's showers. The overnight rains had moved on and now billowy clouds raced across the sky like sailboats on a blustery day.

This morning, everyone had gathered to hear his tale.

"It's hard to know where to start." His voice was flat and his shoulders sagged. "I guess the beginning is as good a place as any."

Genevieve wondered if he could muster the energy to tell his story.

"I grew up in Cornwall, in Falmouth. My family lived there for generations. My dad and his brother had a family business, Weatherington Bespoke Yachts. They designed and built custom-made boats. When I was eighteen, I went to Cambridge. During the summer before my last year at university, I stayed in Cambridge to work." His hands shoved deep in his pockets, he stood looking out of the library windows, seeing nothing.

"An American family was in Cambridge for the summer,

George and Katherine Conway and their three children: a seventeen-year-old daughter, Becca, who was starting at Harvard in the fall; and two boys, Conner and James. The dad asked me to coach the boys. He wanted them to spend most of their time on the water, honing their rowing skills. It was a smashing opportunity." Pausing, David took a long, slow drink from his water tumbler.

"After two weeks working with them every day, they were getting quite good. They loved learning everything and even loved maintaining the shell. Anything to hang around the club and the rowers. At the end of the second week, Mr. Conway asked if I could also work with Becca. She was already a decent sailor but wanted to make the Harvard team. He thought if I worked with her, she could sharpen her skills and become more competitive. In retrospect, I imagine Mrs. Conway said to him, 'You find something for Becca to do or I'm going to kill her!' It turns out Becca was precocious, whip-smart, desperate to be sophisticated, and a challenge for her parents."

"That's Ella in a few years," Philip said, drawing a laugh from the room.

"What do you mean, Dad, in a few years?" said Duncan.

Another round of laughter filled the library.

"I hope not," David said. "At seventeen she was stunning, one of those girls you can't take your eyes off. Though she was from Kentucky, she was every Brit's idea of the perfect California girl: tan, long limbs, blond hair. If I'd known what I was getting into, I would have told Mr. Conway my schedule was too busy. But it seemed like another amazing opportunity. I was making a ton of money and doing something I loved. It was a dream summer—until it turned into a nightmare." David ran his hands over his face as if to wipe away the memory. "That first day when I arrived at the marina, Becca was waiting for me in a bikini bottom and no top."

The men in the room looked more shocked than the women.

"What the hell did you do, David?" Philip asked.

"My first inclination was to turn around and walk away, but I quicky decided it would be an opportunity to teach this young girl a lesson in a safe environment. Very mature of me, wasn't it?"

The five men agreed. The two women rolled their eyes.

"So, how did you handle it?" Duncan asked.

"I stepped onto the Firefly, the dinghy we were using that day, picked up a life jacket, tossed it to her and said, 'You'll need to wear this. Let's go. We need to shove off.'"

Comments poured forth from David's audience:

"Absolutely brilliant!"

"How very clever."

"Good thinking, David!"

"Well done, Man."

David shook his head. "I was sweating buckets."

"So?" Darlington said. "What did she do?"

"I can honestly say if looks were daggers, I would have been dead on the spot. Seventeen-year-old girl-women are terrifying. I bruised her ego and I guess that's about the worst thing a person can do to a teenage girl. It was the beginning of years of Becca storming in and out of my life, always leaving chaos and trouble in her wake."

David ran his hands through his thick hair. He laced his fingers behind his neck and dropped his head back, trying to relieve the tension running across his shoulders.

Julia leaned forward on the edge of a loveseat cushion, her elbows on her knees. Vibrating with curiosity, she asked, "What in the world did this girl do to you?"

David smiled at Julia's lusty enthusiasm and went on. "The entire summer, Becca tried to entangle me in a romance. Well, romance is the wrong word. She tried to lure me into some pretty lurid sex games."

All eyes were wide, waiting for David's next revelation.

"She was seventeen. I was twenty-one." He shivered. "One night when I got home from the pub, I found Becca naked in my bed. She got into my flat by telling my landlady it was my birthday and she wanted to surprise me." He sighed and shook his head. "She surprised me alright. She threatened that if I didn't make love to her, she'd tell her father I raped her." Little beads of perspiration glistened on David's upper lip.

"Jeez, David. What the...! That's terrifying." Philip took a deep breath, unable to imagine what he would do in that situation. "How did you handle it?"

"The only thing I could think of was to call her bluff. I reached for the phone to ring her parents. With that threat, she grabbed her clothes and scrambled out the door. This kind of sexual blackmail went on the whole summer until British Airways took Becca and her family back to the U.S. at the end of August. God, that was a happy day." David swiped the back of his hand across his lips. "When she got home, she wrote daily letters, dripping with teenage despair, which I ignored. They trickled to weekly. Then, thank God, they stopped.

"After my final year at Cambridge, I headed to Boston for my next big adventure in Harvard's MBA program."

Duncan walked to the sideboard, put his cup under the spigot and filled it almost to overflowing. "Whoa! David, you have me so distracted I can't even pour a cup of coffee. This is quite a story."

"To paraphrase Al Jolson: 'You ain't heard nothin' yet'. My first week at Harvard, I was at a party thrown by Henry Fitch, the same Henry Fitch who is now part of your legal team. He was in his second year of the MBA program."

"Small world," Philip said.

"No question." David uncrossed his legs then eased his ankle onto his knee. "An hour and three beers into the party, I was in deep conversation about the EU with a couple of econ wonks who were dazzled by their own intellects. As I was about to pull the plug on their theory, I felt a hand on my shoulder. Lips pressed to my ear and said in a seductive voice, 'Hello, Darling,' followed by teeth tugging on my earlobe. A hand slid down my back and into the pocket of my jeans."

David interrupted his story to clear his throat. He looked around the library. Each person was leaning forward, eager for him to continue. Even the three seasoned Scotland Yard policemen were rapt.

"Who was it, David?" Genevieve's eyes were wide with excitement.

"It was Becca, of course," Julia said.

David resumed. "It *was* Becca, with her perfect heart face, bow mouth and intense, blue-violet eyes. She flashed a wicked smile and tugged my lower lip between her teeth. To say I was surprised to see her was an understatement. For the last year, I had thought about Becca once in a while, always with a sense of dread. But I hadn't worried much about running into her. It's a big campus. I was a grad student, and she was an undergrad. Maybe it was my pleasant, boozy buzz or Becca's breathtaking sensuality, but that evening I was excited to see her."

Julia narrowed her eyes. "Honestly, David. After all she did to you. How could you have even tolerated being in the same room with her?"

David put his hands up. "I know. I know. I have no defense. She looked amazing and knew her way around the room. She was a sophomore, but she knew most of the people at the party. She introduced me to the most interesting and influential students, and by the end of the evening I had met a lot of Harvard's movers and shakers. After the initial shock of seeing Becca, I was feeling pretty full of myself that she still had a thing for me. You know, I was twenty-two." He cocked one eyebrow and shrugged his shoulders.

David paused to take a long drink from his water glass.

Clouds had moved in again and the light in the library had faded to dusky shadows. Only the glow of the crackling fire brightened the room. David rose from his chair, stretching to release his muscles, tight from sitting. The day was intense, and fatigue was weaving its way among the people in the library.

As he settled back into his chair, David said, "I am not a

believer in regrets. but in this case, if I could change what happened next, I would." Remorse swept across David's face, his eyes glistening with emotion. "The decision I made that night was made by a twenty-two-year-old boy, so filled with hubris he thought he could have what he wanted, without consequence.

"Before I left with Becca, Henry warned me. He said Becca had a well-deserved reputation for exacting revenge against anyone she felt slighted her. I thought he must be drunk, or jealous. I was an idiot. It was just over a year since she spent the summer trying to lure me into bed. Every time I rejected her, she had threatened to ruin me. How soon one forgets when heavy drinking and the prospect of sex with a sensual woman are involved. That's all I wanted. What I got was a terrifying night with a wicked, beautiful sociopath."

Chief Superintendent Darlington cleared his throat to interrupt. "Sir David, are you suggesting you slept with a lass and, I assume, never called her back, so she attempted to kill you, twice, twenty years later? I'm sure you're irresistible to women, but…." His voice trailed off, leaving skepticism hanging in the air.

"I don't know why Becca was obsessed with me. Maybe we met when she was the perfect age to fall deeply in love and I was the one who was there." David's voice cracked. "Cambridge is a romantic place, and the summer was full of idyllic interludes." He looked beyond Darlington, his eyes glazed. "Sailing is a seductive sport: the sun, the breeze, long, tan legs, warm nights, Champagne to celebrate every race. I'm sure her infatuation had little to do with me and everything to do with the environment and circumstances."

David looked at his hands, folded in his lap. His words hung in the air for several seconds, the crackling fire and ticking clock the only sounds in the room.

"David!" Genevieve shook him with her voice. "David!"

When he looked up, David's eyes glistened with tears and exhaustion. For the last half hour, Darlington had been assessing David's fatigue and emotional state. He glanced at his watch. "I think we should call it an evening and resume in the morning. Sir David, we've been at this a long time and I'm sure you're tired."

David nodded.

"Whatever you say, Chief." Philip stifled a yawn and stretched his arms overhead. "I'm sure I speak for everyone when I say it's been a riveting day.

Darlington walked across the library to where he had draped his Harris tweed jacket across the arm of a chair hours ago. "Tomorrow the forensic team is coming back to go over everything one more time." He patted the elegant box that had arrived earlier. "This little gift of mead from the courier will, no doubt, be our best lead."

"Do you think they'll find any more evidence?" David asked.

Darlington tugged on his jacket and buttoned the middle button. He shot his cuffs, and said "In my experience, Sir David, there's always one more piece of evidence to find."

Philip smiled at the dry response. "What time will the forensic team arrive?"

"They'll be ready to start by half eight." Darlington motioned to his two subordinates to gather their equipment and files. "We appreciate your hospitality."

"Of course," Genevieve said. "Anything we can do to help, you just have to ask."

"Chief Superintendent, when do you think Julia, the children and I can leave?" Duncan slipped his arm around Julia's waist. "We're trying to talk my parents into coming with us, and David if he would. I think they'd be a lot safer in the States. Don't you agree?"

Darlington snapped his briefcase closed. "At this point, I'd like to think Lord and Lady Crosswick, and Sir David, are safe at Wilmingrove Hall. But since we don't know who the murderer is, whom they're trying to murder or why, I think you'd better make that decision on your own." He picked up his case and headed to the door, then stopped and turned back to Duncan. "We should be finished here tomorrow. You could probably plan to leave the day after, on Tuesday. We know how to get in touch with you if we need to speak while you're in the States, and you could come back, if needed, correct?"

"Of course. Thanks." Duncan shook Darlington's hand and nodded.

Philip escorted the Scotland Yard team to the door and returned to the library. There wasn't an ounce of energy in the room. No one had the strength to move.

Desperate to get into a hot bath, Genevieve stood. "I'd suggest anyone who's hungry should raid the kitchen. I'm sure there's plenty in the fridge. Mrs. Lomax and her staff are off on Sunday evening so you're on your own. David, you must be bone tired."

"I didn't realize it until Darlington suggested we stop for the day, but I am absolutely knackered."

Genevieve rolled her shoulders. "Julia, Duncan, kiss the kiddos for me, please. I'm outta here!"

"I'll be up in a minute." Philip kissed Genevieve's palm.

Genevieve threw kisses, leaving behind silence except for the ticking of the clock and the simmering of embers on the hearth.

"David, your story's unbelievable." Julia yawned as she spoke. "You're sure Becca's behind all this, aren't you?"

"When you hear the rest of the saga, I know you'll agree. Given her obsession with me and her history of threatening behavior, it's hard to think anything else." David heaved himself from his chair. "Shall we see what Mrs. Lomax left in the kitchen?"

"I need to go find our children. They were supposed to be having a picnic in front of the fire in the study, but who knows what that's evolved into. Duncan, could you make me a sandwich or whatever? I'll be upstairs in a minute."

"You bet, babe."

The three men headed to the kitchen to forage, while Julia went in search of two small picnickers.

Half an hour later with everyone tucked in their rooms upstairs, no one heard the house phone ring: four rings, five rings, six rings, until voicemail answered. It wasn't until the next morning anyone listened to the message.

TWENTY-SIX

"**S**IX, SEVEN, EIGHT, nine, ten. Ready or not here I come." Alex peeked between his fingers as he finished his count. "Ella, where are you?"

Lightening flashed as he looked around the music room, followed immediately by a crack of thunder.

Startled, he jumped and thought he saw the drapes move. He dashed to the rain-sluiced window and yanked back the silk curtains, sure he would find his sister. Nothing. He turned, his eyes riveted on a wide pedestal where a marble ballerina stood en pointe.

Stealthy as a cat, he crept across the room until he was close enough to hear Ella breathing on the other side of the column. He eased around the column's edge and peered directly into her gaze.

She screeched.

He shrieked in return.

Thrown off balance by surprise, he fell forward, clawing the air. As he tumbled toward the floor, his hand hit the ballerina.

Instead of falling off the pedestal, the dancer levered back, and a wall panel slowly, silently opened. Alex and Ella gawked at each other, eyes bugging and mouths open, stunned into silence, not knowing what to do next. Still on the floor, Alex crawled toward the opening in the wall while Ella sat cross-legged watching her brother.

The music room filed with another explosion of lightening and crash of thunder. "Alex, don't!" Ella shouted.

On all fours, Alex turned his head to look at his sister. "Come on. I want to see what's in there."

"But, what if there's a monster or a ghost?"

"Don't be silly. You know monsters aren't real."

"But what about a ghost?"

Alex sat back on his haunches considering the possibility. "I don't think there's a ghost in there." He chewed on his hoodie drawstrings, unsure. He hopped up, offered Ella his hand and pulled her to her feet. "Let's just peek in."

They clutched each other's hand and tiptoed to the black opening. Alex pulled her behind him. "Let me go first."

"Why?" Ella's chin jutted, eyes defiant.

"Because I'm older." Before Ella could object again, he stepped through the gap and into a dusty corridor, lit only by the gloomy light from the music room behind them.

"It's okay. It's just a hallway."

Ella was already at his side. "This isn't scary at all." She walked a few steps along the narrow passage then stopped as the light quickly faded. "Where's that flashlight you always carry on your belt?"

Alex's pocketknife jingled against his mini torch. He loosened the small carabiner from his belt loop and slid his flashlight off the fastener. He switched on the penlight and shot a small, bright shaft at the wall. A spider scurried into a narrow gap between two ancient beams. Unfazed, the two explorers crept on, Ella's hand on Alex's back. As they inched forward, he swiveled the column of light back and forth like a lighthouse beacon. They took step after cautious step until the torch shone on a thick door with two beveled panels, daring to be opened. Alex stopped and Ella smashed into his back, her nose taking the brunt of the crash.

"Ack!" she said with a sniff.

"Shhh! Be quiet!" He turned to see Ella's face scrunched, preparing to sneeze. He grabbed the bridge of her nose, pinching it tight. "Don't sneeze," he hissed.

Ella tugged his hand away and wiggled her nose. She looked over Alex's shoulder. Her eyes flew wide. "Are we going in there?" her little voice quivered.

Needing to be brave for his sister, Alex took a deep breath and turned the jiggly doorknob. The knob played on its spindle a quarter turn before it caught and unlatched.

They looked at each other. Her breathing was rapid and shallow. His eyes were wild with excitement. "Here we go." He held his breath and squeezed his eyes closed. As he pushed the door forward, he opened his eyes just enough to peer through slits.

A moaning sound filled the air.

Alex froze, holding his breath.

The moaning stopped.

Realizing it was just the sound of creaking hinges, he started again, pushing until the door was wide open. The room glowed with tiny green lights, some flashing, some emitting a steady gleam. Alex danced the flashlight beam around the curved walls of the small chamber, the light bouncing off one computer screen after another—three, four, five—a bank of six computers, all hibernating, waiting for someone to wake them.

"What the, what the…?" Alex moved further into the room, walking to the semicircular console. Ella stood in the doorway, ready to bolt at any second.

They heard a rumble in the distance; the storm's first wave. "Alex, we should go," Ella whimpered, teetering on the edge of tears.

"Don't be a scaredy-cat," he taunted. "I just want to see if these work." He wiggled a mouse, and the lower middle screen sprang to life. On the monitor, Elsie Lomax bustled in the kitchen, pulling trays of bread from the oven. The children watched as Lottie pushed through the swing door, picked up a china coffee pot and dashed back out.

Her curiosity overtaking her caution, Ella eased to Alex's side. She grabbed his arm, unable to take her eyes from the screen. "We should leave."

"It's okay. I just want to see what's on the other screens."

Ella sniffed, then sniffed again. "Hey, do you smell something? Something sweet? Like the roses Mommy and Daddy gave me on my birthday."

Alex glanced at her and then back at the screens, engrossed in all the tech. "Nah, I don't smell anything." He woke another monitor.

"Look! There's Mommy!" Ella's smile broke through her fear.

"Shhh," Alex warned. They watched Julia descend the staircase and walk out of the camera frame toward the grand salon. On the next screen, the library was empty. The fourth screen showed several people coming in and out of the reception hall. Some people stood talking to each other; some gawked at the grand environment. Some wore police uniforms; some were in civilian clothes.

Their mother strode into the picture and shook hands with a man they recognized from yesterday. She pointed, nodded, then walked out of the room.

Forgetting her fear, Ella sat in the desk chair, fascinated by the action. Alex stood behind her, like a commander on a starship's bridge watching his fleet's tactical maneuvers.

"What's on the other two screens?" Ella bounced her knees up and down, her excitement mounting.

Alex brought the next display to life. In the conservatory, Duncan, Philip, and David sat around a table eating breakfast. Duncan rested his elbows on the table, cradling a cup of coffee and listening to Philip. Talking and gesturing, Philip picked up a triangle of toast and poked the pointed end at David. Philip said something, David shook his head and both Duncan and Philip laughed.

"It looks like they're having a good time," Ella said. "What's on the last one?" She wiggled in her chair, wanting more.

"I guess you're not scared anymore." He smiled at her and moved the final mouse. An image of the stables filled the screen.

Ella stopped bouncing. "I was never scared," she snarled. "Hey look! It's Missy." She saw the girl who helped saddle her horse and guided her on a lunge line when she trotted around the ring. "I like her."

Missy was hanging tack on the appropriate pegs, dressed in riding breeches and a long-sleeved green t-shirt. Her high ponytail swished back and forth as she hung the last bridle and looked around as if making sure no one was watching.

She shrugged into her barn jacket, pulled a small spray bottle from her pocket, held it up, checking the contents, then tucked it back into her coat as she walked out of the screen.

"Wonder what she has in the bottle?" Alex had been leaning into the screen to get a better look.

"Alex! Ella!" They could barely hear their mother's voice calling them.

He froze, his face still inches from the monitor. "We've gotta go!"

He grabbed Ella's hand, dragging her out of the chair and through the door. He stopped, spun around, and pulled the door until it latched. Pushing in front of Ella, Alex shone the flashlight down the hall to where the faint light seeped in from the music room. "Come on, Ella," he growled over his shoulder as they scuddled toward the opening.

Her ragged breath was hot on his neck. They didn't break their stride until they shot out of the secret passageway and into the comforting glow of the music room.

Alex ran to the ballerina, cradled her head in his palm and pulled the statue upright. For a moment, nothing happened.

Then, without a sound, the panel swung back into place, filling the gaping hole in the wall. As the panel latched with a soft click,

Julia sailed into the room to find her two children panting and flushed.

"I've been calling you two. What have you been doing?"

Alex shot Ella a withering glance. "Just playing hide and seek." He affected an angelic smile, oozing innocence.

"Yeah, hide and seek," Ella mumbled, staring at her shoes.

"Well, come on and have some breakfast. You must be starving!" She took Ella's hand and leaned to kiss the top of her little girl's head. She draped her other arm over Alex's shoulders. "You kids should log some screen time this morning. You don't want to lose your computer skills while you're here." Alex and Ella exchanged funny faces behind Julia's back then ran ahead of their mother, hoping there would be chocolate chip pancakes waiting for them.

TWENTY-SEVEN

RAIN DRUMMED AGAINST the bedroom window. A low rumble of thunder encouraged Genevieve to pull the duvet over her head and burrow further into her pillow. She stretched her leg behind her, searching for Philip, but felt nothing but the cool of linen sheets.

She opened one eye and looked at her watch. Nine o'clock. Even though she had slept deeply for twelve hours, she felt herself floating back into a luscious twilight. Her mind wandered through the mist of the last three months, drifting to life before the phone call which heralded so many changes for the Warwick family. Before unimaginable wealth, before murder, and mayhem.

Just as she floated over the edge into sleep, the nutty fragrance of coffee brought her back. A hand caressed her face and lips tickled her ear. "Good morning, pretty girl," a voice whispered.

"Mmmm. Come back to bed, Philip. I'll make it worth your while," she murmured.

"Not possible." Philip swatted her backside through the covers. "The forensic team has been here over an hour. I let you sleep as long as I could, but you need to get up now. The Scotland Yard boys are on their way."

Eyes still closed, Genevieve enjoyed a luxurious stretch.

"Come on, kiddo, let's go. Do you want Mrs. Lomax to bring you a breakfast tray so you can eat while you get dressed?"

"I don't need a tray. I'll be down in fifteen minutes." She threw a pillow at Philip's retreating back. "You're brutal."

"And you love it, don't you?" He tossed the pillow back. "See you in a minute."

"Philip."

He stopped in the doorway and turned around.

"How is David this morning?"

"He's in great spirits. We had breakfast together and he told me that he feels some control over his life again, for the first time since the shooting. As he said last night, he's positive his old nemesis is somehow involved in this. He's also anxious to get the rest of his story on the record. It's going to be another busy day, so let's go." Philip clapped his hands, encouraging Genevieve to pick up her pace.

Twenty-four hours after they first gathered, the group reconvened in the library, except for Chief Superintendent Darlington. Everyone looked refreshed, but no one as much as David. Nattily dressed in a crisp white shirt, camel shawl-collar sweater, and tweed pants, he settled into a roomy down-cushioned chair, ready to resume his story.

"How was the Wilmingrove Inn?" Philip asked Chief Inspector MacTavish and Inspector Franklin.

"It's very nice, but we didn't have an opportunity to enjoy it."

MacTavish offered a sheepish grin. He was dressed in the same suit as the previous day but with a new shirt and tie. "I was hoping for a good meal and early night, but the Chief Superintendent had a different idea. We were on conference calls for two hours, first with the forensic team then with the Commander. That pretty much took care of the evening. By then, a sandwich was all we could get out of the kitchen."

Genevieve grinned at the two young officers and pointed to the sideboard, piled with pastries. "Please help yourself."

"Thank you, Lady Crosswick. All of you have been so hospitable," said Inspector Franklin, who had spoken little since arriving at the Hall yesterday.

Genevieve noted how chatty he was in the Chief's absence.

Chief Superintendent Darlington entered the room, rubbing his hands together in anticipation of the day's events. "All right, is everyone ready to get started?" He wore a black pinstripe suit, white shirt, and blue and black repp stripe tie, all pressed, starched, and knotted to perfection. Genevieve couldn't help smiling at how dashing he looked.

"I'd say we're all caffeined-up and anxious to hear the next installment of David's riveting tale." Duncan gave David a nod, then savored a sip of his steaming Sumatra.

"Let's see. Where was I?"

"You were about to leave the party with Becca." Julia prompted David.

"Ah, that's right. Henry was trying to warn me off getting involved with her and I was too barmy to heed his excellent advice."

"Yup, assuming barmy means crazy." Julia said. She leaned forward in anticipation.

"I needn't go into detail, but suffice it to say, the night was sleepless and filled with the most inventive and intense shagging I'd ever experienced." Even the Americans in the room understood what David was saying. "The next morning Becca started talking about setting a date for our wedding. She asked me how many children I wanted. At first, I thought she was taking the mickey out of me, but I realized pretty quickly, she was serious." David's eyes narrowed. "I remember I laughed and said that was a great joke, trying to lighten the mood. That was the wrong thing to do. Becca flew into a fury. She came at me like an animal, clawing and hissing. She scared the hell out of me. The night before, she had been wild, demanding, and aggressive, but under the circumstances, it was exciting. In the light of day, however, her behavior was terrifying. I finally got hold of her, sat her in a chair and warned her that if she got up, I would call her parents and tell them how she was behaving. That always seemed to work. She was either afraid of them or didn't want to disappoint them. Either way, it was effective.

"Desperate to leave, I told her there was no future for us. I assured her she would find a great love someday. She wasn't having it. In the end, she left me with a chilling warning. She said I should carefully consider my decision to push her away. She said if I chose not to love her, I would be sorry. Three days after that, Weatherington Bespoke Yachts, my family's boat building business, burned to the ground. The police confirmed arson. From the beginning of the investigation, there wasn't a doubt in my mind. Becca was behind it, and I told the police that's where they should look."

With no other sound in the room, the rain pounding against the windows was deafening.

"But, David, how could Becca have been involved in the fire?" Genevieve looked skeptical, furrows deep between her brows.

"I know it sounds like the ravings of a madman, but some things one simply knows. And, in the end, my gut feelings were born out."

"The police confirmed the fire was Becca's doing?" Philip uncrossed his legs and sat forward. "They found evidence she was guilty? Did she go to jail?"

David held up both hands, palms out. "Whoa! Hang on just a minute. Let me explain. Using CCTV and a thumb print left on the backdoor lock of the building, the police tracked the purchase of the accelerant, gasoline, to a petty crook and minor drug dealer from Cambridge, a guy named Michael Greyson. They verified he had met Becca the previous summer while she was in Cambridge. According to his mates, she bought marijuana from him throughout the summer. The trail came to a dead end, however, when he was killed in a car crash returning to Cambridge from Falmouth. His brakes failed and he crashed into a tree."

"Was there any foul play regarding his brakes?" Darlington asked.

"As far as I know, the police didn't check. They're not that concerned with how drug dealers die. The police found no money trail, and no correspondence between Becca and Greyson.

Greyson didn't have a computer, so any email communication between Becca and him would have been sent from someone else's computer."

"What about cell phone records?" Everyone was anxious to ask a question.

"The police never found a cell phone. At that time not everyone had a mobile. The police reached out to Interpol, hoping they would inquire about Becca on their behalf."

"Wow! Interpol!" Julia said. "Did they help?"

David shook his head. "They declined to investigate the daughter of a wealthy American businessman when there was no evidence of her involvement in a crime, just vague suspicions. The case was closed with Michael Greyson listed as the guilty party."

"You were right there on campus with Becca for another year. Did you ever accuse her of hiring Greyson?" Julia asked.

"Not then," David said. "While the case was open, the police insisted I have no contact with her. After the case closed, however, I did confront her."

Darlington's eyes flashed with surprise. "And what happened?"

"I saw her in one of the campus haunts the Friday night after the police closed the case. She was with a group. When I caught her eye, she walked over to me, put her arms around my neck and kissed me on the lips. I grabbed her wrists, drilled into her eyes, and asked if she had anything to do with my family's fire. She smiled an eerie smile and said, 'Remember, I told you to consider your decision carefully.' It was chilling. That was the last time I saw her. It was, however, not the last time I felt her presence."

Darlington had been pacing around the library as he listened to David. At this, he stopped. "Were you surprised by Becca's response?"

"I was not."

"Did you believe her?"

"I did."

"Did you tell the police about the exchange?"

"Of course."

"And what did they say?"

"They said the case was closed. They said there was no evidence that Michael Greyson had any accomplices. The thing they couldn't resolve was Greyson's motive, but with the physical evidence confirming him as the arsonist, they didn't need to look further. They felt they had done their job."

"Understandable, I suppose." Darlington massaged the bridge of his nose, then his forehead. "What do you mean by 'felt her presence'?"

David stood at the rain-streaked windows, watching the storm. After several minutes, he pulled his focus back to the room. "Seven years after the fire, Hannah Montgomery and I decided to get married. Hannah was a brilliant actor and quite the toast of the West End. I had been at Holmes Fitch Smythson Morrow for a couple of years. Our engagement party was brilliant, until it wasn't. About an hour into the party our host suggested we open our gifts. I remember Hannah's beautiful face, cheeks flushed with excitement. When we were about halfway through the pile, we chose an elegantly wrapped package which looked like artwork; ideal for our new flat. Hannah grinned like a kid as she began to read the card which came with it, but then, her voice trailed off and she looked up at me, confusion replacing joy. I took the card from her and read the calligraphy message." David paused to settle his racing pulse.

Genevieve couldn't stop herself from asking, "What did it say?"

"It said, 'David, darling, you will know what this means. Still loving you, B.' I could feel the blood drain from my head. When we first met, I told Hannah about Becca's obsession with me and how I believed she was responsible for the boat factory fire, so I didn't have to explain who she was."

"What did she send?" Duncan asked.

Looking down at his lap, David folded then unfolded his hands. He took a long breath before he spoke. "It was a skillfully replicated painting of Salome holding a platter with John the Baptist's head on it. But instead of John the Baptist's, the head was Hannah's, looking out from the canvas with dead eyes and blood dripping from her shredded neck. Holding the head, fingers entwined in Hannah's hair, instead of Salome, was Rebecca Conway, aka Revy Harris."

"Rebecca Conway?" Duncan and Julia cried in unison. "Rebecca Conway, the heiress to the Harris Distilleries?" Duncan asked.

"One and the same. When I think about it, I can't believe it took so long for the lightbulb to go on, but when I saw her photo on the desk at Margrave House, it hit me like a lightning bolt. For years Rebecca Conway has been mucking about with my life."

"Who the hell is Rebecca Conway?" Clueless, Philip waited for someone to fill him in.

Julia jumped in. "Maybe you've seen the ads on TV or in magazines for Harris Distilleries. Rebecca Conway is the beautiful blond who's not just the spokesperson for the company, but the owner as well. Third generation."

"Of course!" Genevieve said. "I know who she is."

"Could I have read about her in *Fast Company*?" Philip began to show signs of recognition. "Doesn't she have a lifestyle company?"

"She does." Duncan said. "I don't understand, David. She's the person who's trying to murder you? She's a pretty prominent businessperson."

"I actually said I believe she's the person *behind* the attempts on my life, and now Mark's murder. She would never get her hands dirty, but she has plenty of resources. I'm positive Rebecca Conway is somehow involved."

TWENTY-EIGHT

T HE LIBRARY EXPLODED with a bolt of lightning and deafening clap of thunder. Lamps flickered, dimmed, went out. Gloom crept into every corner of the room. No one spoke. No one could. The shock of David's revelation rendered everyone mute. The only sound was sleet tapping against the library windowpanes until a loud rap at the door startled everyone.

Chief Superintendent Darlington bolted from his chair and strode across the room. "Excuse me. I'll be back," he said, closing the door behind him.

Genevieve looked at David, his shoulders slumped, his head cradled in his hands. She ached for what he was going through. What a wrenching experience this must be for him. It was hideous enough someone had tried to murder him twice, but to relive Becca tormenting him for so many years must be agonizing.

"David, how are you holding up? This has to be excruciating for you." Philip seemed to read Genevieve's mind.

"I'm okay," David said, looking up. "It's exhausting, but quite therapeutic to share this saga." He flashed a sweet smile that made him look like a young boy.

Julia stood. Reaching her arms toward the ceiling, she stretched her angular frame. "What do you suppose Darlington's doing?" She bent to touch her toes. "All this sitting is making me creaky."

"I've noticed he's been texting a lot the last half hour," Duncan said. "Maybe the forensic team found something. Maybe the smoking gun." Duncan blew imaginary smoke from his index finger.

Another rumble of thunder and groaning gust of wind announced the storm was still very much alive. The electricity flashed back on, lamps again flooding the library with a welcome glow.

With the break in the morning's session, everyone snatched the opportunity to take care of waiting tasks. Duncan and Philip buried their noses in their phones, responding to messages received in the last few hours. David sat, fingers steepled, gazing into the fire. Julia dashed upstairs to check on the children, and Genevieve went to the kitchen to make sure lunch was organized.

After about ten minutes, Wallace entered the library. "Sir David, Chief Superintendent Darlington requests you join him in the study. The Chief Superintendent suggests the rest of the group adjourn for lunch."

David exchanged a bemused look with Philip and Duncan as he left, all three wondering what was coming next.

The storm continued. The temperature dropped. Rain turned to wet snow and began sticking to the library windows.

Philip and Duncan sauntered together into the conservatory,

where the table was set for lunch and a fire blazed on the hearth in cozy contrast to the howling tempest outside.

"This doesn't look promising for us leaving tomorrow, does it?" Duncan said to his dad. According to the UK's national weather service, the unusual weather system was going to sit over Yorkshire for the balance of the day and well into the night. Several inches of snow were expected by morning and winds gusting to forty miles an hour would continue throughout tomorrow. It didn't look as if anyone would go anywhere anytime soon.

"I know you're anxious to get back to D.C., but I'd say tomorrow is not going to happen." Though Philip knew Duncan and Julia had many things to do on the other side of the pond, he loved having them at Wilmingrove Hall and was in no hurry for them to go back to the States. "You know it's going to kill your mother when you leave." Philip examined the pattern in the carpet. "I...um... I might miss you guys a little bit, too."

Duncan rested his hand on Philip's shoulder. "Dad, we'll be back in a month for the holidays. You know I still think you and Mom should come back with us."

Philip frowned and started to speak, but Duncan held up his hand. "I know. I know. You're going to see what happens today, then decide."

Philip gripped Duncan's hand and squeezed. "Exactly. David's become like a member of our family. And we need to be here to help him through this.

"Of course, I get it but I'm still worried about you staying here."

From down the hall, children's giggles could be herd approaching the conservatory. "Brace yourself, Dad," Duncan said, with a note of joy.

Like two colts escaping their paddock, the children stampeded into the conservatory, Ella in hot pursuit of Alex.

"You're cheating!" Ella shrieked at her brother. "You got a head start!"

Alex stopped, causing Ella to slam into his back for the second time that day. Turning around, he towered over his sister. "I did not cheat. You were just slow off the starting line!"

"Well, I won in sardines!" Ella howled, now on the verge of tears.

"Okay. Okay, you two." Duncan snatched Ella by the waist just as she was about to shove Alex in the chest. He tucked her under his arm and her rage turned to delight, arms and legs flailing as her father tickled her, showing no mercy.

"Daddy, stop! Stop!" Ella gasped between giggling convulsions. Duncan turned his daughter upside down, holding her by her ankles. Her thick mane cascaded toward the floor.

"Is this better?" he asked the wriggling child.

"No! Daddy, put me down!"

Duncan lowered her until her hands touched the floor and he guided her into a gentle somersault. "Do it again," she said, still laughing.

"Absolutely not," he said. "What have you two been doing all morning?"

"We played hide and seek then we had chocolate chip pancakes then we played sardines," Alex said. "Do you know what that is?"

Duncan and Philip both shook their heads.

"Let me tell!" Ella was ready to take center stage.

"Hold on, Ella, I'd like to hear Alex's version." Philip pulled Ella into a hug.

"It's a cool game. It's like Hide and Seek, only in reverse," Alex began. "One person hides then everybody else tries to find them. When you find the person hiding, you hide with them, so everybody's packed in the hiding place like sardines. Get it? The last one still looking loses and is the one to hide in the next game. I don't understand why the last one is called the loser because the one to hide is the lucky one. It was hard to play with just two of us."

Ella wiggled from Philip's arms. "We found an awesome hiding place this morning nobody else knows about."

"Ella!" Alex shrieked, snatching an apple from a bowl on the sideboard and throwing it hard at Ella, smacking her in the stomach.

"Ugh!" Ella grunted, staggered backward and plopped to her bottom, the wind knocked out of her.

"Alex!" Duncan boomed. He crossed to Alex in two long strides and grabbed the little boy by the arm. "Why would you do that?" He loomed over his quaking son. "Why would you hurt your sister?"

"I...I...I was just kidding around." Alex's lower lip began to quiver, and his eyes welled up.

"That did not look like kidding around to me. Go upstairs to your room. I'll tell you when you can come down."

Wounded by his father's disappointment and embarrassed by

being scolded in front of his grandfather, Alex dragged himself across the room, head hanging. He turned back to face his dad, tears staining his flushed cheeks. "I was just playing, Dad. I'd never hurt Ella."

Duncan pointed at the door. "Go upstairs and think about what you did."

Alex sniffed, wiped his nose with the back of his hand, turned and shuffled out of the room.

Philip squatted beside his little girl, who remained on the floor. She was now breathing normally but was still shaken. "Are you okay, sweetheart?"

She wrapped her arms around her father's neck and squeezed. Her lips close to Duncan's ear, Ella whimpered, "Don't be mad at Alex, Daddy. He was just reminding me not to tell our secret."

"What secret?"

Releasing her grip on Duncan's neck, she leaned back and giggled. "Daddy, I can't tell you. It's a secret."

"Of course, darling. Good for you. It's important to know how to keep a secret." He gave her a noisy smooch on her perfect little cheek. She puckered her lips, kissed Duncan's nose, then jumped up, fully recovered, and skipped out of the conservatory.

Standing just outside the conservatory door, Wallace patted Ella on her bouncing curls as she flounced out. He walked into the room and cleared his throat. "My lord, Chief Superintendent Darlington and Sir David have returned, and the Chief has requested you join them as soon as it's convenient."

Pushing back their chairs, the diners stood and drifted away from the coziness of the fire.

"Is there coffee in the library?" Genevieve asked Wallace.

"Of course, my lady."

"Um, Wallace." She shifted her weight from one foot to the other then back again. "I know you don't eavesdrop, but have you heard anything?"

"Well, my lady, I have overheard a few things." He took a step closer to Genevieve and lowered his voice. "The house maids were furious this morning after the police went through all the rubbish bins outside the kitchen. The place is an absolute tip. And after crating all that mess, I don't imagine they found anything, do you? After all it's been three days since Sir Mark was...," Wallace pressed his lips together, "well, you know."

Genevieve leaned toward Wallace, her hand on his arm. "Not exactly information that's going to crack open the case is it, Wallace?"

"Are you saying, my lady, that's not what you were looking for?" he said, eyes twinkling.

"Wallace, you scoundrel. You did hear something." Genevieve buzzed with excitement. "Tell me. Tell me."

"I believe I heard the Chief and his men talking about mead residue on a server's shirt."

"Oh, Wallace, you are an excellent spy. What would we do without you?"

"It would be a struggle, my lady." He maintained his sober demeanor, though Genevieve detected a slight upturn of the corners of his mouth. "I imagine, however, you and Lord Crosswick would manage...somehow."

TWENTY-NINE

CHIEF SUPERINTENDENT DARLINGTON stood with his back to the newly stoked fire, hands clasped behind him. It was evident from the grim line of his mouth that he had significant news. To his left, David sat stone-still, staring at the floor, brow furrowed.

"We had several developments this morning," Darlington began. "We have been reviewing the findings with Sir David for the last couple of hours and are anxious to share them with the rest of you in the hope you can help us piece the puzzle together."

Genevieve glanced around the room. Philip, Duncan, and Julia all strained forward in their chairs, eyes riveted on Darlington. Genevieve willed her clamped jaw to relax. She caught Philip's eye and, together, they breathed in, then exhaled. Philip sat back in his chair, rotating his head in a gentle circle to relieve the taut muscles in his neck.

Darlington continued. "This morning the forensics team found two significant items when searching the rubbish bins. The first is a glass container with mead residue. The team was able to lift a near-perfect print off the jar. The second is a shirt similar to those worn by the catering staff on the night of your party. There is a small stain on the cuff which we believe is mead, indicating it was worn either by the person who made the drink or the person who brought the drink to Sir David. We may be able to pull some DNA off the shirt. The items have already been sent to our labs in London. They left this morning before the storm picked up."

Genevieve smiled to herself feeling smug that she heard about the shirt first.

"I'm thrilled they found evidence in the bins." Philip shook his head. "What was the killer thinking? It seems like a bonehead move to put anything in the garbage cans."

Darlington pressed on. "The other important development is a message on the house phone. It was left last night at 9:47."

"I wonder how we missed that," Philip said. "I guess we had all gone upstairs by about nine thirty."

"And, because it was Sunday night, the staff wasn't here," said Genevieve. "Who was it?"

"It was Rebecca Conway calling for Sir David," Darlington said.

"What?" Duncan gripped the arms of his chair, his knuckles turning white.

"Are you kidding?" Julia's voice cracked.

Philip looked from David to Darlington then back to David. "I don't understand. What in the hell did she want?"

David looked up from the carpet. He gazed around the room, looking dazed. "We don't know what she wanted."

"Franklin, play the message," Darlington directed.

A strong, polished voice filled the room. "This is Rebecca Conway. I'm trying to reach David Weatherington. I have reason to believe he is at this number. David, please call me as soon as you receive this message. It's critical I speak to you. I have important information that may save your life."

David looked at Philip, then Genevieve.

"I'm assuming you haven't returned the call yet." Genevieve walked to David and put a hand on his shoulder. "David," Genevieve squeezed his knotted muscles, "do you have any idea what this means?"

David looked up at Genevieve, eyes warm with gratitude. "I do not. I've heard nothing from her since we received that wretched, insane painting fifteen years ago at our engagement party. " He paused, looking at his clasped hands before continuing, "that's not exactly true. Three years ago, when Hannah died, Becca sent a card. It was a combination 'I'm sorry I made your life a living Hell, and condolence' card. I was stunned at the kind message."

"I bet," Julia scoffed.

"She said she could never apologize enough for her terrible behavior. With the card, she included a copy of a poem, 'The Hopi Prayer'. She said her heart broke for my loss and she hoped my years with Hannah had been as wonderful as I deserved. It brought me to tears."

"Did you believe what she said?" Like Julia, Duncan was skeptical.

"No, I did not. But as long as she left me alone, I didn't worry about it. A psychopath has the spectacular ability to bend the truth to suit his or her needs. When this chaos started, I was pretty sure her remorse was a smoke screen. I thought she was most likely lying low until she found the right moment to cause me the maximum amount of pain. That may be true. It may not. But what is true is the next step is ours. Chief Superintendent Darlington, would you like to tell our band of amateur detectives what happens next?"

While the snow deepened and the winds continued to howl, Chief Superintendent Darlington shared what they knew about Rebecca Conway's phone call.

"By using voice recognition, we verified the caller was indeed Conway. The call came from a land line at Harris Distillery in Lexington, Kentucky. Rebecca left a cell phone number for David. Nothing about the call appears to be threatening, but before he returns it, I want to be sure Sir David is well prepared.

"David, isn't talking to Rebecca going to be horrible for you?" Genevieve frowned and chewed her lower lip.

"It may sound crazy, but I'm anxious for the conversation, particularly if she can shed light on what's been happening the last few weeks." David drummed his fingers on the arm of his chair, the only sign of any nerves.

"Her message sounds as if that's why she's reaching out. My team is preparing for Sir David to call Ms. Conway three hours from now, at six o'clock, one o'clock in Kentucky." Darlington uncrossed and recrossed his legs. "We're setting up recording equipment, and Chief Inspector MacTavish and Inspector Franklin are creating a list of the information Sir David will try to extract from Ms. Conway."

"David, what do you think you'll get out of all of this?" Philip asked.

David straightened in his chair and took a deep breath as if to gain strength. "Perhaps Becca can lead us to whoever is playing this demented game. Or if she's responsible for all of this, she may tip her hand. I think that's what you're expecting, isn't it, Chief Superintendent?"

"I try not to have expectations. I find they can cloud my vision. It's best to keep an open mind and follow the trail of evidence to the end. And, as of this morning, we have some excellent evidence."

"Let's hope she has some relevant information, and this isn't just another effort to disrupt Sir David's life." Philip nodded at David.

"Regardless of the outcome, we'll be a step closer to a resolution." Darlington rose. "Do any of you have other questions before Sir David and I return to the study to prepare for the call? We just wanted to bring you up do date with this morning's revelations."

Julia, flushed from sitting near the fire, looked at David with laser focus. "David, do you want one of us to be in the room with you when you call Becca?"

Surprised and touched, David smiled. "Thank you, Julia, that's not necessary, but I appreciate the offer. It's sweet of you. Don't worry. I promise I won't fall apart." David rolled out of his chair sprawling onto the floor.

Laughter filled the library at David's antics, brightening the mood in the room.

"All right. All right. I get it. You're tough as nails."

"Just let us know if there's anything we can do to be of help." Philip stood, indicating they should let David and Darlington get on with their preparation. "We'll be waiting to hear, needless to say." Philip shook David's hand then pulled him in for a hug.

"Here we go," David said as he followed the Chief Superintendent to Philip's study.

David sat at the desk and listened to Chief Inspector MacTavish and Inspector Franklin.

"After you tell her how much you appreciate her call, you need to—"

"Wouldn't it be smart to let her play the first card?" David interrupted. "Couldn't I just treat her as an old friend and see what she has to say?" David raised his eyebrows.

"Our goal is to control the conversation. By the end of the call, we want two things. First, we want to discern if she's behind the attempts on your life and the death of Sir Mark. Second, if it sounds as if she's not directly responsible, we want any information she may have that will lead us to the assailant."

It may have been fatigue, it may have been stress, but David felt prickles of annoyance rising to the surface. "Why don't you blokes just piss off! You know I'm a barrister. I've led hundreds of witnesses through testimony to my desired end." David looked at the ceiling, let out a deep breath, then looked back at the three coppers. "Look, Inspector, I'm not demeaning your skills, but I know how to talk to Rebecca Conway, who, I'm assuming is a hostile witness." David rose and headed for the door. "I'm going to have a lie down. I'll be back by half five."

Franklin and MacTavish looked at each other, panic in their eyes. MacTavish rang Chief Superintendent Darlington who was with the forensic team.

"Don't worry about it. He'll be fine," Darlington said. And that was that.

THIRTY

THE CLOCK IN the grand salon bonged six times. David cradled the house phone and punched in the international code for the U.S. followed by the number Rebecca left on her message. His hand tremored, and his breathing was shallow and rapid. After a long pause, the line connected and began to ring. David willed himself to slow his breathing. On the fourth ring, a refined voice said, "Hello, David."

"Becca? Is this Rebecca Conway?" David didn't recognize the voice. He struggled to steady his own. His heart pounded in his ears.

"Yes, David, this is Becca. Are you all right? You sound strange."

To his relief, David heard himself laugh. He wiped his sweaty palms on his woolen pants and took a drink of water. "I guess I'm a bit nervous talking to you after all these years. You must admit our relationship hasn't always been smooth."

Now it was Becca's turn to laugh. "That's an understatement. I cringe to think of my deplorable behavior for so many years. If it hadn't been for my parents having me committed so I could get psychological help, I would be dead. Or, at the very least, in prison." Becca sounded detached, as if she were talking about an acquaintance rather than herself. "I hated them for years after they placed me at Winthrop Hills, but it was a perfect place for me. It took a long time to forgive them and finally thank them for making the hard choice to place me there." She cleared her throat. "But, David, I didn't reach out to tell you my woeful tale. I called because I know about everything that's happened to you since you were shot, and I think I know who is responsible for the attempts on your life and for Mark Holmes' death."

"I don't understand." David's shoulders tensed. "How do you know what's been happening?"

"Henry Fitch and I have remained friends since Harvard. We speak every couple of weeks and knowing how you are has always been important to me. Please don't be angry with Henry. I promise, he only kept me apprised of your health and happiness. I was heartbroken when he told me you lost Hannah. You two seemed so in love and so happy. The year before she died, I was in London on business and saw her in *The Importance of Being Ernest*. She was spectacular. It was easy to understand why you fell in love with her."

At the mention of Hannah's name, David felt the sting of tears. He cleared his throat, careful not to break Becca's verbal stride. He barely breathed, afraid he would spook her and cause her to end the call. Softly and slowly, he inhaled as she continued.

"When Henry told me someone shot and almost killed you, I was shocked. But it didn't take long for me to realize who might be responsible. I would have called sooner, but I've been doing a lot of sleuthing. I didn't want to raise suspicions if my feelings had no basis in fact. And then when Sir Mark died from poisoned mead meant for you…" Becca couldn't finish the sentence.

"And what did your *sleuthing* reveal?"

"I checked on the whereabouts of the person I suspected and, I'm sorry to say, she wasn't where she was supposed to be."

Silence filled the line.

"Becca. Becca, did I lose you."

"No. I'm still here." Becca's voice cracked. "David, assuming you're still in Yorkshire, I think it's best if I come to Wilmingrove Hall to talk to you in person. I'm sure I can be of some help to the police. My pilot told me earlier today you're having a strange late-fall storm, but the weather looks good for the day after tomorrow. I could be there Wednesday morning. What do you think?"

Chief Superintendent Darlington handed David a notepad with a scribbled note written in black ink:

Yes! Ask her who she thinks is trying to kill you.

"Becca, there's no question it would be helpful if you came here. I'd be grateful for any information you can give the police. Do you really have an idea who might be behind all of this?"

"Yes. I'm quite sure I know who it is."

"It just seems strange that you would know anything about this. You're four thousand miles away and we haven't had any contact for almost twenty years. Why in the world would you have any idea who's trying to kill me?"

"When I tell you, you'll understand."

"You said 'she wasn't where she was supposed to be. It's a woman?"

"Yes. Her name is Olivia."

"I don't know anyone called Olivia."

"Olivia Conway."

David's eyes widened. "Is she related to you?"

David heard Inspector Franklin's rapid-fire keystrokes as he googled "Olivia Conway." Franklin scribbled a note and handed it to David.

She's 20 years old. Last known address, London

"Becca, Olivia Conway is only 20. I don't think I know anyone in their twenties. I'll ask you again. Is she related to you?

"She is. David. She's my daughter.

A drop of sweat hung from the tip of David's nose. He sent it flying with a flick of his finger. "I don't understand. I didn't know you had a daughter. Why in the world would she want to kill me?"

There was silence at the other end of the line. David held his breath. "Becca, are you still there?"

"I'm here, David." Becca's voice was husky with emotion.

"Becca, why would Olivia want to kill me?" He was angry now.

Because, David, she believes you're her father and she hates you for it."

THIRTY-ONE

WEDNESDAY MORNING DAWNED cloudless and calm, the storm finally over. Snow piled high, lining the runway edges at Yorkshire's Leeds Bradford Airport. As the wheels on Rebecca Conway's Airbus touched down, the House of Crosswick's Bombardier waited second in line for takeoff. Julia and the children were heading home, leaving Duncan behind. Duncan and Julia had decided he could not leave his parents and David alone with the woman who might be responsible for their recent nightmare arriving.

In their short week at Wilmingrove Hall, they had been engulfed by Philip and Genevieve's new world of great fortune. It was hard to comprehend until you stepped onto your family's luxurious private jet. Only then could you begin to grasp the reality of jaw-dropping wealth.

The plane rolled forward. "We are next in line for takeoff." Captain Bruni's sensual Italian accent came over the intercom. They would soon be on their way.

Julia glanced out of the window and saw the Harris Distillery logo on the side of the Airbus. She pressed Duncan's number on her cell.

One ring and he answered.

"She's here."

"How do you know?"

"I'm looking at her plane. She's taxiing to the terminal. Wow. I thought *we* had a fancy private jet!" Julia smirked. "Becca's plane makes us look like a poor relative." She broke into a full-throated laugh, amused at her ridiculous complaint.

As the Harris Distillery aircraft rolled toward the terminal, Rebecca Harris Conway breathed deeply, hands folded in her lap. She appeared serene, self-possessed. She turned her head to look out of the window and her beveled blond hair swung just above tense shoulders. She looked younger than her forty-two years, even with the small lines at the corners of her ice-blue eyes. Her olive skin and full mouth were gifts from her mother's Italian heritage.

Butterflies fluttered from her stomach into her throat at the thought of seeing David after so many years. She didn't really need to fly to England. She could have told David and the Met detectives when they had spoken on the phone why she suspected her daughter of terrorizing David. But she couldn't resist seeing him in person. So, she offered, and they agreed she should come to Wilmingrove Hall.

A woman used to making hundreds of decisions daily, Becca had labored over what to wear for her initial meeting with David and the Scotland Yard team. She had changed her clothes four times before settling on a black cashmere turtleneck, slim black jeans, and a camel and black herringbone tweed hacking jacket. She finished the classic look with black leather boots with a two-inch heel. She kept jewelry to a minimum, with large gold studs in her ears and on her right ring finger a square-cut ruby surrounded by two rows of diamonds.

Becca didn't doubt for a moment that she was doing the right thing. After her conversation with David, she had spent half an hour on the phone with Chief Superintendent Darlington. The Chief had been cordial, offering her the department's gratitude for coming forward with information, and traveling to York to help. Now, about to depart the safe haven of her plane, her temples throbbed, and her stomach continued to churn.

"You need to be here," she said to herself. "This is the only thing you could do. You owe David a great debt and you may be saving his life."

The plane slowed to a stop as her captain said over the intercom, "Ms. Conway we have arrived at Leeds Bradford Airport. The local time is 8:27 a.m. and the temperature is forty-two degrees Fahrenheit. The stairs will be in place shortly for your disembarkment."

Becca walked back to her sleeping cabin, slipped into her wool trench coat, gathered her handbag, and walked forward to the exit door. Captain Marshall had come from the cockpit to see her off and stood with Marion and Edward, the two flight attendants.

"Thank you all for an uneventful flight. It was most appreciated." Becca offered a genuine smile that crinkled her eyes. "I'll keep you posted regarding my schedule, but in the meantime, enjoy yourselves."

Edward eased open the exit door, allowing a blast of cold air to push into the cabin. Across the tarmac stood three men. There was no doubt these were the men from Scotland Yard. The officer standing in front was several inches taller than the other two. If appearances counted for anything, he was the alpha male. Becca ran her tongue over her lower lip as she admired the man's rugged good looks. Even at this distance, she could appreciate his chiseled jaw and full mouth. The sun glanced off his aviator shades.

Becca had not had a serious relationship since ending her engagement eight years ago. Her former fiancé was an attractive, kind, Lexington tax attorney who bored her to tears. After many years of tumult, she had been lured by the idea of stability and a life without drama. But one deadly dull year later, she realized she would be happier alone than in a colorless world filled with colorless people. However, she still appreciated an attractive, interesting man, and at a distance Chief Superintendent Darlington looked very interesting indeed.

Standing at the top of the stairs, Becca pulled on calfskin gloves and filled her lungs with chilly morning air. Descending the stairs, she, too, hid behind dark glasses.

"Chief Superintendent Darlington?" Alighting from the last step, Becca held out her hand. "It's good to meet you."

"Ms. Conway, as I told you when we spoke, we appreciate you coming across the pond to help."

"Chief Superintendent, as I told you, I'd prefer to deliver my information to David in person." Shoving her sunglasses to the top of her head, Becca turned her focus to the two other men standing with them. "And who are these fellows?"

"May I introduce the other two members of our Met team: Chief Inspector MacTavish and Inspector Franklin." They exchanged handshakes and cordial smiles. "Lord Crosswick's people are handling your luggage and paperwork. Unless you need something from your aircraft, we can go directly to Wilmingrove Hall."

"Thank you. If someone is taking care of my luggage, I'm ready to go. Is Wilmingrove Hall far?"

"It's about a twenty-five-minute drive." Darlington ushered Becca into the back seat of a black Range Rover, which had been left running. The warmth in the car was a welcome relief from the biting chill of the morning. Conversation was spirited during the drive from the airport to the Hall. A lover of bourbon, Darlington pelted Becca with questions about running a world-renowned distillery. He surprised her with his knowledge about her lifestyle program, *The Most Interesting Woman in The Room*.

"I haven't watched too many episodes, maybe four or five." He offered a sheepish smile. "But my favorite was the one about reinventing yourself."

"Aha," Becca nodded. She placed her gloved hand on the Chief's arm and leaned into him. "I assume you were doing research on me?"

"Guilty as charged. At least that was why I watched the first couple of episodes. When I saw the show about how people could change their lives, I realized it was personal for you." Darlington's eyes held Becca's. "Particularly the part about how even terrible people can take their lives down a very different path. Do you honestly think that's true?"

Becca's hand slipped from his arm. "Yes, Chief. It was a *very* personal show. And yes, I do believe people can transform their lives. But they have to be repentant." She broke his stare and slid back to her side of the car. "It's why I've come to help."

After passing through the charming village of Wilmingrove, the Range Rover turned off York Road onto Wilmingrove Lane to the Hall, stopping in front of a high iron gate. Inspector Franklin rolled down the driver's window, reached out to press the button on the intercom, and announced their arrival into a security camera perched atop the fence. The gates parted, and they proceeded down the allee toward the house.

Becca had spent a lifetime in elegant surroundings, but she had never experienced an entrance quite like that of Wilmingrove Hall. Silver birch lined the quarter-mile drive, autumnal gold leaves shimmering in the mid-morning breeze. At this time of year, the trees mirrored the color of the Hall's glowing Yorkshire stone. On either side of the lane, the fields overflowed with the brilliance of yellow tansy, purple-pink heather, and the vibrant lavender of spear thistle, all of which had survived the storm and were pushing their sturdy heads through the remnants of the melting snow. In late fall, much of the thistle was morphing into seed heads, blanketing the fields with a ghostly cast as the thistle seeds waited for a gust of wind to lift them onto the breeze and take them to parts unknown. At the lane's end the car emerged from the shelter of the birch, arriving at the circular drive and Wilmingrove Hall.

For the past half an hour, Becca had been deep in conversation then dazzled by the drive to Wilmingrove Hall. She hadn't been considering what was about to happen. But as the door to the Hall opened, blood rushed to her head. Her vision blurred and sweat popped out on her forehead.

As he stepped from the massive doorway into the sunlight, David looked just as Becca remembered. His build was still athletic, but a bit leaner now. His hair was gray at the temples and more styled, but he was as handsome now as he had been twenty-five years ago. Her heart raced and she noticed she was holding her breath.

"Are you all right, Ms. Conway?" Darlington turned in his seat to look at Becca.

"I, uh… I'm fine," she stammered. "Much to my surprise, I'm a bit overwhelmed seeing David. Who knew?" Trying to make light of her nervousness, she gave a laugh that came out as a snort, causing her to giggle. Realizing Franklin was holding her car door open, she pulled herself together and scooted out of the Range Rover.

"David!" Becca strode toward him, her hand outstretched.

"My God, Becca!" Desire, dread, anxiety, gratitude all overwhelmed David as he shook Becca's hand. "We can't thank you enough for coming forward with your ideas about this mess. This can't be easy for you. If your theory about your daughter is correct, this will be hellish for you."

"David, knowing what I know and believing what I believe, there is no way I could stay silent. I'm just grateful you don't think *I'm* behind these attempts on your life."

David said nothing.

Becca held his gaze as she continued. "As you well know, there was a time I would have been the logical suspect. In fact, there's a time I might have been the culprit. It doesn't surprise me at all I was the first person you thought of when you started wondering who's causing all this," she fluttered her hands, "all this trouble. I'm relieved you and the police are taking my suspicions seriously."

"Well, you're here and I'm grateful." Taking her elbow, David ushered Becca into the grand salon. Becca grinned, looking up at the coffered ceiling inset with frescos. "To coin a phrase from my youth, David, this is awesome. If Lord and Lady Crosswick are as wonderful as their home, I can hardly wait to meet them."

"You need wait no longer because here we are, the wonderful Philip and Genevieve Warwick." The couple crossed to where Becca stood with David.

Becca peeled off her right glove. Philip proffered his hand formally. "Welcome to Wilmingrove Hall, Ms. Conway?"

She flashed a warm smile. "Please call me Becca," she said, putting her hand on Philip's arm.

Genevieve blanched and swayed as the blood rushed from her head.

"G, are you all right?" Philip grabbed his wife's arm and led her to a chair. "Sit down?"

"Genevieve, I'll get you a glass of water." David dashed toward the kitchen.

"Darling, put your head between your knees."

Genevieve waved all the attention away. "It's the ring," she said. "Becca, you're wearing Victoria Laney's ring.

Becca stared at her hand, frozen in place. Seconds passed before she blinked and said, "It was stupid of me to wear this ring before I told you about my relationship with Jonathon. I'm so sorry."

No one knew what to say. Becca looked from Genevieve to Philip to David, then back to Genevieve. "Perhaps I should stay in the village," she said pulling her glove back on.

Genevieve collected herself "Don't be ridiculous. I'm the one who should apologize. It was just a shock seeing the ring in reality after seeing it in your photograph and in Victoria's portrait."

"My photograph? What portrait?"

"I'll tell you all about it later." Genevieve almost smiled. "Welcome. We're grateful you're here. We've been anxious to meet the infamous Rebecca Harris Conway!"

"Infamous indeed!" Becca exhaled, looking relieved. "From the moment I knew I had to reach out to David, I've been terrified how I'd be received—by David, by the police, by the two of you—apparently for good reason. I've been here five minutes and almost gotten myself thrown out!"

Becca stuck her gloves in her coat pockets and David held the collar of her coat as she slipped her arms out. "I'm sure David told you about my horrible, sometimes felonious, behavior. From the moment I met him, David became the object of my narcissistic obsession. Thank goodness my parents intervened and got me the help I needed."

"That must have been quite an experience, working through a serious psychological issue. You deserve a lot of respect for all the years of hard work." Philip's voice was filled with admiration.

"That's kind of you Lord Crosswick, but—"

"It's Philip, please."

"Of course, Philip. It's kind of you, but I was lucky. My parents had means and spared no expense getting me the best help possible. There are so many people who suffer from mental health issues but are left on their own." Becca's eyes misted. "One of the first things I did when I left Winthrop Hills, was to volunteer with a grassroots organization in Lexington: NAMI, the National Alliance on Mental Illness. I began fundraising for them and now sit on their national board. And I'm going to stop lecturing now!" Smiling a self-conscious smile, Becca blushed and looked down at her elegant boots.

"As they say, 'I knew you when'. And to say you have come a long way appears to be an understatement." David put his arm around Becca and gave her a squeeze. "If you can help solve this case, all will be forgiven!" Stepping back, David grinned and gave Becca a chummy punch on the arm. "How are your brothers?"

"They're terrific." Becca's smile oozed pride. "Conner is a psychiatrist in Boston. Considering my past, it's wonderful to have a shrink in the family." Becca's laugh filled the salon. "He's married to a concert pianist, Calliope Stanhope, and has two spectacular boys, Max and Henry. My brother James has been at the distillery since he graduated from business school. When Kentucky legalized same-sex marriage, he and Michael, the man he's loved since they were undergrads, had a big wedding at our farm. Best wedding I've ever been to. Sadly, Mother and Dad missed seeing James happy. They died in a plane crash nine years ago. I had been Harris Distilleries Vice President of Marketing for several years, so took over as CEO and James became CFO. We're a good team. It's wonderful to be in business with people you know, love and trust."

"I remember reading about the plane crash." David's face clouded. "I liked your parents very much. They were good to me that summer in Cambridge."

"It's been a long time. I'm just happy they saw me come out the other side of a very dark period in my life."

Striding into the grand salon, Duncan added his greetings. "Ms. Conway, welcome. I'm Duncan Warwick, the son," he said, shaking Becca's hand.

"The resemblance is striking. What lucky girls we are, Genevieve! We're surrounded by handsome men!"

"Aren't we? Not only are they hunky, but they're pretty nice most of the time. Come on, I'll show you to your room" Genevieve led the way through the grand salon toward the stairs. "You and David will have plenty of time to catch up over the next few days. Chief Superintendent Darlington wants to gather at two o'clock, so we'll have lunch at twelve thirty. Are you exhausted or did you sleep on the flight?"

"I'm fine. As much as I travel, I find I sleep as well on my plane as anywhere. You'll have to give me the grand tour of Wilmingrove Hall. I spent a lot of time with Jonathon at Margrave House, but I've never been here. It's magnificent. From the moment we turned down the driveway, I've been mesmerized."

"I'd love to, and we'll bring our head housekeeper, Mrs. MacIntosh, with us. She's the Hall's docent. You'll love her! She knows everything about every thing in the house. And, who knows? We might even meet up with Charlotte!"

"Oh my God! Charlotte. I haven't thought of her in years. How is the old girl?"

"She seems to have come with us to Wilmingrove Hall. I smelled her just the other day."

The two women headed up the grand staircase side by side, chattering like old friends.

✦ ∷ ✦ϾƆＣϾ✦ ∷ ✦

Watching the two women walk up the steps, a wave of exhilaration swept through her. It wasn't part of the plot, but what if they both tumbled down the stairs at the same time, bouncing, smashing, cracking. Then there could be two more beautiful ghosts wandering through Wilmingrove Hall.

THIRTY-TWO

B Y THE TIME everyone gathered in the library, the sun had disappeared behind banks of clouds that had rolled in during the early afternoon.

Becca sat next to the fire. She had changed into a starched white shirt topped by a camel cashmere sweater-jacket. Brown and camel tweed pants draped her long legs. Only someone born into wealth could have such natural authority and appear so comfortable in the old-money environment of Wilmingrove Hall. She sat calmly, hands folded in her lap.

On the other side of the fireplace, in direct contrast to his old nemesis, David's nerves danced close to the surface. His body was taut and the ankle resting on his knee bounced. After a moment, he uncrossed his legs, reversing his position, then finally put both feet on the floor and rested his hands on his knees.

Seated on the sofa in front of the hearth, Philip patted the cushion next to him as Genevieve entered the room. He inhaled the hint of the perfume she had worn for forty years. He could not smell the aroma without thinking of his wife. He placed his hand, palm up in the space between them. Genevieve reached

MONEY, MURDER, MAYHEM

out, intertwining their fingers without looking at him. Sneaking a sidelong glance, Philip could see a smile just for him pulling at the corners of her mouth.

Each man on the Met team was in his place. Chief Superintendent Darlington had exchanged his suit pants for more casual cuffed wool trousers. He no longer wore a tie and had pulled a heavy, collared sweater over his dress shirt, which was now open at the neck. Becca couldn't help wondering if all Scotland Yard coppers dressed so nattily. Then she looked at Chief Inspector MacTavish and Inspector Franklin and had her answer. No, they did not.

"Are we ready to begin?" Chief Superintendent Darlington looked around the room. In return, each person nodded. "MacTavish, Francis, are you ready?"

"Yes, sir," they said in unison.

"If I may, I'd like to give a brief recap of events starting when Sir David was shot six weeks ago. I think it would help focus our conversation today."

"I know I would appreciate it," said Philip. "So much has happened since then."

"Needless-to-say, as the late-comer, it would be very helpful to me." Becca's voice was low and steady.

Darlington nodded to Franklin. "Inspector."

In the silent room, a soft click could be heard as Franklin pressed the record button.

Chief Superintendent Darlington started with the shooting in September and droned on about the events until he got to the findings two days ago, excitement crept into his voice. "Since

Monday, forensics has been analyzing the shirt we found in the rubbish bin. They found a short black hair inside the collar."

"Well, that's exciting, isn't it?" David sat straighter in his chair.

"We hoped they could extract DNA from it," Darlington continued. "But the hair is synthetic, no doubt coming from a wig."

'Well, crap," Philip said.

"It's not all bad news. No doubt it means the person who prepared the mead was in a disguise. We believe that was the barmaid."

"But you can't find her," Duncan stated.

"True, we've had no luck so far. But Ms. Conway coming here and sharing her theory about the murderer could very well be the break we need. With that said, Ms. Conway, could you please start from the beginning? This is your official statement, so please don't leave anything out. Is there anything you need before we begin?"

"Thank you, Chief Superintendent Darlington. I'm quite comfortable, maybe a little nervous."

"There's no need to be nervous, Ms. Conway. We can take a break at any point. Just say the word."

A soft smile curled her lips and Becca began. "Two months after my graduation from Harvard, I came to England." Becca paused, glancing at David. "By then, David had been back here for two years and, I'm sure, hadn't given me a thought during that time. I, however, was still obsessed with him. I intended to stalk him until he fell madly in love with me." Becca nodded at the smirks and sly smiles around the room. "No, really," she pressed. "There was no doubt in my mind I could bend David to my will. Delusional? Yes." She stopped for a moment, chuckling. "I had won a Laney Museum of Fine Arts Fellowship."

She gestured to Philip and Genevieve. "You both know what a plum grant that is. My parents were thrilled. Little did they know that I had applied and been accepted under the name of Revy Harris."

Genevieve asked, "Why did you do that?"

Becca sat forward in her chair, her elbows on the arms. "Because I didn't want anyone to recognize my name."

Philip looked puzzled. "Why would they recognize your name?"

"Before she married my father, my mother's name was Katherine Robeson."

Gasps and questions filled the room.

"Katherine Robeson was your mother?" Duncan snorted a laugh. "This just keeps getting curiouser and curiouser."

"Doesn't it just," Becca confirmed.

"Who's Katherine Robeson?" Darlington asked.

"Katherine Robeson had once been engaged to the 12TH Earl and I didn't want anyone to find out she was my mother."

Questions began to fly.

"Was the 12TH Earl your father?" Philip couldn't ask fast enough.

"No. Jonathon was not my father."

"When did Katherine marry your dad?" Genevieve asked.

"About a year after Jonathon sent her back to the States, she met my father, who was a wonderful man. They dated for a couple of years before they got married.

"How did you find out your mother was engaged to the Earl?" Duncan wanted to know.

"I found a letter to Jonathon my mother wrote and never sent, telling him how devastated she was when he broke off their engagement.

"I don't understand, Ms. Conway. Why didn't you want the Earl to know your true identity?" Darlington looked puzzled.

"I was afraid if he realized I was Katherine's daughter, he would have me thrown out of the fellowship program. Then, much to my surprise, I was chosen to help catalogue Lord Crosswick's collection at Margrave House. It wasn't what I wanted to do," Becca shrugged, "but in the end, it turned out to be spectacular for me."

"So, you spent your time at Margrave House organizing the collection?" Chief Superintendent Darlington asked.

Becca inhaled and gave a soft laugh as she breathed out. "Yes, Chief. I did a little cataloguing, but I spent most of my time flirting with the Earl. With great success, I might add. Not long after I started working at Margrave House, he and I started having intimate dinners, and eventually we became lovers."

The statement was so matter of fact, it almost went unheard, then Genevieve gasped. "You were lovers with your mother's ex-fiancé?"

"I know," Becca rolled her eyes. "Hard to imagine a daughter would do that, right?" "Wait a minute!" Duncan shook his head. "Wait just a minute. I thought Jonathon was, um, well you know, um, paralyzed."

"He was paralyzed, but he wasn't impotent. In fact, he was a very good lover." Becca took a long drink from her water glass. "Of course, like everything else about my story, it's complicated." Pushing herself from her chair, Becca strode to the windows to admire the acres of green dotted with remnants of snow.

"During my years of therapy, I learned the motive behind my rebellious behavior was to hurt my parents my kind, loving parents. I excelled at fulfilling that goal. I've always been a high achiever." She turned to the group and smiled a melancholy smile. She began to wander around the room. "When I realized I could have an affair with my mother's former fiancé, I couldn't believe my luck. I was drunk on the idea of how much pain I could cause her." She caught David's eye and held his gaze. "It even took my mind off you."

Pink crept up David's neck and into his cheeks until even the tips of his ears were blushing. "So, that's why you stopped stalking me. Better offer, better pedigree."

"Better return on investment." Becca wiggled the ruby on her finger.

Everyone laughed at the witty parry and thrust.

Philip had said little since Becca began telling her story. He cleared his throat before he spoke. "Did Jonathon ever realize you were Katherine's daughter?"

"You know, Philip, I didn't think so at the time. But in retrospect, it may have been one of the reasons he broke off our relationship." She picked up a tiny bronze statue of a hunting dog. She turned it over in her hand, running her fingers back and forth over the cold, silky surface of the belly. "A month before my fellowship was up, Jonathon told me I needed to go home as soon as it was finished. I was shocked. I was furious." She looked at David. "You remember how angry I could get."

David blanched.

Becca closed her fist around the bronze puppy until her knuckles whitened. "He said all the right things: that I was young and had my life ahead of me, that he was too old and feeble. I didn't want to hear any of it. I didn't want any of his self-sacrifice."

Draped in sadness, Becca drifted back to her chair and sank into the cushion. "I had fallen in love with him. Deeply. But there was no changing his mind. The last time I saw him, he gave me this ring." She looked down at her hand. "And he thanked me for all the joy I had given him." Tears trailed down her cheeks, dripping from her chin onto her sweater.

Genevieve walked to Becca, squeezed her shoulder, and offered unused tissues from her pocket.

"Thinking about Jonathon still brings me to tears." Looking down at the carpet, Becca blew her nose. "But that's not the worst part."

"What could be worse than unrequited love?" David asked.

Becca looked at him through wet lashes. Outside, the sun played hide-and-seek as the clouds broke apart and raced across the slate-gray sky. The library filled with a golden glow, then darkened into dusky gray before brightening again.

Becca took a sip of her cold coffee. Setting her cup back in its saucer, she looked around the room. "When I got home, I was out of control. I was angry. I was mean. I was hateful. I took out all of my fury on my parents."

"As you said, I've been on the other side of that anger and it's not a good place to be."

"You're right, David. I even frightened myself. For a month my mother and father tried to deal with me alone, but it was impossible. After consulting with the medical staff at Winthrop Hills, a psychiatric clinic, my parents decided to commit me. Two weeks after I was committed, I learned I was pregnant with my mother's ex-fiancé's baby. Welcome to *Days of Our Lives*, Rebecca Conway style."

No one in the room spoke. There were no words to be said. The stunned silence lasted until Darlington said, "Please go on, Ms. Conway."

Becca nodded. "My daughter was born six weeks after I left Winthrop Hills. My parents were extraordinary and by the time I moved home, I was beginning to understand my misplaced anger toward them. They doted on Olivia. Olivia Harris Conway. She was a beautiful little girl: blond curls and blue eyes ringed with violet. But even as a toddler something about her worried me. She was never warm and cuddly. She never wanted or needed my approval like most babies. Something about my beautiful child haunted me.

"I refused to tell my parents who the father was. Can you imagine how horrified my mother would have been? Even I couldn't do that to her. My father implored, threatened, begged. My mother convinced him, after several weeks, to stop haranguing me. I think she was relieved they wouldn't have to deal with a father who might cause problems. Several times I wanted to call Jonathon and tell him about Olivia, but I always thought better of it. The only person I ever told was my brother, Conner."

Becca stood up and walked to David. With tears in her eyes, she took his hand in both of hers. "David, I'm so sorry. I believe what I'm about to tell you is what set everything in motion to bring us to where we are today. If I could, I would change everything."

Nearly growling, David said, "What in the world did you do?" He felt the old sense of dread creep into the pit of his stomach. Déjà vu swept over him in a wave of nausea.

Becca moved away from him to face the fire, her back to the room. She stood motionless until Darlington asked, "Ms. Conway, are you all right to continue or would you like to take a break?"

Becca turned around to face the room. Her eyes glistened and her cheeks were moist with tears. "I, um… I didn't expect this would be so emotional." She smiled and sniffed. Reaching into her pants pocket, she pulled out a tissue and dabbed at her eyes. "This is embarrassing," she said, offering a weak smile.

Genevieve moved to Becca with outstretched arms. Holding Becca by her shoulders she said, "You're telling a roomful of strangers an incredibly personal story. I think you're remarkably brave!"

"And I think a brandy would be helpful." Philip went to the sideboard, pulled the stopper from a decanter, poured generous servings into snifters, and passed them around. He sat down, handing a glass to Genevieve.

"Becca, would you please get on with it?" David snarled. "I'd like to know what you've done to put my life in danger."

"David!" Genevieve shot him a scathing look.

"It's all right, Genevieve," Becca said. "I deserve David's anger, and so much more." She took a fortifying drink. "I'm not proud of what I'm about to tell you. But then, I'm proud of very little I did in my youth. But I never imagined what damage my actions would cause.

"I had several photos of David from the summer in Cambridge and a couple at Harvard. Some were of him alone; some were of us together. I lived in those pictures and created an entire life for the two of us, in my head. Scary, isn't it?" Becca said, looking at David. "I never told Olivia you were her father in so many words, but I let her draw her own conclusions."

David slumped in his chair. As Becca spoke, he stared at her, shaking his head back and forth, seeing only the Becca who terrorized him for years.

"When she was little, it was easy. She just saw lots of pictures of a very handsome man and some pictures of that man with her mommy. As she got older, she began to ask about her daddy. I simply told her that he didn't live with us.

"When she was almost seven, Olivia began to show signs of some disturbing behavior. One day the housekeeper found a dead cat in her toy chest, dressed in some of Olivia's doll clothes. She had brought one of the stable cats into her room for a tea party. When the cat objected to being dressed up and scratched her hand, Olivia strangled it trying to make it more compliant. My parents and I immediately called in a child psychologist. The psychologist wasn't as concerned about the act of strangling the cat as she was about Olivia's lack of remorse at what she had done."

"That must have been terrifying." Genevieve couldn't imagine having to deal with such a thing.

"With my history, red flags were waving all over the place. Olivia began to see a therapist once a week. By that time, I was working at the distillery and rebuilding my life. I felt strong and healthy, but as time went on, I became concerned that my neuroses had transferred to Olivia. There's no question that narcissistic personality disorder can be genetic.

"By the time she was eight, she started obsessing about her father, whom she thought was David. Even if her classmate's parents were divorced, most of the kids had fathers in their lives. There were father-daughter dinners at school and father-daughter dances at cotillion. I should have told her from the beginning that her father had died, but by then it was too late. She constantly asked me questions about him: how did we meet, where did he live, why didn't he live with us, when would she meet him, did he love her? It was easier for me to build my answers around David than to tell her the truth. I didn't realize I was enabling her fixation on a man who didn't even know she existed."

Becca unclasped her hands in her lap and placed them on the arms of her chair. "We spent two years with psychiatrists, psychotherapists, behavioral psychologists... anyone we thought could bring our darling Olivia back from her place of darkness. No one could help. All I could imagine was Olivia spending her life in an institution. We were at our wits' end when we met

Miriam and George Conrad. They came from England to buy a horse at a neighboring farm. During their visit, they came to tour Harris Distilleries. Because all the guides were busy, the front desk called me. It was serendipity. They were charming, funny, and full of life. We spent a wonderful afternoon together and we stayed in the tasting room until early evening. It turned out Miriam, Dr. Conrad, was the head of the Langston School, a boarding school for children with challenges in Burnstall."

"Burnstall, England?" David asked, surprised.

"Yes."

"But that's only about twenty miles from here," David said.

"Ironic, isn't it? I thought I had heard all there was to hear about new therapies and cutting-edge approaches but the more we talked, the more interested I became in their program. The school specialized in highly intelligent children with emotional and psychological problems. It was academically rigorous, which gave the students a focus beyond their mental issues and an opportunity for success. Every student was required to master a wide range of sports: riding, archery, shooting, cross-country running, swimming, skiing. When they were not studying or in therapy, their bodies were working hard."

David looked incredulous. "I've known about the Langston School for years. They have an amazing reputation for success. Several well-known writers graduated from Langston, and even a couple of MPs. I can't believe Olivia went there. I can't believe your daughter has been right down the road all this time."

"Quite a coincidence, isn't it?" Becca swirled the last of her brandy then tipped it to her lips. "When Miriam finished telling me about Langston, I was convinced it was the right place for Olivia. The next day my parents, Olivia, and I flew to England. The school had a two-year waiting list and extensive testing program before accepting a student, but a child Olivia's age and with Olivia's profile had just been asked to leave. Understanding our desperation, Miriam was kind enough to offer the place if testing proved it was the right school for her. It did. Within the week I left my nine-year-old daughter at a boarding school four thousand miles from home." Becca looked at David. "I know you English consider that normal, but I'm an American. We don't do that. Even though it was a relief, it was also agonizing.

"Since that day eleven years ago, Olivia has been home only six times, one of which was when her grandparents died. She distanced herself from me more and more each year. After the first four years, she chose to spend her holidays with friends or at school. She was an excellent student and excelled at every sport, but it's questionable how mentally stable she was. She would make good progress, then regress. Periodically there were incidents that indicated Olivia was more fragile than she appeared. But nothing was ever significant enough to cause the therapists serious concern. In retrospect, I don't believe her mental health was improving. I believe she was becoming masterful at hiding her psychoses; a useful skill with a treacherous outcome."

"In her last year at Langston she decided to take a gap year before going to Oxford. She had been an excellent student, and reports from all her teachers and therapists weren't glowing but were positive enough. Miriam's one serious concern was that in her last year, Olivia had become obsessive about the man she thought was her father. She had been spending a great deal of her therapy time talking about how she needed to connect with her father, discussing the importance of father figures, parental rejection, and the consequences of being raised by a single mother. In my opinion she should have been thinking about everything that her single mother had done for her." For the first time since Becca began her statement, her voice filled with anger. Though her composure was intact, fatigue was creeping into her eyes and her shoulders were beginning to droop.

"Becca, do you think we should take a break?" Signs of Becca's weariness had not escaped Genevieve's notice.

"No. I want to get through this. Bear with me, I'm getting to the end."

Genevieve slipped off her shoes and pulled her legs onto the couch, so she was sitting crossed legged. She wiggled her shoulders into the down-filled cushion behind her until she was comfortable.

Anxious to finish her statement, Becca pressed through her thickening exhaustion. "During her years at Langston, Olivia developed into an accomplished writer. She had an idea for a novel and wanted to spend her gap year working on it." Becca sat taller, summoning the last of her energy. "I was thrilled at the prospect of her doing something creative, delving into something she loved. Her plan was to live in London and work with a successful murder mystery author, S.J. Smythe. Smythe was her best friend's mother and agreed to mentor Olivia for the year, reading and critiquing her work.

I went to England as soon as she finished her exams to help her move from Langston to London. I hadn't seen her since the previous September and was thrilled at how healthy she seemed, both physically and mentally. We spent two weeks together, settling her into her cheery apartment in Holland Park." Becca smiled as she reminisced about helping Olivia set up house.

"We had Indian food delivered, drank wine, and sang to rock and rap music blasting from her new speakers. We laughed. We talked. We shared. We cried. For the first time, I felt the loving bond with Olivia I had longed for since my daughter was born. When it was time for me to leave, I didn't want to go, and it appeared Olivia wanted me to stay. But we agreed she needed to get on with her project and I needed to get back to work. We pledged to FaceTime and visit each other as often as possible. I have wondered every day since: if I had stayed, would things have turned out differently? Those two weeks were the most cherished two weeks of my life. I'll never know if they were precious to Olivia or if she was playing me the entire time." Becca looked around the room, smiling an exhausted smile.

"Call me cynical, but yes, I was suspicious of how genuine Olivia's feelings were. What stunned me, however, is Olivia took her gap year to write a terrifying piece of fiction that she is turning into reality." Becca reached into her tapestry tote at her feet, pulled out a book with violent red ink splashed across the dustcover, and put it on the coffee table.

Everyone leaned forward to see the volume. There was an audible gasp as people read the name of the book and saw the name of the writer. It was the same book Fenton Morrissey had found in the library weeks ago. *How I Killed My Daddy.* The author's name emblazoned across the bottom was Olivia H. Conway.

<hr />

For well over an hour, she barely moved a muscle. Now, watching people drift from the library, she could breathe again. Euphoria flooded to the very tips of her fingers and toes. She heard nothing but the blood rushing in her ears.

Now everyone would marvel at how clever she was. Reaching into her pants pocket, she pulled out a small squirt bottle. She spritzed the air once, twice. Sniffing, she smiled.

Out of the corner of her eye, she noticed Harrington moving onto the stables screen. He looked around, walked to the office then walked back down the aisle. She could tell he was calling out.

She grabbed her jacket, doused the lights, and dashed out of the room, down the secret passageway and out onto the back path.

THIRTY-THREE

Anxious to review Becca's testimony and immerse himself in Olivia's book, Darlington suggested they call it a day and the Scotland Yard trio headed back to the village and Wilmingrove Inn.

Remaining in the library, Philip uncorked a bottle of Bordeaux and began to pour. Before he could pour the fifth glass, Becca stood, fatigue shadowing her eyes. Succumbing to jet lag and the stress of the day, she excused herself to take a nap before dinner.

Philip, David, Duncan, and Genevieve watched Becca retreat to her room, shoulders drooping, exhaustion slowing her pace. No one spoke until everyone was sure she was out of earshot.

"So, what do you make of all of this, David?" Philip massaged his temples. "Do you think Becca's story is real or invented?"

Genevieve jumped in. "Before you answer, I have a million questions. The first of which is the big one. Why would anyone planning a murder write a book telling the world 'I'm going to commit murder and here's how I'm going to do it?' That's crazy, isn't it?"

Looking bewildered, David set his glass on the table next to him. "The whole thing's crazy. I don't know what I was expecting, but it wasn't all of this." He flailed his hands to emphasize his confusion. "If there is an Olivia, she's a maniac! She must be clinically mad. And all her life she has believed I'm her father. I... I... I'm speechless." David shook his head, then shrugged. "I don't think Becca is making this up... do you?"

"If she is, it's a complicated lie." Philip said. He drained his wine glass. "I have no idea what to make of her story."

"Mom, I think your question's a good one." Duncan stretched his long legs in front of him. "Who details their plan to murder their father in a book she then publishes? I'm assuming it wasn't just a mockup. It looks real enough."

"Oh, I know!" Genevieve grabbed her phone from the coffee table and typed furiously.

"What are you doing?" Philip leaned forward to look at Genevieve's screen.

"I'm checking Amazon to see if they have *How I Killed My Daddy*. Give me a second." Genevieve punched search and realized she was holding her breath. "Voila! Here it is! It was just published in September." She scrolled down and clicked on customer reviews. "I don't believe it. *How I Killed My Daddy* has sixty-eight reviews and four and a half stars." She looked up from her phone. Philip and David were staring at her. "Am I getting off track?" she asked, sheepish.

"Maybe a little," Philip said.

"That's interesting, though. The murder plan is selling well. Not many authors can make that claim," David laughed.

"David, on a different subject, how do you feel about seeing

Becca after all this time?" Genevieve had been wondering what was going through David's mind since Becca arrived. Today's Rebecca Harris Conway was an elegant, accomplished, woman, seemingly kind, and remorseful about her misspent youth. Genevieve wondered if David could embrace the Becca who had flown four thousand miles to come to his aid, or did the specter of Becca's old self overwhelm who she was now?

"I must say, I'm on a bit of an emotional rollercoaster. When I first saw Becca, I was wary, but relieved by her warmth and how guileless she seemed. As she began her statement, old feelings of dread and fear crept into my psyche. Then, when she described how she encouraged Olivia to believe I was her father, all the distrust and suspicion I've felt since I met her came flooding back. I think everything she said is probably true. Between Becca believing her own child could be a murderer, and Olivia's book outlining all the events, I think it's the best explanation we have."

THIRTY-FOUR

I F *HOW I KILLED MY DADDY* proved to be the guidebook
for this case, the mystery just got a great deal easier to solve.
Becca's testimony, however, came first. Drinking pints from
the bar and gobbling crisps from a bag, Chief Superintendent
Darlington, Chief Inspector MacTavish, and Inspector Franklin
huddled in a small meeting room in the Wilmingrove Inn,
slogging through Becca's lengthy recorded statement.

They listened to Becca's steady, polished voice for several
minutes, then clicked off the recorder. Darlington asked a
question, MacTavish and Franklin offered an opinion, then the
three discussed the point, and jotted down follow-up questions.
It was a slow, methodical process, one each of them had executed
hundreds of times over their careers.

"There was an element of fiction to Ms. Conway's story that's
nagging at me." A small piece of crisp danced at the corner of
the Chief's mouth as he spoke. "As genuine as she seems, could
anyone spend years as a highly dysfunctional youth and evolve
into such a productive adult?" he posed. He believed in the

effectiveness of therapy. He had seen it in his own family, but he wasn't sure he believed in miracles.

"Do we need to bring our psych people in to interview her, sir?" McTavish said.

"I've encountered my share of psychopaths, schizophrenics, people living with all kinds of neuroses, and I've been duped more than once by a clever criminal. In our business, it doesn't take long to develop a healthy skepticism of humanity and a respect for the capacity of humans to lie, but," Darlington picked at a piece of skin on his thumb and chuckled, "in my gut I believed every word of Becca's testimony. I think we're okay for now," he said.

Everyone at Wilmingrove Hall seemed helpful, forthcoming, and truthful, but somewhere in all the polite willingness to help, someone was lying. It may be just a small untruth, or even an unwitting inaccuracy, but it could be the loose bit of string that would unravel the entire ball of yarn. With Olivia's novel, that thread might be easier to find.

"So," he said to himself, "you'd better get to it.

Bleary-eyed from late night reading, Chief Superintendent Darlington nursed his first cup of coffee. Nearly alone in the inn's cozy breakfast room, he looked out over a field of late autumn weeds, browned by the recent freeze. A seasoned cop of thirty-two years, he could say, without reservation, that he had never experienced anything like this case. Lying on the table was the novel that not only reviewed what had already happened but showed how the story would end. He should be confident about the swift resolution of this case, but instead, a sense of dread sat in the pit of his stomach.

"Good morning, sir."

Darlington looked up into the earnest face of Inspector James Franklin. A tiny piece of toilet paper stuck to his skin just above his shirt collar, blooming red from a razor cut. He tapped *How I Killed My Daddy* with his index finger. "What did you think of the book, sir?"

"I'm about three quarters of the way through. What about you, Franklin?"

"I finished it."

"Really?" Darlington was impressed. Sales had gotten quite a boost yesterday when everyone downloaded the book.

"I love reading and I'm fast." He flashed a proud smile. "Wasn't it amazing to read about what's already happened? The two crimes in her story didn't turn out like she wrote them. I bet she was surprised when she found out she actually hit Sir David rather than just shooting into the car like she said in the book." Franklin's pace sped up with each word. "And when she killed Sir Mark, wow! Do you think that frightened her or was she excited to see a twist on her own story? Maybe she decided she shouldn't carry out the rest of the book. You know, we haven't heard anything from her since Sir Mark's death… except when she delivered the tankard of mead, of course," he corrected himself. Pausing to take a breath, Franklin realized Darlington was staring at him. "Sorry, sir. As you can tell, I'm excited to be working with you on this investigation."

"No, no, Inspector. Please go on. Coffee?" Darlington caught the server's eye and mimed pouring coffee, then turned his attention back to his young protege. "Tell me more. What do you think will happen next?"

Thrilled his boss was asking his opinion, Franklin offered it. "Olivia is cunning, probably brilliant, and she seems to have mastered the art of disguise. She's a chameleon who can blend into the woodwork one moment and be blatantly obvious the next, whatever the situation calls for." Stopping to gulp his coffee, Franklin looked at Darlington for any sign of approval.

The Chief nodded his encouragement.

"I'd say the most dangerous thing about Olivia is she has no moral compass. She believes Sir David is her father and he abandoned her. Nothing will stop her from revenging this slight. Thanks to her book, we know how she plans to do that and when."

The Chief sat upright as if he'd touched a live wire. "We know when she'll kill Sir David?"

"Ah, right." The lightbulb switched on. "You haven't finished the book. In the last chapter, Olivia reveals that Bonfire Day is Doomsday."

"Jesus! That's in a couple of days!" As if on cue, Darlington's phone vibrated on the table. 'Rebecca Conway,' the screen announced.

Keeping his voice calm, he answered. "Good morning, Ms. Conway. You're up early. Jet lag?"

"Good morning, Chief Superintendent. No. I was awakened by a text from Olivia." Becca's voice was tight. "I thought you'd want to know immediately."

'What did she say?"

"The message said, 'How wonderful we're on the same side of the pond, my darling mother. It's been too long. Shall we get together? How about we see each other at the funeral?'"

"Well, that's quite a message. Did you respond?"

"I did not. Should I?"

"Don't do anything until we get there. I'll be at the Hall within the hour." He swiped his napkin across his mouth as he stood. "We should be able to pull a lot of information from the text. Ms. Conway, it may not seem like it, but this is excellent news."

"Oh, Chief!" Darlington could hear Becca stifle a sob. "We have to find Olivia before she can do any more harm. She's my daughter, but I have no illusions. She's a sick, dangerous young woman. The worst thing we could do is underestimate her."

Darlington signed his bill and strode back to his room as he continued his conversation. "Ms. Conway, give me ten minutes and we'll be on our way."

Thirty minutes later, the team gathered in the library, which had turned into investigation headquarters. As two digital forensic experts arrived, Rebecca walked in holding her phone. "Anyone looking for this?" She raised the mobile for all to see.

The forensic officers looked as if Becca were about to give them a bag of gold, eyes bright with anticipation.

As Becca handed the prize to Officer Simons, the data specialist, an incoming message sounded.

A chill shot through Becca. "Should I check the text?"

"Simons, take a look," the Chief ordered.

"Ms. Conway, what's your passcode?"

"204279."

Simons unlocked the phone and tapped the message icon. He scrolled to the most recent text, then handed the phone back to Darlington. As he silently read, furrows marched across Darlington's brow.

"Chief Superintendent, is it from Olivia?" Becca gasped, realizing she had been holding her breath.

Darlington paused. When he spoke, his voice was brittle. "It is."

"And?"

He looked at Becca, then back at her phone. "She says, 'Mommy, I'm disappointed you're with Daddy and didn't invite me. I bet the makeup sex was hot! Enjoy it while you can because he won't be around much longer. By the way, I love your red cashmere pants and sweater. Blood is my favorite color.'"

Becca gasped and looked down at the crimson trousers she was wearing. "What the hell?" she whispered.

Darlington laid a notepad on the table in front of Becca. He rose from his chair and said, "I'm going to get my briefcase. I left it in the car." He strode from the room.

Becca glanced down at the pad. Written in a hasty scrawl it said:

> *Follow me in five minutes.*
> *I'll meet you in the Range Rover.*

Becca noted the time on the library clock and mentally added five minutes. She stood and walked to an imposing giltwood mirror hung above a low, upholstered bench next to the library doors. She surveyed her reflection, looking at her vivid sweater and matching trousers, tears burning her eyes, fear pulsing through her.

Her daughter was here, in Wilmingrove Hall. Somehow Olivia had seen her this morning. Terrifying, simply terrifying. For years, Becca had feared Olivia might be capable of violence but had clung to the hope that her child was not that damaged. But now, knowing what Olivia had done to David and to Sir Mark, an innocent bystander, she could no longer ignore her daughter's criminal insanity. Olivia was watching the residents of the Hall like ants under a magnifying glass and planning how and when she would turn the next chapter of her novel into non-fiction.

Becca glanced at her watch. Knowing Olivia might be watching her at that very moment, she pulled her shoulders back, jutted out her chin and walked out of the library.

THIRTY-FIVE

"**W**HAT PAGE ARE you on?" Genevieve closed her Kindle, laying both hands on top. "Finished," she said.

Not included in the morning meetings with Darlington and his team, she and Philip knew nothing of how things had progressed since last night. Understanding they would not be needed at all today, they had buried themselves in the book.

"I'm on page two ninety-seven. You're a faster reader than I am. I'll be finished in an hour. From your expression, I'd say this novel doesn't have a happy ending." Philip chuckled.

"I'm overwhelmed by how the plot mirrors the last two months. Hurry up and finish." Though she was sitting close to the fire, and had a coverlet thrown over her lap, Genevieve shivered. What she had just read chilled her. Cradling her mug in both hands, she took a long drink. The Stroh rum in her tea, helped it slide down easily.

The Grand Salon clock bonged once. Genevieve rose, folded the lap robe, and placed it over the back of her chair. She walked to Philip, who was sitting on the opposite side of the fireplace buried in the story. She needed to be close to him right now.

She took his reader from his hands and set it on his side table. Putting her hands on each arm of his chair, she leaned toward him until her lips were only a breath from his. "I'm going to take a shower." She closed the tiny gap between them. "Would you like to join me?"

"You wash my back, I'll wash yours," he said, then gave her a noisy kiss.

"Good idea." She pulled Philip out of the chair. "I think we should finish this in the shower. I'd hate for Mrs. Macintosh to pop in on us with a lunch tray. She'd never recover!"

"You're probably right. On the other hand, she may have secrets that would shock us! You realize this interruption will delay me from finishing the book."

"A small price to pay, I'd say." As Genevieve turned to walk to the bathroom, Philip gave her a hearty smack on the bottom. She stopped, looked over her shoulder and said tempting him, "I dare you to do that again, I just dare you."

Philip shot out of his chair and the chase was on!

Hair piled into a damp knot on top of her head, cheeks flushed from her romp with Philip, Genevieve was refreshed, relaxed, and energized. Black jeans hugged her lean frame, her long legs stretching from under an oversized camel sweater. She trotted down the grand staircase, anxious to see what Mrs. Lomax was cooking in the kitchen.

"Nothing like shower sex to stir up your appetite," she said out loud.

"I wouldn't know," David said from the bottom of the stairs, mischief sparking in his eyes. "At least not recently."

"David!" Heat rushed into her cheeks. "I didn't see you there... obviously!" Laughter bubbled up from deep in her throat. "I'm expecting attorney-client privilege to apply here. We shall never speak of this again, right?"

David mimed locking his lips, then threw the imaginary key over his shoulder.

She linked her arm through David's, and he matched his stride to hers as they headed to the kitchen. "Any idea what's been going on this morning?" She assumed David would have the up-to-the-minute developments.

"I know nothing."

"Really?" Genevieve pulled back in surprise and narrowed her eyes.

"No. Really. I've heard nothing. I've been in my room reading the book just like you and Philip. Well, not exactly like you and Philip." David wiggled his eyebrows and grinned at Genevieve.

She responded with a sharp punch to his arm. "Behave yourself!" She failed at looking stern and laughed in spite of herself.

"I must say, it's fascinating to read about myself being terrorized, then barbecued. Olivia is a terrific writer, but I didn't particularly like the way I was killed. Too bad her editor didn't suggest something a bit less gruesome."

"David," Genevieve looked at her friend. "We're joking about Olivia and her crazy plan, but it's a deadly serious matter. You can't be as calm as you appear."

"The whole thing seems too much like a novel to be real. I

understand I was shot in the head and Sir Mark died from Olivia's handiwork…" David's voice trailed off. "Hmm. When I say it out loud, it does sound rather sinister, doesn't it?"

"It does, indeed."

As they approached the kitchen, the smell of freshly baked bread assaulted the two famished readers. Red-faced from pulling loaves from the oven, Mrs. Lomax beamed at Genevieve and David.

"Good afternoon, my lady, Sir David. As long as you're hungry, your timing is perfect."

"We're starving!" Genevieve and David said in unison.

"We're just setting luncheon for the Chief Superintendent, his team and Ms. Conway in the library. They're going to work while they eat. Where would you two like to dine? Or is it three? Will Lord Crosswick be joining you?"

"Let me check." Genevieve pulled her phone from her jeans pocket and tapped in a text.

Almost instantly, the phone pinged.

She glanced at the screen. "Yes, Elsie. Lord Crosswick will be joining us. Let's eat in the conservatory, in front of the fire. Will that work?"

"Of course, my lady."

"Thank you, Elsie. And could you ask Mrs. MacIntosh to come see me when she has a moment, please?"

As Genevieve and David walked through the kitchen, David tore a piece of fresh baguette from a loaf and popped it into his mouth. He groaned a note of pleasure, bringing a smile to Mrs. Lomax's face.

"Still warm from the oven," David said. "Oh Elsie, will you marry me?"

"Of course, Sir David. Just let me finish up here." Still smiling, Mrs. Lomax turned back to the job at hand.

⸻ ♦ ⠸ ⸺⟡●ᗞ●ᘒ●⟡⸻ ⠸ ♦ ⸻

Sitting in front of a bank of screens, Olivia's wide, violet eyes watched every movement of everyone in the Hall. Her flawless skin was marred only by a slight crinkle between her brows.

She watched Daddy and Genevieve walk away from the camera toward the kitchen. Her eyes darted to an adjoining screen as the twosome came through the swinging door and into view. She could almost smell the warm bread as she watched Mrs. Lomax pull baguettes from the oven. Saliva flowed into her mouth at the thought of the steaming, yeasty flavor. She took a bite out of a pear and, with the back of her hand, wiped a trickle of juice as it slid down her chin.

And there was Duncan, alone in the library, reading her book. Thank God he hadn't left with Julia and the kids. Ahh, Alex and Ella. She missed them. Though they weren't originally in the book, she had decided to add them to the real-life plot. And then they left...too bad. Maybe next time.

She began making small alterations in how she would execute the real-life *How I Killed My Daddy.* Her mother's arrival had thrown a wrench into the scheme. After all, her mother wasn't a character in her book. She could have included Becca in the murder scheme, but her creative integrity wouldn't allow it. She would have to work around this inconvenience. It might be fun to see how much pain the sight and smell of burning flesh would cause her mother. She smiled at the thought of Becca sobbing, realizing there were no limits to the horrors her clever daughter was capable of committing. This could be fun. All the cunning psychological tricks and physical skills she had honed over her brief life were serving her well.

She wanted them to be dazzled by how brilliant and skilled she was. She wanted them to be awed by her. Just days before the climax of her story, the volcano inside her was about to erupt. She leaned back in her chair, pulled at her blond, pixie hair with both hands, and screamed, "I'm special! Love me, damn you!"

THIRTY-SIX

ENEVIEVE'S FULL-THROATED laughter wafted into the grand salon, making Becca smile as she walked through the vast entry hall.

"They're just finishing lunch." Mrs. MacIntosh sensed Becca was looking for Philip, Genevieve, and David, and directed the American beauty to the conservatory. "Should I have Lottie bring you coffee, Ms. Conway?"

"Thank you, Mrs. MacIntosh." Becca flashed an irresistible smile. "You are pretty wonderful."

At the outset Mrs. MacIntosh hadn't known the full story about the anguish Rebecca Conway had caused Sir David over many years, but she knew enough to dislike the woman. Now, Mrs. MacIntosh was surprised how she was warming to Becca, despite her initial reservations. The more she got to know the American, the more she liked her.

Becca opened the conservatory door and stepped into the cozy room. Giggling, Genevieve stopped long enough to drain her wine glass and hold it out for a refill. The three people seated around the table looked up in unison.

"To the illustrious American who's here to save my life." David raised his glass toward Becca.

Not to be left out, Philip and Genevieve hefted their glasses to join in. "Here, here," they chimed.

"Where have you been? What have you been doing, beautiful lady?" David's cheeks and the tip of his nose looked as if they had been kissed by crimson lips.

Taking in the tipsy scene, Becca's eyes widened. "Are you three drunk?"

"Drunk? No." Philip straightened in his chair. "A little mellow, maybe, but drunk, absolutely not."

"Join us?" Genevieve shoved a chair out from under the table with her foot and motioned for Becca to sit.

"It appears I have a lot of catching up to do." Becca took the goblet David offered her, swirled the ruby liquid, then took a drink. "You realize, while you three have been eating, drinking, and leading slothful lives, I've been working like a demon to figure out if my daughter is executing her novel as she wrote it or writing a new chapter as we speak?"

"You're right," David said. "While you're doing the difficult things, we three are drowning our fears."

There was a loud knock, and the door opened before anyone could say, "Come in." Chief Superintendent Darlington and Sean Harrington strode in, carrying Olivia's book and filling the room with tense energy.

"Is something wrong, Chief Superintendent?" Philip stood, his wine buzz vanishing.

"I wouldn't say 'wrong.' We have some new information that

could explain the mystery behind the Purdey rifle that was used to shoot Sir David. Mr. Harrington, please." Darlington pulled a chair up to the table, sat, and motioned for Harrington to do the same.

"Lord Crosswick," Harrington began. "Do you remember in September, just before Sir David was shot, a police officer came to Wilmingrove Hall to start the transfer of all the gun licenses from the former Earl to you?"

Completely sober now, Philip squinted his eyes, thinking. "Yes, yes, I do. It was the day we arrived at the Hall. It seems like years ago."

"Remember, Philip, I was in the middle of the tour of the house, and you called me to join you."

"Right." Harrington pointed to Genevieve and nodded. "As I remember, the police officer had all the appropriate identification and was very professional. She wanted to see where the shotguns are secured, where we keep the key to the gun safe and how many duplicate keys there are. She asked all the right questions about gun maintenance, who used the guns and how often they were used. All the questions the police routinely ask."

Genevieve recalled that day with a roll of her eyes. "She spent at least fifteen minutes lecturing on procedure and gun safety. She went on and on and on."

"The first time we interviewed Mr. Harrington," Darlington explained, "he told us about the visit. If it weren't for Olivia's book, we would never have circled back to him. But what he told us mirrors the chapter in Olivia's book."

Slack-jawed, Philip looked at Darlington. "I read the part about how she got the Purdey rifle. How did I not connect the dots?"

"In all fairness, darling; we had just arrived and were pretty overwhelmed with just being here. And that was quite a while ago."

"I agree with Lady Crosswick. But I do need you both to think back." Darlington pressed on. "How did she get a key to the gun safe? Mr. Harrington told me his recollection of how it could have happened. I need for you, Lord Crosswick, to search your memory for any opportunity she had to make an impression of the key. As I understand it, you went back to the house, Lady Crosswick. Is that correct?"

"Yes."

"Lord Crosswick, please tell me what you remember."

Philip rested his elbow on the table and cradled his chin in his hand. Looking at nothing, he tried to recall that day in the estate office. Light flickered in his eyes as he began to remember. "As I recall, I went with you, Sean, to help Andrew Frazier with one of the Harris hawks. Kafritz would have been alone in the office then. When we left, she was checking the inventory list against the guns in the safe and the key was on the desk. We were gone ten, maybe fifteen minutes, plenty of time for her to take an impression of the key. When we got back, she had finished the inventory. She stayed long enough for Sean to sign a couple of forms, then she left." Philip sat back and laid both hands on the table palms down.

"Do you remember what she looked like?" Darlington gave no hint of whether or not he already had a description.

"Oh! I can tell you exactly what she looked like." Genevieve jumped in. "Without a doubt, she was one of the homeliest women

302

I've ever seen. She had mousy brown hair, and she wore thick glasses that looked a bit like she had an artificial nose attached to them. Her police uniform was too big on her small frame."

Darlington smiled at Genevieve's vivid description. He pulled a photo from the pocket of his jacket and handed it to her. "I took this from the dust cover of Olivia's book."

"I'm anxious to see what you think, Lady Crosswick," Harrington said. "When the Chief showed me the picture of Olivia, I couldn't believe it was the same person."

Genevieve's eyes hardened. "Oh, yeah. Olivia could change her hair. She could make her nose bigger. She may even have altered her teeth somewhat, but that mouth. Kafritz had the same mouth."

"Exactly!" Harrington shouted. "I was gobsmacked what sexy lips she had, especially for such an, um, uh, unattractive woman." He looked at his shoes, hoping his words weren't too coarse.

Genevieve smiled at him then passed the photo to Philip.

He gazed at Olivia's mouth. "I think you're right, Sean. Becca, do you think this is possible?"

"Of course, it is." Becca's shoulders slumped. "My daughter's always been good at changing her appearance and she's very clever."

"She is that, Ms. Conway." Darlington had the rapt attention of the people around the table. Each leaned forward, elbows balanced on the table's edge.

"When I finished the book this morning, I wondered how much you can trust Olivia's novel to be her actual plan." Becca's mouth drew down at the corners. "Do you think she'll stay true to her plot, or do you think she'll deviate from it?" Becca asked. "What's your best guess?"

"Ms. Conway, your daughter is a shrewd adversary. She's talented and smart and, I fear, has skills that will make it challenging to disrupt her plan. According to our forensic psychologists Olivia will follow her plot as closely as possible. The shrinks said she feels her novel is flawless, so her ego won't allow her to alter it, unless there's a compelling reason. Our strategy is to follow the storyline and snare her before the climax."

Darlington pulled himself away from the door jamb where he had been leaning. He looked down at his well-buffed brogues, then at the group. "As I told you last week, we appreciate how you have all done your utmost to cooperate, which leads me to extend an invitation for this evening. Would you all please join me for dinner at the Lion and Lamb?"

"Oh, I love that pub!" Genevieve clapped her hands in delight. "That would be wonderful. You will be off duty, right?"

"We will, indeed. It's just a small thank you for your hospitality."

"Totally unnecessary, but we look forward to it. Thank you," Philip glanced at Genevieve. "I think there's more to this invitation than meets the eye," his arched eyebrow said.

"Shall we say half seven?' Darlington shrugged on his overcoat. "I'll take my leave now. I have some calls to make, but I'll see you all this evening."

At that, Philip, Genevieve, Duncan, David, and Becca raised their glasses and with a hearty "cheers," toasted to the night ahead.

THIRTY-SEVEN

C HIEF SUPERINTENDENT FRANCIS Darlington, Chief Inspector Morris MacTavish, and Inspector James Franklin walked through the door of the Lion and Lamb at 7:15 p.m., fifteen minutes before their guests would arrive.

"You old plonker!" A stout, ruddy-faced man greeted Darlington like an old friend, which indeed he was. Reid Moore, the publican, wore slouchy tweed pants and a cabled turtleneck sweater that had seen better days. He had spent thirty years with the Met before retiring to the Yorkshire Moors, where he had grown up. After a year's search for the ideal English village, he fell in love with Wilmingrove and bought the Lion and Lamb. Dating from 1789, it was a picture postcard pub, long cherished by the county and beyond. With a thatched roof and ivy-covered stone, the alehouse sat in the middle of an untidy English garden, which provided a haven for butterflies, bees, and hummingbirds all summer. But now, as the autumn wound down, tight pods of spent blossoms clung to browning marigold stems and the last roses of the summer faded almost as soon as their buds opened. As the weather cooled, ferns that filled the gaping mouth of the fireplace throughout the summer were replaced by the glow of fire in the grate. In the place of honor, just to the right side of the hearth, a round table was set for six, bearing a 'reserved' sign that was hard to miss.

"Reid, this is perfect. Thank you, mate." Darlington slapped his friend on the back. "Did you know Lord and Lady Crosswick like your little hole in the wall? They were pleased when I told them where we were having dinner."

Reid beamed. "They've been here four or five times. It isn't bad for business to have our county peers pop in now and then. The locals get excited about brushing elbows with the rich and famous."

Chief Superintendent Darlington pulled Reid into an alcove and spoke in a low voice. "It was brilliant of you to suggest we meet here, mate. It's possible we could snare her tonight." Since he arrived in Wilmingrove over a week ago, Darlington had dined most evenings at the Lion and Lamb, discussing the details of the case over bangers and mash and a good local stout. Using his years of experience, Moore had given his perspective on the investigation. Fresh eyes were always welcome.

By 7:30, the pub was full of drinkers and diners, many of whom had been loyal supporters of the Lion and Lamb for generations. When he purchased the landmark pub, Reid had given every wall a new coat of paint and polished every piece of wood and brass, giving the watering hole a sparkle without changing the essence of the classic tavern. The menu still provided standard pub grub, but his talented chef peppered the bill of fare with gourmet specialties, resulting in an influx of younger diners. The expanded wine list became an attraction as well.

Surveying the three connecting rooms, Darlington took an inventory of the patrons. Most tables were filled, with about eighty-five to ninety people packing the alehouse. The seven waitstaff were all attractive, young, and each wore a white shirt with the pub's logo on the left breast pocket, black jeans, and a knee-length black apron.

"They've all been working for me since I bought the pub, so Olivia can't pose as a waiter," Reid told Darlington. He had confirmed the kitchen staff as well, all five being long-term employees.

Darlington's sharp eyes moved from table to table, person to person. He saw withered and fresh-faced, smart, and dowdy. At most tables, people were enjoying themselves, full of laughter, smiles, and energy. Faces glowed from drink and the warmth of the rooms. People flirted and leaned into each other for intimate conversations. He saw two women, heads together, sharing gossip while their partners had a heated Premier League discussion about the merits of Leeds and New Castle. In a corner booth a family of five laughed at their toddler, face smeared with shepherd's pie.

The Chief Superintendent ducked, walking through a low door into a smaller dining room with six tables, each a four top. Two of the tables had been pushed together to accommodate a party of six. The room had three small windows along the wall to his left, that overlooked the carpark. At the far end was a small fireplace where embers waited for a few sticks of wood to spark them back to life. Darlington identified no one as suspicious.

He looked into the taproom, where about forty people, mostly men, gathered near the bar, some playing darts, others dealing cards. He noticed one young woman of Olivia's build, but her hair was long and raven. It could have been a wig, but her features were coarser than Olivia's. She was in a brutal battle at the pool table with a lad whose tattooed arms told the story of Lady Godiva and her infamous horseback ride.

"I don't think that's our girl," Darlington said to himself, turning back to the main dining room just as his guests walked in.

Two beautiful women and three handsome men coming through the door were enough to capture the attention of the diners within view. For a moment, there was a sharp drop in conversation as patrons swiveled their heads to observe the newcomers. Many people recognized the Earl and Countess of Crosswick, and the brief silence turned to an excited buzz.

Much to his surprise, Darlington found himself warmed at the sight of his five guests. He moved across the room, hand outstretched. "Welcome! Welcome. I'm pleased you could come tonight."

Reid came up behind him and slapped his back. "Lord and Lady Crosswick, the Lion and Lamb is so happy you're spending the evening with us, thanks to my old mate, Francis."

Darlington beamed as he explained his connection to Reid. "We've known each other since we were young, dashing sergeants together at the Met. I've been using Reid as a sounding board on this case, tapping his keen cop mind to help us think outside the box."

"I had no idea you two knew each other." Philip's expression was a mix of surprise and delight. He liked each man and was comforted knowing they were both looking out for David's welfare.

Darlington completed the introductions and Reid escorted the group to the fireside table.

"Reid, this is perfect." Genevieve admired the blazing fall centerpiece. "What stunning flowers. I can't imagine a more inviting setting."

The pub owner beamed. "Thank you, Lady Crosswick. I'm pleased everything is to your liking. My wife will be delighted you like the posies. She attends to all the details that make the Lion and Lamb a special place."

"Is she here? I could tell her myself."

"She took the night off. Her sister is visiting from Gretna Green. If they come in, I'll be sure to introduce them." Reid was the quintessential host, just the right amount of familiarity, charm, and warmth. "Unless you object, Francis has asked our chef to prepare a tasting menu for you. Is that all right with everyone?"

Agreement was unanimous.

Two servers approached the table and filled each Champagne glass with Veuve Clicquot.

"Oh my!" Genevieve's eyes sparkled. "My favorite!"

Becca held her glass aloft. "Mine, too," she said. "We have a

French friend whose family has been supplying grapes to Veuve Clicquot for six generations. When you ask him if he would ever drink Dom Perignon, he says, 'Perhaps I would drink Dom Perignon if all the Veuve Clicquot were gone and if all the water were tainted!'"

The table roared with laughter.

Darlington stood to offer a toast. "To an extraordinary case and its successful conclusion. But most of all to the House of Crosswick and all who dwell within."

With resounding "Cheers," everyone clinked glasses and drank.

With his back to the fire, Darlington scanned the room. He had a full view of the main dining room. Though people kept glancing at their table, the attention appeared to be curiosity rather than malice. He was about to sit when he noticed a woman he had not seen earlier. Seated alone near the door to the taproom, she was plump with graying brown hair pinned into a topknot. Her clothes, though dowdy, were clean and tidy. Next to her on the floor was an oversized tapestry bag. Rimless, rose-tinted glasses hid her eyes.

Darlington excused himself. "I'll be back in just a moment," he said. Before he reached the kitchen, Reid came through the swinging door carrying a tray of amuse bouche.

"I need to talk to you." Darlington snarled. "I spotted someone, and I need to see if you know her, if she's a regular."

Reid stopped a server heading into the kitchen. "Michael, take these to the Crosswicks' table." He handed off the tray and turned his attention to where Darlington nodded.

He squinted at the frumpy diner. "I don't recognize her," he said. "Let me see if she had a reservation or is a walk-in. We only had one or two tables unreserved for this evening."

He sauntered through the lounge, stopping at tables, chatting with patrons on his way to the hostess stand. Glancing over the reservation list, he saw table four, where the woman in question sat, had been reserved earlier that day. A definite red flag.

Reid walked to the table next to number four, where a couple was in the midst of a lively conversation. He asked them if they were enjoying themselves, the woman said something witty in response and the three laughed.

He turned and sauntered to table four. "Good evening."

Hunched over her meal, it took the woman several seconds to realize Reid was addressing her. When she glanced up, she looked startled, her eyes magnified by her thick glasses.

"I'm Reid Moore, the proprietor of the Lion and Lamb. I believe this is your first time dining with us, isn't it?" Reid smiled and leaned casually on the table.

"I—I—I'm having a brilliant time, thank you," she mumbled. She looked up at Reid, offering a shy smile. "It's my birthday, you see, so I thought I'd give myself a special treat. I've always wanted to come to the Lion and Lamb, but one doesn't like to dine alone."

Caught off-guard by the woman's lack of guile, Reid took her hand. "We're honored you would choose to spend your birthday with us. May I ask your name?"

Color bloomed in her cheeks. "Mary. Mary Sloan." She smiled. "I'm hoping my daughter can join me in time for pudding. She works late at the hospital but thought she could get away."

"I'll cross my fingers that she makes it. Thank you for honoring us this evening, Mary Sloan. I hope it's the first of many more occasions you share with us. If there is anything you need, please let our servers know. And I am always at your service." Reid squeezed her hand, nodded, and turned away from her table. As he headed back to the kitchen, he stopped a waiter. "Take a glass of Champagne to table four. It's complimentary." Reid wanted to make certain Mary Sloan felt special tonight.

"Well, she's not Olivia," he said to himself. He caught Darlington's eye as he walked by the Crosswick's table and subtly shook his head.

Darlington nodded in response but couldn't resist confirming Reid's conclusion for himself. As he sauntered toward Mary's table, she pulled her cell phone from her tote. He stood by the hostess stand and heard her say, "Oh, pet. I'm so disappointed. I was looking forward to you joining me. The restaurant is just lovely, and the proprietor has been so nice to me."

Darlington could see disappointment cloud her face and he dismissed her as a threat. He and Reid were a good team.

At the fireside table, the courses came and went, each perfect morsel more delicious than the last. Wine flowed and laughter came easily. Around the table, there was a sense of release after so many days of intense conversations and fear of the unknown. The group was loud and jolly and enjoying themselves. By eleven o'clock, they were alone in the dining room.

Ready to bring the revelers back to reality, Chief Superintendent Darlington began to review the events of the last two days. He talked about Becca receiving the texts from Olivia and about the cameras planted throughout Wilmingrove Hall.

"We thought Olivia would come to the Lion and Lamb tonight in disguise, but it doesn't look like that happened," Reid interjected.

With each disclosure, the light-hearted mood of the evening faded a bit more and the reality of imminent danger came clawing back.

Her eyes glossed with tears, Genevieve brought her hands to her cheeks. "Chief, reading Olivia's book has made a grisly ending seem inevitable. You can't let anything happen to David."

Before he spoke, Francis Darlington, sat straighter in his chair, took a deep breath, then released it. It was difficult to read the look on his face. When he spoke, his voice was measured, steady, and firm.

"We cannot for one minute assume Olivia Conway's objective is anything but homicidal. She has twice proven her intentions, so we must believe she will not be satisfied until Sir David is dead. If she continues to execute her plot, then we can expect her to lure Sir David to a bonfire on Guy Fawkes Day, November 5TH and incinerate him. *Our* goal is to prevent her from accomplishing that."

Darlington's candor sobered the group.

Silence blanketed the table until a server approached. "Excuse me, Reid," the young man said. "A woman left these for you." He held out a beautifully wrapped package about the size of a book, and Mary Sloan's tapestry bag.

"Interesting." Reid looked at Darlington then down at the bag.

Always prepared, Darlington pulled a pair of plastic gloves from his jacket pocket and tossed them to Reid, who put them on and unlatched the satchel.

"Jesus," Reid said, peering into the bag.

"What is it?" the others asked in unison.

Reid pulled out a thick notecard. He read it then handed it to Darlington.

"What does it say?" Genevieve's eyes were wide with dread.

"It says, 'Thank you for the glass of Champagne. It was a lovely touch. O'"

Next, Reid held up a brown and gray top-knotted wig, then a frumpy flowered dress and last, a pair of tinted glasses. "Shit," he said under his breath. "Shit."

"Open the package, Reid," Darlington directed.

He ripped the crimson paper off, tossed it on the table, and held up a copy of *How I Killed My Daddy*. He opened the book to a notecard, which marked the first page of the last chapter. The notecard read:

It was such fun seeing you all tonight.
You looked like you were having such a good time.
The story is almost over
and you know how it ends...
in a blaze of glory!
Yours ,
Olivia

Intoxicated by power, Olivia raced her Ducati down dark lanes through the Yorkshire countryside, banking around curves toward her secret command post in the walls of Wilmingrove Hall. Swaying with each bend in the road, she slalomed from side to side and relished the wind ruffling the short locks on her helmetless head. She laughed into the bank of air, exhilarated. She had them all fooled. They were confused and frightened with no idea what to do next. She was smarter than all of them and they were her stupid little pawns.

She geared down as she approached the back lane to the stable. The engine's throaty rumble sent a thrill up her spine. This had been a good night.

With the surge of adrenaline waning, a sudden wave of exhaustion swept over her. She rolled her Ducati through the narrow entry way to the abandoned storage shed. She pulled a tarp over the bike, piled three bales of hay around it, and closed the door behind her as she walked out. Overwhelmed with fatigue, she could barely drag herself up the stairs to her cozy room over the barn. Too tired to pull back her bed linens, she collapsed onto her bedspread. Within seconds, she was deep in a dreamless sleep.

THIRTY-EIGHT

WHILE CHIEF SUPERINTENDENT Darlington called his Met team from their beds and ordered them to gather at the Lion and Lamb, MacTavish, Franklin and three local constables escorted the three Warwicks, David and Becca to Wilmingrove Hall. To confirm Olivia was not lurking in the house, the police swept the Hall before allowing the residents to go in. To assure no one could enter or exit without their knowledge, officers were posted at each door.

Bustling about, preparing a hot toddy for herself, Mrs. MacIntosh looked up from the tea kettle as five frightened people walked into the comforting warmth of the kitchen.

"This is the perfect place to be right now." Genevieve pulled out a chair and plopped down with a heavy thud, propping her elbow on the table, her head in her hand.

"You all look dreadful," Mrs. MacIntosh said. "The evening was a bit botched, was it? Sit down, all of you. I believe a cup of tea is in order." Mrs. MacIntosh was in mother mode, chiding everyone to be seated. She delivered tea to the table along with a bottle of Dalmore Scotch. "For medicinal purposes," she said.

"We're absolutely gutted, Mrs. Mac," David said. "Olivia was at the restaurant the entire evening in a disguise. All the coppers were looking for her, thinking she might show, but none of us had a clue that the middle-aged frump at table number four was Olivia."

"My goodness. What a shock for all of you." Mrs. MacIntosh patted David on the back and handed him a cup of tea.

Becca stared into the room. "What kind of mother doesn't recognize her own daughter?" Tears filled her eyes, a lone drop plopping in her lap.

David covered her hand with his and squeezed. "I won't allow you to fault yourself for not knowing that a dowdy, forty-something matron was your beautiful twenty-year-old daughter. That's absurd!" He was gentle but firm.

"But—" Becca started.

"But nothing," Duncan interrupted. "David's right. Unless you sat with her and had a conversation, there's no way you could have known. And even then, you may not have realized it was Olivia. That girl is talented!"

"She should have been on the stage!" Genevieve agreed. "The productive thing to do right now is figure out ways to help Darlington find Olivia before she does any further harm. Focusing on that will make us all feel better."

Philip leaned forward in his chair. "The Crosswick family motto is 'Garde Le Roi.' Guard the king. In this case, David, you're the king and we're here to guard you. Of course, the real line of defense is the Met. They're good, David, really good."

THIRTY-NINE

C HIEF SUPERINTENDENT DARLINGTON sat with his back to the fireplace, a stoked blaze sparking back to life on the hearth. Around the table were six groggy forensic specialists, including two technology experts and Reid Moore.

Every muscle in Francis Darlington's body tensed. A toxic combination of frustration and anger throbbed in his temples. Olivia's wig, her dress, and spectacles lay lifeless as a corpse in the middle of the table that, less than an hour ago, was surrounded by high energy, laughing people. Next to the pile, the dustcover on her novel screamed, "How I Killed My Daddy!", taunting the group of seasoned detectives.

Glancing around the table, Darlington began. "Here's what we know. Olivia Harris Conway was on the premises tonight for at least two hours. During that time, she was disguised as a middle-aged matron treating herself to a birthday dinner. Always the consummate host, but sadly not a very clever chap, Reid gave her a glass of Champagne on the house!"

"Way to go, Reid!" The group hissed, booed, and banged on the table, razzing the former detective.

Darlington allowed himself a robust laugh, reveling in his mate's embarrassment, then he held up a hand. "Okay, okay, lads. Settle down. We've all read Olivia Conway's book. Assuming she follows her story, we know how she intends to proceed."

Darlington reached across the table and picked up the copy of *How I Killed My Daddy*. Next to it, Olivia's wig looked like a curled-up cat. "Franklin, you've thought a lot about this novel. Or should I say, autobiography. I think it would be useful if you read the last couple of pages to everyone. Do you mind?"

"Of course not, sir." Surprised by his Chief's suggestion, Franklin took the book from Darlington's outstretched hand. "You know, sir, this is going to be weird, because it's written in first person."

"That's fine, Franklin. You don't have to read in a lassie's voice." A wave of laughter circled the table.

Pulling his glasses from his rumpled shirt pocket, Franklin cleared his throat and began to read.

The night is perfection—black as the inside of a buried coffin. I'm waiting. I'm waiting for my Daddy. Every few minutes the sky explodes with fireworks, turning the night to day. I flatten myself into the shadows so I can't be seen. Aha, here he comes. He still has my note in his hand. It's hard to believe someone so clever could be stupid enough to fall for my little ruse, but curiosity is a powerful drive. 'Come meet me behind the bonfire.' I wrote. 'I'll make it worth your while.' Then I signed it with lipsticky lips. I thought maybe that was too much, but it worked. By now, I'm sure he wants to know who his temptress is.

"Hello, Daddy," I say. I'm impressed how much I sound like Mommy.

He's still walking toward me. He's just a few feet away now. I put the dart blower in my mouth. I inhale and taste the bitter fumes from the curare, then blow out with all my might... thwap! Right in the neck. Just as the sky cracks with a kaleidoscope of reds, greens, yellows, he sees my face. The shocked surprise in his eyes makes me laugh. He wafts to the ground like a pricked balloon.

Now for the fun. My very own grownup doll. My tapestry satchel holds everything I need. Here's the black cape, black hat, and wig. The creepy Guy Fawkes mask is the cherry on the sundae.

"Daddy, I need you to sit up so I can drape the cape around your shoulders. Oh, my. Hi. It didn't occur to me that you'd be looking at me. Of course, you're not dead...yet. Let's get your mask on so I don't have to see you watching me. Now the wig. The hat should be at a jaunty angle, don't you think? Let's put the elastic under your chin. Ooo. Sorry. I didn't mean to snap it like that, but you can't feel it anyway, can you? You look good."

I fold my tongue into my lower lip. My piercing whistle cuts through the noisy night and four local tipsy boys pop out of the shadows. It's amazing the talent a few quid and a *nickel bag will buy you.*

"Okay, boys. Let's get this mannequin on the bonfire. You, there. You with the Man City t-shirt and you with the tats, take his arms. And you two each take a leg. Let's go! I'll watch you from here."

The climax is so close now I can taste it. I can taste the metallic tang of blood. My heart is beating so fast, I gasp for air. I'm trying to count the thuds pulsing in my neck, but it's impossible.

As I watch the four lads carrying Daddy to the back of the bonfire, I don't know how they're staying upright. They're staggering, they're stumbling. But they are moving forward and are there at last. Now if they can just get him onto the pile.

Here we go.

One swing.

Two swings.

Three swings and up. Good for them!

And the timing is perfect. On the front side where all the people are standing, the mayor is touching his blazing torch to the pile, unaware Daddy is lying helpless on the opposite side.

The bonfire bursts with color and heat. The flames dance and surge higher and higher, devouring leaves and twigs and branches. It's creeping toward him.

I plop down on the ground, so dizzy from the thrill I think I may faint. I sniff the air for the telltale sign the raging beast is devouring Daddy. His sweet smell wafts to me on the night air. As the life leaves his body, I feel his spirit come to me, infuse me with all that he was.

I look one last time at the inferno, pick up my satchel and walk back into the black of the night.

Inspector Franklin closed the book and laid it on the table. No one spoke. His throat parched from reading aloud, Franklin took a long swallow of water. "Sir, if Ms. Conway adheres to her storyline, we have to find her before Bonfire Day. That's tomorrow."

FORTY

GENEVIEVE AND BECCA trotted across the meadow on a matched pair of black Friesians, Onyx and Dutch, drops of frosty moisture spraying from their hooves, as they pranced through the pasture. After spending days cloistered in Wilmingrove Hall putting the pieces of a bizarre mystery together, it was a joy to breath crisp air and feel the chill of autumn.

The women whooped with laughter as they nudged their horses into a gallop. The release was exhilarating. They raced along a ridge overlooking the Hall, until they came to a stream that flowed into the dense forest at the eastern border of the estate. They reined their steeds to a halt. The magnificent horses tossed their heads, anxious to continue.

"That was the best thing I've done in days!" Genevieve gasped.

Becca had to catch her breath before she spoke. "My God! I haven't ridden like that for years! I've forgotten how spectacular it is to fly across the earth on a gorgeous animal like Onyx."

Genevieve pulled on her reins to turn Dutch around, then pressed her calves into his side to spur him forward. Over her shoulder, she yelled to Becca, "Last one to the river buys breakfast!" and she streaked off down the slope toward the riverbank.

FORTY-ONE

S TILL DOZING, WAFTING in and out of fragments of dreams, Duncan heard his phone ping, announcing a text. He ignored it. A few seconds later it sounded again, urging him to look at the message.

Eyes still closed, moving as few muscles as possible, he groped the side table until he felt the coolness of his iPhone. He opened one eye and looked at the screen. He blinked, opened both eyes and read:

"Duncan, we're at the stable. Come ASAP. Darlington discovered information that will lead us to Olivia."

He read the text twice, then glanced at his watch. It was 7:30 a.m.

He stumbled out of bed and into the bathroom, where he splashed water on his face, brushed his teeth, and patted water on his bed-ruffled hair before pulling his clothes on. He wrapped a muffler twice around his neck and tucked the ends into his black wool duffle coat as he loped down the grand staircase.

He couldn't imagine what Darlington had discovered between midnight and seven o'clock this morning. But, given the serious character of Francis Darlington, Duncan assumed whatever had been uncovered was important. As he dashed onto the terrace, he passed Lottie coming in from the herb garden.

"Lottie," he said, keeping his pace. "If you see Lady Crosswick, would you please tell her I'm meeting Chief Superintendent and my dad at the stable?"

"Of course, sir. I'll tell her as soon as I see her." The fresh-faced kitchen helper was always eager to please.

He headed for the series of stairs leading down the hill to the stable and saw Genevieve and Becca on two black stallions, trotting across the field away from the barn. They had talked last night about going on an early ride. He smiled, watching them canter toward the ball of sun, inching above the horizon.

Deep in thought, Duncan walked into the stable, glad he'd stay at Wilmingrove Hall until everything was resolved. It took him several seconds to realize the only sounds in the barn were the normal rhythms of horses eating oats, swishing their tails, blowing raspberries and the occasional whinny. There was no sign of Darlington or Philip.

"Chief Superintendent Darlington," Duncan called out. At the end of the double row of stalls, a horse snorted.

"Dad," Duncan bellowed, hoping to hear a response.

Behind him, a sweet voice cooed, "Hey cuz. It's wonderful to see you."

Duncan whipped around at the saccharine sound, just as he heard the whistle of a dart pierce the air, followed by a sharp pain under his jaw. In an instant, his muscles began to relax. He gasped and took a tentative step forward, discovering he had little control over his body. He hovered for a moment, then crumpled to the wide-planked walnut floor. Though his body had abandoned him, his mind was even sharper than usual. He forced himself to focus on Olivia's angelic face and knew his terror must be evident in his eyes.

Olivia dropped to her knees beside Duncan's limp body. She leaned down on all fours until her cheek was on the floor and she was nose to nose with Duncan. She said nothing, just stared into Duncan's panic-filled eyes until, at last, she whispered, "I bet you're so surprised." She lingered for what seemed like forever, a demented smile curling her blood-red lips. "I have an exciting morning planned for us."

Duncan's mind raced to Olivia's book, trying to remember why he was paralyzed and why he—and not David—was here with Olivia.

As if reading his mind, Olivia said, "Curare, Duncan. You're paralyzed by curare. I don't know how long it will last. I tried to give you a dose that would just paralyze you until I can get you on my little bonfire. You're going to make a beautiful blaze!'

Olivia sat up, clapping her hands with glee. "I bet you thought David was going to be the Burning Man!" She cackled, eyes wide and blazing. "Let me tell you a little story. For such a long time I thought David was my father. I ached for him to love Mommy and me, he didn't even know I was alive until I got his attention. I know that now. My book was published before I knew about you and your very perfect family. Your perfect parents and perfect Julia and perfect little Alex and Ella. You all make me sick." She shook her head as if to refocus. "After my Uncle Conner read

How I Killed My Daddy, he sent me a long letter explaining that David wasn't my father. He said he was the only one in the world, besides my mother, who knew Jonathon Laney, the 12ᵀᴴ Earl of Crosswick, had sired me, as they say in your circles. Conner's a psychiatrist. I think he was afraid I was going to execute my book and he was right, of course. But when he told me the truth, well," she shrugged her shoulders, "I had to change my plot a bit. It didn't take long for me to realize you're the one. You're the one who has to go. There can only be one special one in the Crosswick line and I'm it. Besides, I'm the real heir." She clinched her teeth and growled. "Wilmingrove and all of this belongs to me, not to you."

The more she spoke, the more frightened Duncan became, her madness filling the stable like a suffocating vapor. Breathing as deeply as he could, he tried to calm himself. Keeping his wits might be his only chance to survive.

"Well, our moms will be back soon, and we don't want to run into them. And, since I'm not sure if I've given you too much or too little curare or if it's just the right amount, I'd better get busy." Olivia hopped to her feet. She jogged down the aisle toward the far end of the stable and was gone.

"What the hell?" Duncan's mind raced. "Surely somebody will come before she moves me or I die, whichever comes first." Duncan listened for any sound but heard nothing.

At last, he felt, more than heard, a faint rhythm on the wood floor. The rumble of tires? Maybe it was Darlington or one of his men. He closed his eyes and focused on the intensifying rhythm of whatever was coming. The low whomp, whomp, whomp morphed into a soft hum, then amplified into the gentle whine Duncan recognized as an electric motor. The sound bore down on him until it came to an abrupt stop. Then, slowly, it jerked toward him until he sensed a nudge in his upper back and thighs.

"Damn! I don't quite have the hang of this yet." Olivia sounded annoyed. She walked around and squatted in front of him. Grabbing his jacket in her right hand, his jeans in her left, she pulled him toward her until he was balancing on his left side. "That should do it," she said, giving Duncan a pat on the cheek. The engine started again. There was another nudge, and again, Olivia bent over him, but this time she rolled him away from her, so he was on his back.

Olivia could see the confusion in Duncan's eyes when he realized what she was doing. "Can you believe it, Duncan?"

Her open-mouthed grin filled Duncan with horror.

"You're going for a ride on a forklift. La, la, la, la, la, la." She sang a little ditty while she figured out how to raise the forks. "Just give me a minute and we'll be on our way. I love this little forklift. It's perfect for doing things in the stable, but it isn't as easy to drive as I thought it would be. Not to worry, practice makes perfect. I know it's not for outdoor use, but I think it will be just fine to get you down to the river. Next stop, your blaze of glory!"

Olivia started the forklift, put it into gear and rolled slowly toward the stable door. Duncan lay on his back like a ragdoll, limp legs hanging over one prong, the other tine supporting his back. He lolled back and forth with the rhythm of the lift, his head hanging back between his arms, elongating his neck, and exposing his throat.

Once out of the barn, Olivia turned left, away from the Hall. She accelerated onto the gravel path, which sloped to the river's edge. For the last few days, the Wilmingrove Hall grounds staff had been gathering forest debris, which they would float down the river and add to the town's ever-growing pile. Little had they known they were creating a funeral pyre right here at the Hall.

She was unhappy about having to change the timing of her storyline. She loathed having the blaze during daylight but, knowing Darlington was closing in on her, she didn't feel she had a choice. The fire wouldn't be as glorious during the day as it would be at night, but it was the best she could do under the circumstances. Sometimes you had to make concessions, just like she had to change her victim.

As they bumped along, Olivia belted out the words to the primal rhythm of Talking Heads' "Burning Down the House". She pumped her shoulders, her left hand pounding out the beat on the steering wheel.

FORTY-TWO

T HE SKY STILL blushed with a hint of pink when Philip set out on an early morning walk to survey the Wilmingrove Hall grounds. In his green Barbour jacket and wellies, he looked like an ad from *Horse and Hound*. With him were King George and Prince Albert, the matching pair of Labrador Retrievers Harrington had trained to perfection.

The dogs raced ahead of Philip, barking, and chasing each other. Circling back, they would streak by their master before shooting out again across the field. The more Philip wandered the estate, the more he could feel it in his blood. He was getting to know the hills, the valleys, the fields, the streams, and had befriended a two-hundred-year-old tree on the property. His love for his family's land grew each time he ventured out. Standing on a knoll surveying his estate, he saw Becca and Genevieve on horseback, walking through a meadow. He pulled his phone from his pocket and was just about to take a photo of the two riders just as it rang.

Julia's picture filled the screen and he answered.

"Thank God, Philip! I've been trying to get ahold of Duncan and he's not answering."

Hearing the alarm in Julia's voice, Philip was on high alert. "What's the matter? What's happened?"

"Listen, Philip. This is important."

"I'm listening, Julia."

"Last night when I walked into the playroom, the kids were playacting they had a room full of computers and they were watching everyone in Wilmingrove Hall. They had set up boxes, pretending they were monitors and they were describing what was happening on each screen. When I asked them where they got the idea, Ella said it was like the room inside the walls in Wilmingrove Hall." Her panic reached across the ocean. "Philip, there is a statue in the music room that opens a panel in the wall. The ballerina."

Philip whistled the dogs to him and raced toward the Hall. "The surveillance equipment is somewhere in the walls?"

"I believe Olivia set up a room of monitors and has been watching our every move from inside the house."

"Julia, I've got to call Darlington. I'll call you as soon as I have anything to tell you."

"And have Duncan call me as soon as you see him."

Lungs on fire, Philip burst through the Hall's kitchen door. Mrs. Lomax stopped midway through pulling a tray of cinnamon buns from the oven, her eyes popping at the Earl's frantic entrance.

"Is Darlington here?" Philip barked, his face crimson.

"I don't know if he's arrived yet." Mrs. Lomax wiped her hands on her apron. "If he's not here, he's on his way. What's wrong? Something's wrong."

Ignoring her questions, Philip ordered, "I need to see him as soon as he gets here." He pushed through the swinging kitchen door and smashed into Sean Harrington. "Come with me, Sean," Philip commanded.

As the two men bolted to the music room, Philip briefed Harrington on his new information. Philip walked straight to the ballerina, pulled backward on the statue and the panel slid open.

"Did you know we had secret passages in the Hall?"

From Harrington's look of surprise, Philip guessed the answer.

"I did not, my lord." A bark of laughter escaped Harrington's throat. "This is absolutely brilliant!"

"I don't think we should go in until Darlington gets here." Philip was trying his best not to storm headlong into what might be disaster. "Let's wait for him in the grand salon."

"I just got off the phone with him. He'll be here any minute. His men have been doing a drone search through the night and he has some results."

"I need to call Genevieve and tell her and Becca to get back here. Assuming Olivia is on the estate grounds, I want everyone here in the Hall. I guess David is still asleep. And I don't know where the hell Duncan is." They left the study and headed through the hallway, where the library clock struck eight. The hour was still early and so much had already happened. A pit in Philip's stomach warned him that it was only the beginning.

FORTY-THREE

THE WIND WHISTLED around Genevieve's riding helmet, her body an extension of the thundering black stallion beneath her. She could feel Becca pressing forward on her left and smiled at the competitive surge spurring her on. The howling wind and the pounding hooves filled her ears.

"You haven't won yet," Becca laughed into the wind. Thirty yards to the bank of the river. Thirty yards for Onyx to champion her to victory. Eager for just a bit more speed, she softened her hands on the reins and increased the pressure of her calves and heels around the horse's girth. She inched closer to Genevieve and Dutch, now only half a length ahead.

"Come on, you magnificent boy!" Becca urged her steed forward, her body flowing with the movement of her horse.

With twenty yards left, the Friesians and their riders were in a dead heat, racing at a breakneck pace. At ten yards they each reined in their mounts to a canter then slowed to a trot until they stopped near the river's edge, breathless and exhilarated.

Genevieve unstrapped her helmet and pulled it off. Shaking her head, her hair fell from the band holding her ponytail. She ran her free hand through her mane, allowing the breeze to lift the ends.

"I've never ridden that fast!" Genevieve's eyes flashed from the thrill of competition.

Becca couldn't stop grinning. She leaned down and patted Onyx on the neck. "What a gorgeous ride you are, my man." She smiled at Genevieve. "Have you ever had so much fun? Thank God neither one of us has to buy breakfast! What a perfect finish to a spectacular race, my friend!"

"Speaking of breakfast, what time is it? I'm starving!"

Becca looked at her watch. "It's 8:10. I bet Mrs. Lomax has something wonderful just coming out of the oven. I can just taste her cinnamon buns! I'd suggest we race back to the Hall, but I'll be lucky to make it at a slow walk."

Genevieve pushed her hair behind her ears and pulled her helmet back on. "I'm with you, Becca. I can't imagine how sore I'm going to be tomorrow.

"I bet I won't be able to walk by this afternoon," Becca laughed.

"Small price to pay, though. Wouldn't you say?"

Turning their horses away from the river, they started ambling toward the Hall. It had just come into view in the distance when Becca pulled abruptly on her reins. She squinted across the field toward a path leading out of the woods. "What the hell is that?"

"That's the pile Harrington's men cleared out of the forest. They're taking it down to the village today for the Guy Fawkes bonfire tonight."

"No, not that!" Becca was becoming more and more agitated.

"There! There!" She pointed beyond the huge pile of branches and twigs. Something moved toward them.

"What the hell, indeed!" Genevieve focused on the small image bumping along the ground. "It looks like a forklift carrying a big bundle."

They watched for a few seconds as the figure approached and they could see her better. The blinding sun glanced off the driver's short white-blond hair.

"Jesus!" Becca growled. "Jesus, Genevieve. That's Olivia and I bet you any amount of money, that's David on that forklift!"

FORTY-FOUR

PACING THE GRAND salon waiting for Chief Superintendent Darlington to arrive, Philip finally heard the crunch of tires on the gravel drive. The slam of two car doors was followed seconds later by the creak of Wilmingrove Hall's massive front door. Looking short on sleep and long on stress, Chief Superintendent Darlington burst into the cavernous room, accompanied by Michael Flynn, the head of the tech squad. Darlington's usually manicured appearance was disheveled, his short hair sticking up at the crown of his head and his clothes rumpled.

Dispensing with all pleasantries, Darlington opened his mouth, but before he could speak, Philip motioned them to follow him to the music room. On their way, he told them what Alex and Ella had found in the wall.

Using his phone as a flashlight, Darlington led the anxious band down the hall to the closed door.

When the door opened, he gave a soft, "Whoa" and flashed his light around the room.

Philip flipped a wall switch, and the room came to life.

"Jesus." Darlington looked around, his mind racing. "Flynn, get your team in here and get to work." His voice was terse and urgent. He motioned for the other two men to head back out the door.

When they crossed back into the warm glow of the music room, Darlington said, "Lord Crosswick, we have drone images of a bonfire pile by the river. Could Olivia have built a pyre without anyone noticing?"

Stepping out from behind Philip, Harrington said, "The pile by the river is from the forest. For the last week, my men have been clearing rubbish from the woods. It never occurred to me that Olivia might use it for her Guy Fawkes bonfire. Holy shite! Do you think that might be her plan?"

"It deviates from her plotline, but she has to adjust details as she goes, doesn't she?" Darlington's brow furrowed as he rubbed his temples with his thumbs "When our forensic psychologists told us Olivia would follow her plan, they didn't take into consideration how many circumstances have change since she wrote her book.

"We need to get David down here." Until now, Philip had been silent, but now he was anxious to account for his friends and family. "Chief Superintendent, I want Becca and Genevieve back here. The Hall may not be as safe as we thought, but at least I want us all together until this is over. They're out riding. I called Genevieve about ten minutes ago, but she didn't answer. I think David's upstairs and I want Duncan here as well."

As the group returned to the grand salon, David sauntered

down the stairs. "Good morning, all," he said, looking remarkably rested for a man in the crosshairs.

"We were just going to roust you out, David. A lot is happening." Philip squeezed David's shoulder. "We want to keep our eyes on you today."

"Excuse me, Lord Crosswick."

"Wallace. Just the man I wanted to see. Could you please let Duncan know he needs to join us?"

"That's what I was coming to tell you. Lottie saw him about half an hour ago. He wanted Lady Crosswick to know he was meeting you and the Chief Superintendent at the stable."

Darlington's face was blank.

"Did you meet up with him, sir?" Wallace asked.

"What the bloody blazes are you talking about? I haven't seen or talked to Duncan since everyone left the restaurant last night. Where would he get the idea I was meeting him this morning at the stable?" Darlington pulled his phone from his pocket, punched one number, and waited seconds before someone answered. "Immediate Priority. All available units to Wilmingrove Hall." His voice was commanding and hard as steel. He mashed another button. "Flynn, get drones to the stable and riverbank straight away! I want eyes on both locations. Lord Crosswick, keep calling your wife. When you get her, tell her and Ms. Conway to come back to the Hall immediately."

He spun around and was out the door, leaving Philip, David and Sean Harrington looking at each other with no idea what to do.

FORTY-FIVE

WITHOUT A WORD to Genevieve, Becca kicked Onyx to a trot and headed toward Olivia.

"Becca!" Genevieve hissed. "Becca, wait!" She moved forward to Becca's side and grabbed her arm. "Stop! We need a plan before we go charging at Olivia."

Becca reined Onyx to halt and looked at Genevieve, eyes briming with anger and tears. "You're right, of course, Genevieve. I'm just so angry I could wring Olivia's neck with my bare hands. I knew this was coming, but a part of me held out hope that she would stop before it went too far. What an idiot I am to keep believing my child is salvageable, to believe she has a soul."

Glancing beyond the wood pile towards Olivia's steady approach, Genevieve reached out, took Becca's gloved hand, and squeezed. "We need to figure out right now how to prevent a troubled young woman from killing our dear friend. I don't think she's seen us yet. Between the sun in her eyes and the woodpile, I think we can stay out of her line of vision until we're close to her. Is there any possibility of reasoning with her?"

Becca barked a single laugh and shook her head. "No!" She snarled.

Genevieve's phone rang from deep in her riding jacket. Pulling her iPhone from her inside pocket, she saw Philip's face on her screen. She punched "accept" and his urgent voice shot through the phone. "G, where are you? You need to get back to the Hall. Don't go to the stable. Get back here!" His rapid-fire instructions took her by surprise.

Looking up, Genevieve saw Becca and Onyx walking on the riverbank's soft edge, trying to stay hidden behind the bonfire heap. She was heading straight toward Olivia.

Turning her attention back to Philip, Genevieve covered the phone with her hand to muffle her voice. "Philip," she whispered. "We're at the river near the big pile of branches."

"Oh shit!" Genevieve could hear Philip's rapid breathing.

"Olivia is heading there on a forklift with David hanging on the prongs. She's done something to David to make him—" She cut herself off. "Of course, the curare."

"Genevieve." A coldness took over Philip's voice. "It's not David."

She narrowed her eyes, laser-focused on the figure bouncing on the forks. "Not David? But in the book—"

"Forget the book."

"But the book outlines what she's planning to do, Philip. It says—"

"It's Duncan."

"Duncan?" she asked, confused. "Why in the hell would Duncan be on he forklift?" She squinted to focus on the body swaying from the forklift, then panic filled her voice. "Oh my God, Philip. You're right! It's Duncan." Tears closed her throat. "What if he suffocated from the curare? Oh Jesus. What if he's dead?" She was barely breathing.

"Genevieve, listen to me." Philip's voice was like a slap. "Darlington and a shitload of cops are on their way to the river. Just stay away from Olivia. They'll be there any minute. Did you hear me?" Raising his voice, Philip yelled at Genevieve to confirm she would stay put.

"I heard you, but I have to get to Duncan! I have to. Oh, Philip, I can't believe this is happening."

"I'm on my way with Harrington and you should see the police any minute. Stay put!"

"Just get here, Philip. Please, just get here." Genevieve ended the call, shoving the phone back into her pocket.

As Becca and her horse moved closer to Olivia, she gasped. She yanked on Onyx's reins, halting him, stunned at what she saw. Duncan, not David, hung from the forks. She turned in her saddle. Did Genevieve know it was her son who was about to become a human torch? Seeing her friend's fear-stricken face, there was no question, she knew.

Olivia was no more than twenty yards away, singing at the top of her lungs and bumping along with Duncan dangling from the forks. Excited about placing Duncan on the wood pile, Olivia had raised the mast to its full extension.

Trying to keep her rage in check, Genevieve breathed slowly and deeply. Nudging Dutch forward, she timed her inhale and exhale with her horse's stride, slowly bringing her anger under control. Moving closer to Olivia with every step, Genevieve assessed what items could serve as weapons. She had her crop and a two-thousand-pound horse.

She reined Dutch to a stop. An idea flashed to mind. It might work. She needed to think for a moment before charging ahead. Genevieve closed her eyes, visualizing her plan. This just might work. This just might startle Olivia into making a mistake.

She leaned forward, patting Dutch on the neck. "Okay, you magnificent beast. My darling boy is relying on us to save his life. We can do this." Her voice was soft, coaxing. She felt the ridged firmness of her crop and she was ready.

Genevieve sat erect, sinking her bottom into her saddle. She took a deep breath and exhaled. Reins in one hand, her crop in the other, she struck Dutch on his hindquarters and drove her heels into his sides. He burst forward like shot from a cannon, skirting the wood pile, flying past Becca, and heading straight for Olivia.

Stunned at the sight of the jet-black horse and rider roaring toward her, Olivia yanked the forklift to the left, driving onto the riverbank.

Genevieve reined Dutch to a sliding halt and jumped out of her saddle to a standing crouch, coiled, ready to strike.

The forklift's small tires stuck in the riverbank's muddy grass, stopping the vehicle's forward motion with the left side just inches from the edge. Olivia sat stone still, moving only her eyes to glance down at the cold water rushing below. Looking up ten feet above her, she could see Duncan starting to move his head and heard his raspy voice as the curare's effects began to wane.

Duncan felt a fork at the joint of his thighs and knees, his muscles coming back to life. "Jesus, Olivia! What have you done?" Like a trapeze artist gripping a high bar, he squeezed the tine as hard as he could with his weakened muscles.

The forklift listed to the left, its weight too much for the soggy bank. In slow motion, it eased onto its side, the mast stretching out into the air above the river, almost horizontal to the embankment.

Olivia froze in the driver's seat.

Hanging out over the icy water, Duncan struggled to pull his dangling arms from above his head, trying to reach the fork pressing against his back. If he could grasp that tine, he could hold on until someone could rescue him.

"Olivia, don't move!" Genevieve screamed. "Stay where you are! If you move, the forklift will go over the edge!"

The buzz of drones and screaming sirens pierced the air. Six police cars, a specially equipped Road Policing Unit, and an ambulance, all with lights blazing, raced toward them from across the field. Overhead a police helicopter shared the sky with the drones, keeping watch over the scene.

With the onslaught of arriving emergency vehicles, Becca and Onyx streaked across the field to join in the mayhem. Becca threw herself off the steed and was running to Genevieve before Onyx came to a full stop.

Coming from the Hall, the fastest way to the river was on foot. Philip, David, and Harrington bolted across the terrace then flew down the stairs, taking two at a time. They raced between the parterre and croquet lawn, past the falconry field, and whipped by the quince trees to the river's edge where all three bent over, gasping for air after their sprint.

Genevieve scanned the crowd of police, looking for Chief Superintendent Darlington. She found him in the middle of a sea of dark blue, barking orders and pointing toward the forklift where Olivia and Duncan teetered.

"Get that forklift stabilized!" Darlington shouted. "Get a harness around Warwick and get your hands on Conway! I want that woman in handcuffs!"

Before anyone could stop her, Olivia pushed herself out of the driver's seat, balanced on the edge of the forklift's frame, then dove into the river. The forklift shuddered, tilting a bit more toward the water.

Duncan's voice could now be heard above the din of all the activity. "Help!" he rasped. "Help me!"

Lying flat on her belly, Genevieve scooched to the edge of the bank until her torso hung out over the water. She extended her hand as far as she could, trying to touch Duncan. Not quite able to reach him, she sucked in a breath. Then, exhaling, she stretched a bit further and grabbed a fistful of his pant leg.

"The police are here, Duncan. It's going to be all right. I promise you," she sobbed. "Everything's going to be all right. Just stay still. Don't move. We'll get you back on the embankment. I promise. You're going to be okay."

Blinking to clear her tears, she felt weight pressing her into the ground. Glancing back, she saw Philip sitting on her butt so she wouldn't fall over the embankment.

She couldn't believe the absurdity of this situation. Duncan was hanging from a forklift, tipped on its side, while she stretched across the ground, torso hanging out into thin air, holding onto their son's pantleg, while her husband sat on her butt to keep her from tumbling over the bank into the water. It would be hilarious if only it weren't so terrifying. Genevieve tightened her grip even more. She vowed to cling to Duncan's pants until he was in the grasp of the police.

The Met team moved a vehicle fitted with a winch into position. They hooked cables to the Mini, one to the frame, another to the mast, stabilizing the forklift. Well-developed muscles straining his black uniform shirt, a SWAT officer crawled out onto the mast to wrap a harness around Duncan. The rescue team pulled the forklift to an upright position and three officers held the limp man as they lowered the fork. When it was four feet off the ground, paramedics grabbed him off the lift and strapped him onto a gurney.

"It's curare," Duncan rasped to the EMT's. "She used a dart to inject me with curare." His voice was stronger with every word.

Within seconds Duncan was in the ambulance. The SWAT officer pounded twice on the closed doors and the hospital wagon took off, bouncing across the field, siren blaring.

In the river, the current and her strong stroke carried Olivia swiftly. Ten feet above her, a police helicopter hovered, its blades whipping the water into white caps. Downstream, a small, inflatable motorboat churned against the current, closing in on her. She bobbed in the waves like a buoy, coughing and sputtering as water rushed into her mouth. The boat slid beside her while two officers hung over the side. One grabbed the collar of her jacket, the other grasped her under her arm.

"We're pulling you out!" one cop shouted above the din as they plucked her from the churning river. They sat her on the bench seat, zip tied her wrists and wrapped a mylar blanket around her shoulders. Rivulets from her drenched hair streamed down her face. She glared at everyone on the riverbank high above her. They were watching her. She saw her mother sobbing and she sneered.

She jumped to her feet and the officer yanked her back down. She shook her fisted hands at everyone on the bank. "It's not over!" she screamed. "Tell Duncan it's not over!"

But it was. The drama of the last two months was over.

FORTY-SIX

BECCA LOOKED AT her reflection in the walnut cheval mirror. Her eyes were ringed with dark circles, confirming her lack of sleep and the tears she had shed since the climax at the river's edge six days before. Dressed in simple navy wool pants, jacket, and a white silk shirt, she was ready to see her daughter for the first time since the police fished her out of the river.

So much had happened since that terrifying morning. After Olivia's apprehension, Becca's first phone call was to Henry Fitch, who had come immediately to represent Olivia. Having an old friend on their side was a great comfort. At Henry's suggestion, her second call was to the director of the Langston School, where Olivia had thrived for so many years. Thanks to Henry and the school, Olivia was remanded to a private psychiatric hospital: Blain Lodge, near York.

After four days of court appearances, helping police tie up loose ends, and fending off the tabloid press, Becca was a cauldron of emotion: anger, frustration, sadness, self-pity, guilt. She was determined to accomplish two things during today's visit with her daughter. First, she would tell Olivia about her father, Jonathon Laney, the 12TH Earl of Crosswick. She wanted Olivia to know how much the couple had loved each other. Second, she would apologize. She would tell Olivia how guilty she felt and how sorry she was for all the years she nurtured Olivia's fantasy that David was her father. After years of her own therapy, Becca knew she had contributed to Olivia's struggles, but this would be the first time she would share just how responsible she felt. It would be a painful meeting.

Becca heard a soft knock on her door. "Come in."

The door opened just enough for Genevieve to stick her head in. "Just checking to see if you need anything. Are you okay?"

Becca offered a joyless smile. "I'm fine, as well as one could expect. But thank you, Genevieve. Everyone's support means a great deal to me."

At that, Genevieve walked across the room and enveloped Becca in her arms. They lingered until Genevieve gave a squeeze and then held Becca at arm's length. "Well, my friend, you look ready to go into battle."

"Let's hope it's only a small skirmish." Becca's laugh was brittle. "Do you know if David is downstairs?"

"He is. He's waiting for you in the car. You're sure you don't want Philip and me to go, too?"

"Absolutely not." Becca gave Genevieve a kiss on the cheek. "David will be there after my visit. He's more than enough support."

During the forty-minute drive to Blain Lodge, BBC Radio York droned on and on, filling the Range Rover with news of local holiday fetes, international news of skirmishes and protest marches and the Prime Minister's latest embarrassing behavior.

Becca didn't hear any of it. Gazing out the window, she stared at the endless fields. Not long ago, they were golden with wheat. Now, resown, they waited for their snowy winter blanket to protect them from the icy months ahead. The cycle of life, Becca thought. Come spring, these fields will be green with new life and hope. She smiled at her musings. It was her first real smile in a week, and it felt good. Deep in her own thoughts, she was unaware the car had stopped until she felt David's hand squeeze hers.

"Becca, we're here."

Nothing registered.

"We're here," David repeated. "Do you want me to walk you to the door?"

Several seconds passed before Becca's eyes sparked. "Wow! I was lightyears away!" She smiled again. "No. No. I don't want you to come in. I'll be fine. I'll be fine." She took a cleansing breath, held it, then exhaled. "I guess it's now or never!"

David walked around to Becca's door and opened it. She grasped his hand and let him help her from the Range Rover.

He held her shoulders, looked into her eyes, and said, "You're one of the bravest people I know. What you did for us, coming here and exposing Olivia, is something few people would have done."

David pulled her into his arm, holding her there longer than he had intended. Before releasing her, he kissed her lightly on the lips. Much to his surprise, she pulled his face to hers, parted her lips and planted them firmly on his. "To be continued," she said.

Becca walked away to face her troubled daughter, head high, back erect. David couldn't take his eyes off her until she disappeared into the building.

FORTY-SEVEN

HAVING NO IDEA how Becca would feel after her time with Olivia, Genevieve wanted everything to be perfect when she returned. This evening she wanted to wrap Becca in a blanket of love. She stood back to admire her efforts.

"Pretty, very pretty," she said to herself.

Set in front of the music room fireplace, with a fire waiting to be lit, the round table was just the right size for an intimate dinner for five. A square damask tablecloth, heavy tassels hanging at each corner topped a floor-length blue, green, and gold plaid cover. Royal Doulton Carlyle china was the perfect dinnerware for the fall with its blue and gold rim and center rosettes. A cluster of Waterford crystal sparkled at each place with the reflection from lamps dotted around the room. Votives and a nest of blue and violet hydrangeas finished the tableau.

In the kitchen, Mrs. Lomax was doing her part to make the evening comforting and special. When they talked menu, there was no question. It would be Beef Wellington, Joel Robuchon's mashed potatoes and Mrs. Lomax's own nutty Brussels sprouts.

Glancing out of the towering widows, Genevieve noticed a

few flakes of snow wafting from low clouds. She heard the crunch of tires on gravel and saw the black Range Rover make its way around the circle, stopping at the front door. She glanced at her watch. 5:30.

Genevieve heard voices before she got to the salon. David and Becca were chatting with Wallace in the cavernous room. She heard laughter. She heard banter. Genevieve frowned, searching for a word to describe how Becca sounded. She listened a bit longer before it occurred to her. Happy! Becca sounded happy! Throughout the afternoon Genevieve had thought about her friend. She thought about all the emotions Becca might be feeling, but not once did 'happy' occur to her.

"You're back!" Genevieve crossed the great hall with outstretched arms. "David, you brought our girl back in one piece. Well done!" She wrapped her arms around Becca. "So, how did it go?" Genevieve pulled back, looking at Becca's face for any clue.

"It was an extraordinary afternoon. Not at all what I expected." The relief in Becca's eyes was genuine. "I'll tell you all about it at dinner. Right now, I want to shower and change. What time do I need to be down?"

"Are we having a party or a wake?" Genevieve asked.

Becca looked at David. "I'd say we're having a party." She looked back at Genevieve, grinning.

"Then the party starts when you arrive," Genevieve said. "Philip and Sean Harrington are in York finishing a few things with Chief Superintendent Darlington. Philip just called to say they're about to leave so there's no rush. And I ordered Duncan to rest so he'll be ready to enjoy the evening. According to Mrs. Lomax, dinner will be served at 7:30, but the Champagne is on ice just waiting to pop."

"Alrighty then. I won't be long. I don't want to miss anything, and I have a lot to share." Becca pressed her lips to David's cheek. "Thank you, David, for your support today. You were wonderful." She swept up the staircase and was gone.

Genevieve looked at David, with amused surprise.

David shrugged his shoulders, a sheepish grin on his face.

"Has something happened between you two?"

"I don't know. Maybe." David started up the stairs, stopped and turned around. "Can we talk about this later?"

"Oh, you can count on it," Genevieve confirmed.

Bubbles teased the top of Genevieve's Champagne flute. "Philip, stop!" Genevieve begged him as he coaxed just a bit more Veuve Clicquot into her glass. He filled his glass then set the bottle back in its silver cooler.

"To happy endings." Philip and Genevieve clinked glasses.

Philip smiled at his wife and took a drink. "Can you believe all that's happened in two short months? The inheritance alone would have been enough to change our lives, but the madness of Olivia trying to kill Duncan... I mean, who experiences such wild events, except in the movies?"

"It's hard to imagine. And speaking of all that's happened," Genevieve lowered her voice and leaned toward Philip, "I think something's going on between Becca and David."

"What do you mean by 'some—'" Philip stopped, seeing

Becca, David, and Duncan in the doorway. Philip raised his glass then took another drink. "Come in. As you can see, we didn't wait."

Genevieve held flutes while Philip poured. The trio took the glasses, and the toasting began.

"Julia's devastated she's not here," Duncan said. "She almost cried on the phone. It's good I'm going home tomorrow."

"Then our first toast is to Julia." Philip raised his glass and the chorus of "To Julia" rang out.

At precisely 7:30, Wallace announced dinner would be served. The diners were very happy indeed, and the Champagne bottle was empty, he noted.

Genevieve rose from the love seat where she and Philip had been sitting opposite Becca and David for the last half hour. "Come on, everyone. Mrs. Lomax is very serious about her meals being eaten hot. We don't want to suffer her wrath, do we?"

"I should say not." David held out his hand, helping Becca to her feet. "She's been very good to me while I've been at the Hall. Lord knows I've overstayed my welcome!"

David slipped his arm around Becca's waist, escorting her to the table.

"Tell me, David," Genevieve said. "Where else would you rather have been? Where else could you have been the center of attention for the last two months?"

David held Becca's chair, scooching her closer to the table "This kind of attention, I could have done without," he said.

When everyone was seated, Wallace led a parade of servers into the music room. Each placed a silver-domed plate in front of a diner. On the silent count of three, they removed the domes to reveal Mrs. Lomax's exquisite meal, which was greeted with "ooh"s, "aah"s and applause.

Wallace poured a splash of Chateau Beaulieu Bordeaux, the Crosswick's own vintage, into Philip's glass. Philip swirled it, admiring its legs, then stuck his nose into the goblet's tapered mouth to inhale the rich aroma. He slurped a taste into his mouth, closed his eyes, then swallowed. "Wallace," he said, "we make a hell of a wine!"

"We do indeed, my lord." Wallace poured the rest of the glasses. When he was finished, he bowed at the waist. "Lord and Lady Crosswick, Lord Crosswick, Sir David, Ms. Conway, may I say, it is with the greatest happiness the staff and I serve you this evening. We could not be more pleased that Ms. Olivia's novel had a happier ending than planned. My lord," Wallace nodded at Duncan. "We are all delighted you did not die." Wallace's sober voice betrayed nothing, but the curl of his lips brought his audience to laughter.

"I, too, am pleased I'm not dead," Duncan deadpanned.

"Lord, Lady Crosswick, just ring when you need me." Wallace caught Duncan's eye and winked as he left the room.

"There aren't many like Wallace," Becca said. "He's in a class all his own. How long has he been at the Hall?"

"He was born here, in the stable," Genevieve said, poker-faced.

"You don't suppose he'd like to come to the U.S. to work, do you?" asked Becca.

"Pull something like that at your peril." Philip pointed his dinner knife at Becca.

"Just testing the waters! I can't imagine Wallace putting up with us insufferable Americans, although he's put up with the Warwick family pretty well!"

"Okay. Okay. Changing the subject." Genevieve gestured toward Becca with her wine glass. "Tell us about seeing Olivia today. Judging from your high spirits, things must have gone well."

Looking around the table, Becca smiled, her eyes brimming with happy tears. "In such a short time I've grown to trust this special group as much as I've ever trusted anyone. Though my own daughter has terrified you for the last two months, you welcomed me into your lives, embracing me from the moment I arrived on your doorstep." She paused, looking down at her napkin twisted in her fingers.

David offered his hand.

She took it and went on. "Dr. Morgan, the lead psychiatrist on Olivia's case, is on the cutting edge of treating mental illness. Over the next month, they'll do a thorough assessment of Olivia's mental state and create a treatment plan. That's all very normal and as I expected. What excites me is Dr. Morgan's success using several of his new therapies. Olivia's only been at Blair Lodge for four days, but already Dr. Morgan seems to have a good read on her. He's not taken in by her guile. He is, however, impressed and interested in her ability to manipulate and influence people. He seems excited to have her as a patient. There's no question she's brilliant and can charm her way out of most trouble. But not this time. I think she's met her match with Dr. Morgan. I can't believe I feel such happiness, such—well—such hope. Over the years there were more than a few times I thought we were on the right track with Olivia, but never have I truly believed Olivia might someday be able to lead a happy, productive life. I may be a fool, but I..." Becca's voice trailed off into silence. For several seconds, the only sound in the room was the crackling fire and the pretty pink marble mantle clock's tic toc.

Still holding Becca's hand, David pulled it to his lips and kissed her knuckles. "I will never understand how such a brilliant mind, who carried out her plotline so well, made such a dog's breakfast out of the climax. Thank goodness she did. Right, Duncan?"

Leaning back in his chair, Duncan's serenity belied the anxiety gnawing at him. Only his fingers tapping on the table's edge gave him away. "When Olivia squatted down beside me and said that she was the special one in the Crosswick line and the true heir so she had to eliminate me, the hate in her eyes is something I will never forget."

Becca started to speak, but her voice failed. She cleared her throat and tried again. "From the time she was born, my parents and I told Olivia how special she was. She was the prettiest, the smartest, the best at everything. Of course, we were overcompensating for her not having a father. What a mistake!"

"But understandable," Genevieve sympathized.

Becca leaned forward, elbows on the table. "Duncan, Dr. Morgan said that watching your loving family over the course of several weeks fueled a jealousy that overwhelmed her. When Conner wrote to her to tell her that Jonathon, not David, was her father, she transferred her rage from David to you. She felt you were trying to take her special place. You had everything she longed for, and she felt by destroying you, she would have your life."

Duncan stopped drumming his fingers. The corners of his mouth lifted, and he said, "If Olivia had executed the end of her story as well as she did the rest of her tale, I'd be toast! I'd be just a bar of charcoal you could use on the grill to cook some ribeye steaks. I trust you'd serve a nice Petrus with that, Dad. I know it's not our vintage, but at least it's a Bordeaux."

Duncan's comic observation pierced the heavy cloud that had gathered, and the room exploded with laughter at his dark humor. They laughed until their eyes streamed with tears. They laughed until their faces hurt. They laughed weeks of tension away.

Surprised and pleased by the jovial mood when he entered the music room, Wallace offered a reserved smile. "My lady, may we serve dessert?"

Still breathless from laughing, Genevieve nodded. "Thank you, Wallace." She dabbed at her eyes, hoping she didn't look like a racoon. "We've been having the most marvelous laugh about everything that's happened over the last two months."

"That must sound deranged," David said.

"Not at all, Sir David. Indeed, laughter is the best release in the world. Let me pour more Champagne. Champagne always helps the laughter bubble up." Pleased with himself at his bon mot, Wallace refilled the flutes as servers placed puffy chocolate souffles in front of each diner.

"Wallace, would you ask everyone in the kitchen to come in, please? And if Mrs. MacIntosh and Harrington are available, please ask them to join us as well." said Genevieve. "We need to give them an ovation for all they've done, not just this evening, but since we arrived. And we'll need glasses for everyone and more Champagne. We always seem to need more Champagne, don't we, Wallace?"

He smiled. "What is life without Champagne, my lady? Everyone will be delighted to come in."

A few minutes later, Wallace returned, carrying a tray of glasses, followed by Mrs. Lomax, Lottie, Claire, and two girls who would have been called scullery maids a century ago. A moment later Mrs. Lomax and Harrington joined the growing crowd.

Brimming with emotion from an evening spent in his ancestral home, Wilmingrove Hall, Philip stood in front of the elegant marble fireplace, fire dancing on the hearth. He was unsure how the Hall managed to be both grand and embracing, but it was. Each day, the connection to the generations of Laneys who preceded him grew stronger. The longer he sat at the helm of this vast empire built by clever, courageous men and women, the more responsibility he felt to secure the continued success of the family going forward. He could envision one day handing the reins of the Laney dynasty to Duncan and Julia, who would continue nurturing the family legacy until ultimately Alex and Ella would take their place as Crosswick heirs. At the thought, his eyes stung with tears.

Philip walked around behind Genevieve and rested his hand on her shoulder. He waited while Mrs. MacIntosh and Wallace organized Champagne for everyone.

Taking a deep breath to get his emotions under control, Philip began. "Just a few months ago, we were all strangers. Genevieve, er, Lady Crosswick and I arrived here out of our depth. We are not unsophisticated people, but as Lord and Lady Crosswick, we stepped into roles that very few people in the world experience. Those who do, are usually born into this wealth and responsibility rather than thrust into it as we were. Honestly, it was terrifying." He looked around at the faces he had grown to know and admire. "After years of managing the estate very well on your own, you could have resented us coming to Wilmingrove Hall, but you didn't. All of you welcomed us with extraordinary grace, for which we thank you. The presence of a new lord and lady would have been unsettling enough but add to that the upheaval of Olivia Conway's attempts on Sir David's and Duncan's lives, and the last few weeks have been quite, um…" Philip searched for just the right word. "Exciting, haven't they?" Giggles rippled through the room.

"Genevieve and I—" this time he did not correct himself, "can't express how much we have grown to love Wilmingrove Hall, and each of you." He nodded to Duncan, David and Becca. "Like the three people sitting here, you are our family. And, like family, we will always be here to support you, protect you and share all of our happiness with you."

Philip raised his glass. "To Wilmingrove Hall and all of you who nurture her. We will cherish you forever."

EPILOGUE

"BUMPA, I'M NEXT, I'm next!" Ready to perform the song she had prepared for the *Christmas Eve Musicale*, Ella danced with excitement. Cocky and self-assured, she stood in front of the guests assembled in the music room, anxious to begin. Genevieve sat at the piano waiting for Ella's nod, while her brother was at the ready with his harmonica.

Ella curtsied, holding the skirt of her red velvet dress in each hand. "Ladies and gentlemen, tonight I'm going to perform my Bumpa's favorite Christmas song, Santa Baby." She looked back at her grandmother and nodded.

Genevieve played the introduction and Ella began to perform.

For years, the Warwick Christmas Eve tradition had been an evening filled with performances by everyone, followed by a sumptuous dinner. The meal's climax was the discovery of *the almond* buried in someone's dessert, which won them a prize. And then, accompanied by sleighbells and booming "ho, ho, ho's," Santa's arrival was almost more excitement than one could bear.

It was an elegant, black-tie evening. Even the children dressed in their best party clothes. Philip and Genevieve made sure this year would be no different. They committed to incorporating their Christmas Eve ritual into Wilmingrove Hall's traditions, offering their own addition to the Laney heritage.

David travelled from London the day before and Becca had flown in a few days earlier to spend time with Olivia. Duncan, Julia, Alex, and Ella had been at the Hall since Thanksgiving and planned to stay until the new year.

Like a scene from a Currier and Ives lithograph, snow floated down just outside the windows, fires crackled on hearths, and as was the tradition of the Hall, Champagne flowed.

David stood to deliver a poem he had written for the occasion. Becca played the guitar and sang "Silent Night" in German. Duncan and Genevieve sang a fractured version of "A Partridge in a Pear Tree" which included the entire group's participation. For the grand finale, Philip and Julia joined their talents lip syncing "All I Want for Christmas is You," which brought down the house.

Just as the applause died and as if on cue, Wallace entered the room and announced, "My lords and ladies, dinner is served."

Accompanied by Alex on his harmonica, Wallace led the parade out of the music room, and across the grand salon to the dining room. With great flourish, he opened the double doors to reveal the room dressed in all its Christmas glory. The soaring tree was decked with a thousand lights and hundreds of antique English ornaments representing generations of Laneys. The magnificent table twinkled and beguiled with sterling and candles and crystal and flowers. No one could imagine anything more holiday perfect.

When everyone was seated, Genevieve stood. Glass in hand, she smiled at each glowing face looking back at her. "Every Christmas is special and every year we say, 'This holiday was the best ever.' This year I believe it's true. As our wise Julia says, 'We have so much we'll never get over, but so much we've gotten through.' With that in mind and knowing how much each of you means to Philip and me, I propose the toast our family has offered on Christmas Eve for many, many years."

She raised her glass and said:

> *"On this happy Christmas tide,*
> *Gathered round our table here*
> *Are those we love and hold so dear.*
> *To you, we wish good Christmas cheer.*

"We love you all and will see you at Chateau Beaulieu after the new year. Please come whenever and as often as you can. We'll drink our lovely Bordeaux and see what mischief we can get into in France. Joyeux Noel!"

Above the clink of toasting glasses and the din of happy voices, the faint sound of jingling bells could be heard. Santa was on his way... and the aroma of Charlotte's Rose Otto wafted through the Hall.

KEEP READING FOR A SNEAK PEEK OF

ART, WINE, AND CRIME

A Lord and Lady Crosswick Mystery,
Book 2

ONE

As they plummeted toward earth, a high-pitched whine and thunderous shudder of the fuselage confirmed these could be their last moments before they slammed into earth and exploded into a million bits. Tears stung her eyes, but Genevieve was calm, dead calm. She looked down at her hand, her fingers entwined with Philip's.

"Lord and Lady Crosswick, brace for impact," Captain Bruni barked over the intercom.

With their heads almost between their knees, Genevieve and Philip held each other's gaze. If these were their last moments, they would cherish each other until they perished in a ball of flames.

Genevieve stretched toward Philip, brushing his lips with hers. Philip's hand cradled the back of her head. He pulled her to him, firming their embrace, probably their last. Each could feel the other's taut muscles and hoped against hope their combined strength might ease the plane safely to earth…and then, the front of the plane nosed up. As they looked out the window, the horizon leveled. The jet engines roared back to life, their thrust slamming Philip and Genevieve back against their seats.

"What the hell," Philip gasped, under his breath.

The hum of landing gear lowering, filled the cabin with its glorious moan.

"Lord and Lady Crosswick." Captain Bruni's voice smiled through the speaker. Philip and Genevieve could hear his relief. "It appears our engines had a change of heart and have decided to take us into Paris rather than dumping us in a farmer's field. We will be on the ground in just a few minutes."

Overcome with relief, Philip and Genevieve's whoops and thunderous applause filled the cabin of their Bombardier jet. They would soon be on the ground, and alive. Still gripping Genevieve's hand, Philip brought it to his lips and kissed each knuckle.

Tears streamed down Genevieve's cheeks, flushed from adrenaline, and she croaked a laugh. "That's quite an entrance into Paris," she said glancing down at her trembling hands.

"After what we've just been through, all I wanted was a few calm months in France." Philip shook his head. "This does not bode well."

Flashing lights from two ambulances clustered in front of the general aviation terminal at Paris-Le Bourget Airport, waiting for the Warwick's jet to ease to a stop. Unsure what to do next, Genevieve and Philip didn't move, didn't release their seatbelts, barely breathed. After what seemed like an eternity, the cockpit door opened. Filling the doorway with his tall, broad-shouldered frame, Captain Francesco Bruni paused before he entered the owner's cabin.

"Well done, Captain Bruni." Philip mopped his brow with a crumpled linen napkin left from lunch. "What the hell just happened?" He motioned for the captain to sit in the seat across from him.

Bruni hesitated, then sat. In his lilting Italian accent, he began. "Lord, Lady Crosswick," he said, hands clasped between his splayed legs, his exquisite face pale from strain. "Until the mechanics investigate, it's difficult to say what caused the flameout, but I wouldn't..."

"Flameout?" Philip interrupted. "What's a flameout?

"This term is often used for any failure in a turbine engine, but it's technical meaning is a power loss not associated with mechanical failure. In this case, though the engines stopped, we were able to restart them."

"For which we are grateful." Genevieve reached out and touched the captain's sleeve, her eyes still sparkling from her tears of relief.

"If it wasn't mechanical, what could have happened?" Now that the unthinkable was behind them, Philip wanted answers.

Captain Bruni cleared his throat. His gaze riveted on Philip. "Lord Crosswick, the problem could have been caused by a number of things such as birds flying into the engine, a compressor stall or..." Bruni glanced at his interlaced fingers. He looked at Genevieve then back at Philip. "...or perhaps water in the fuel. If we find that was the problem, there will be serious consequences for whoever was responsible."

"I don't understand. How does water get into the fuel?"

"Normally it does not. I don't want to speculate, but we're scrupulous about testing before we refuel, so I would say, if that turns out to be our problem, we need to look for the person responsible."

Philip ran his hands over his face, sighing. "Are you saying if the engines stalled because of water in the fuel, someone intended to make that happen?"

"As I stated, I don't wish to speculate. I shall work with the authorities to uncover the problem and, I assure you, we shall discover what happened. Please, leave it in my hands, and I shall report to you as soon as possible. And now, Lord, Lady Crosswick, your car is waiting to take you home. I would suggest you do your best to enjoy the rest of your day."

Genevieve glanced out the window and saw a sparkling silver Rolls Royce Ghost at the ready. She unsnapped her seat belt and gave Philip a nudge with her shoulder. "Philip, there's nothing we can do here. We should go."

"I guess we'll leave you to it, Captain Bruni. And again, thank you." Philip extended his hand, a rare gesture for an earl to a member of his staff. Without hesitation, Bruni gripped Philip's hand.

The door now open, cold January air rushed into the cabin, chilling Genevieve's cheeks as she walked forward. She stood at the open door, looked at Philip next to her and laced her fingers through his. "Here we go again," she said.

Philip slid his arm around his wife's slender waist and pulled her close. "With a start like this, I can't even imagine what France has in store for us."

Genevieve flashed a radiant smile at her handsome husband of forty years. "Well, my darling, let's find out."

Join Lord & Lady Crosswick on their next mystery.

JOIN TANA'S NEWSLETTER TO BE THE FIRST TO HEAR WHEN ART, WINE, AND CRIME IS RELEASED.

WWW.TANALHBOERGER.COM

ACKNOWLEDGEMENTS

WRITING *MONEY, MURDER, MAYHEM*, my first novel, was a wonderful and challenging experience. It's best when you don't know how daunting a task is. That way you just plow ahead and get it done. As long as you surround yourself with people who cheer you on and give you the kind of help that keeps you moving forward, you don't realize how hard it is until you're finished, look back and say, "Wow! How did I do that?"

I'd like to acknowledge everyone who was in my corner from the beginning. During the pandemic when I decided I needed to do something more than put together jigsaw puzzles and learn to cross stitch, I began writing this book. It was a while before I told anyone that I was writing a novel. It sounded too self-important. But, when I finally confessed to my sister and husband that I had written several chapters, they didn't bat an eye. They just wanted to read it! And so it went for over a year. I wrote, Alana Davidson and Tom Boerger cheered me on. They were my sounding board, my tender critics, and my willing accomplices on my flights of fancy. Thank you both.

If I had not had my spectacular editor, Rosie Walker, my initial manuscript would have died a gentle death. Without killing my enthusiasm, Rosie showed me that the first draft of any work is just the beginning. In her very English way, she nudged me, kindly prodded, ceaselessly asked the right questions and insisted that I could do what it would take to transform my initial story from an amateur string of words into a compelling mystery with interesting characters and an exciting climax. Thank you Rosie. You are the best.

To the three other people in my realm whom I allowed to read the manuscript early on, entrusting you with that responsibility was a true sign of confidence in our friendship.

Bucky Holmes, never fails to support me whether it's an encouraging word or unbridled enthusiasm. He's the best cheerleader one could ask for and has spurred me on when it wasn't always easy.

Paul and Kay Zimmerman were there without fail, to assure me this journey would end well. I know their support will endure as long as there are more Lord and Lady Crosswick adventures to be written.

Colleen Sheehan understood immediately and perfectly what cover design would captivate MMM's readers and got it right the first time. Thank you for making it fun and exciting.

And last, but certainly not least, thank you to Cody Boerger who asked me, every time we spoke, how the book was going. It was a great motivator. I moved forward every day if for no other reason than I wanted to give him a good report. Cody, you are my best nudge!

I love you all and now you get to start all over again with the Warwicks next big adventure, Art, Wine, and Crime. Hold onto your hats!

ABOUT TANA

Tana L.H. Boerger is an unapologetic Anglophile. At the age of five, while watching Elizabeth II's coronation, (or as she called her, "my mom,") on a black and white TV in Nampa, Idaho, Tana was convinced she was the newly crowned queen's daughter and fell in love with all things English.

Since then, she has been under England's spell, so it is no surprise the primary setting for her debut novel, *Money, Murder, Mayhem: a Lord and Lady Crosswick Mystery,* is York, England.

She is deep into the second book in the series, *Art, Wine, and Crime: a Lord and Lady Crosswick Mystery,* which will be published in summer 2023.

She lives with her spectacular husband, Tom, in Sanford, North Carolina.

WWW.TANALHBOERGER.COM

f TANALHBOERGER

Printed in Great Britain
by Amazon